Reina Lisa Menasche

The Spirit of Shy Moon Lake

Reina Lisa Menasche

A Novel

CONTENTS

An Unexpected Guest

BOOK TWO:

The Other Side of Normal

No More Barriers

The Wrong Path

Too Many Signs

Broken Circle

A Deceptive Peace

Liking It Here

The End

This novel is dedicated to you, Irene, my big sister. I followed you, idolized you, confided in you, laughed with you, cried with you, and learned with you. I hope that goes on for many more years.

AUTHOR'S NOTE:

From beginning to end, this book is a work of the imagination. My imagination. The town, geography, people, cultures, history, rituals, and ceremonies are all invented by the imperfect mind of this author strictly for entertainment purposes.

"Reina Menasche puts a whole new spin on one of the most famous movie taglines in history: *You'll never go in the water again.* And yet in Ms. Menasche's novel THE SPIRIT OF SHY MOON LAKE, readers learn there is something much worse than a shark in the waters of which she writes. Enter . . . if you dare."

– Alan Russell bestselling author of BURNING MAN

BOOK ONE:

The Reaping

"This is the excellent foppery of the world, that when we are sick in fortune (often the surfeits of our own behaviour) we make guilty of our disasters the sun, the moon, and stars..."

—*WILLIAM SHAKESPEARE, King Lear*

NO SWIMMING

CHAPTER 1

MY PHOTOGRAPHIC MEMORY IS LIKE a GPS unit holding a gun to my head. I go where it takes me and remind myself that it's stronger than I am, so just enjoy the ride.

Mind you, I don't always choose to be a passenger in my own life. For example, after my new husband Charlie programmed our Mercedes minivan's GPS for Shy Moon Lake, I insisted on driving. Taking the wheel helps me get rid of my headaches, the kind that come from too many old pictures in the head. Driving's useful that way; a respite for bleary brains.

Then, just as we reached the foothills, the minivan's GPS unit quit working.

"What the hell." Charlie pressed buttons on the suddenly blank screen.

"Must be broken," I said. "You know these cheap German cars."

He laughed. "Oh well, we can wing it from here. There's only one road up, right? Just follow it."

"Are we *winging it*?" yelled little Jonah from the back.

"Yup," Charlie said. "We drive up the mountain, and at the top we search for a crater lake. Then, if we fall in, we know we got there."

"No, don't fall in!"

"No one is falling anywhere," I said in my wet-sock Mommy Voice.

Charlie touched my bare knee, sending goosebumps up my leg. "Jess, he knows I'm kidding. I think you're tired. Pull over, I'll drive."

Yes, please, I thought. "No," I said. "You had insomnia last night. And this road—"

"Is like a snake?" Charlie said.

I nodded.

"Well, you're right, I did have insomnia. Couldn't stop writing."

"Because you're a poet and sure as heck know it?"

"Mommy said 'heck' instead of the bad word," Jonah yelled.

Charlie laughed again. With his classically straight nose, square chin, deep-set brown eyes—plus that unlikely scar across his forehead—he really did look the part of poet. A little rumpled, a tad disorganized. Often dreamy and impulsive, yet surprisingly traditional. He was the one who had suggested buying a vacation cottage, sight unseen: an example of the impulsive part. On the traditional side, he dreamed of having a big family. He thought I felt the same way. Luckily, we had Jonah.

Triggered by that thought, a familiar flare of pain erupted at the base of my skull—and no, it was not caused by a brain tumor (I'd already checked that out). As usual, a visual flash followed. This time it was of my son after I had woken up from the C-section. Two o'clock in the afternoon. Sunny day, pale yellow walls, a slight glinting off bed railings. The bundle in a basinet next to me. His little hat, striped. His curled fingers. The mewing cry.

And standing to one side peering down at him, the father who would soon vanish from our baby's life…

"I can't wait to see this Mrs. Pattick," Charlie said now, breaking my reverie. "She's the most convincing woman I've ever *not* met."

"I picture her as four feet tall and dressed in polyester," I said. "Kind of an Oompa Loompa."

"Mm, maybe. At least the house looks sublime in the pictures, and you can't beat the price. We have to live a little, right?"

"Or a lot. Which is why I'm driving," I said.

At that, my all-too-cheerful husband snapped open the glove compartment and unfolded a brochure we'd downloaded from the Internet. After some dramatic clearing of the throat, he began to read it aloud:

* * *

Visit Shy Moon Lake

Admire the mountaintop views of this bottomless crater-lake, and

Stroll the streets of our remote little town;

See where star-crossed lovers met their watery fate.

And two cultures collided and fell.

Now a romantic retreat;

The least-known, best getaway in the State,

A wholesome family refuge.

Taste the mystery—young and old!

For Rentals, please call the Visitors Center at 888-555-5876!

SHY MOON LAKE...

A Vacation to Live For; A Place to Live Forever!

* * *

Listening to Charlie's voice, I held onto the wheel carefully, hands at the ten-and-two position. Happily, driving on this road sucked up most of my attention, kept me focused on the present. Shadow and gilded late afternoon light etched road and sky in intricate patterns. It was hard not to stare everywhere at once, and difficult to look at anything in particular.

Charlie folded up the brochure and returned it to the glove compartment. Then he leaned back in his nice warm leather seat and began whistling. He was quite the whistler, my Charlie. Immediately I recognized Vivaldi's "Four Seasons: Spring." Sometimes I whistled along with him—my contribution less like Vivaldi's fluty songbirds and more like tone-deaf pigeons. Today I stayed silent. Miles continued to unfurl, trees and moss and leaves, and the green-gray depths of space *between* the trees distorting space itself. Even the inside of our car felt as rippled as water, as loopy-de-loop as the road. All around us, light flickered, turning the sky into an otherworldly shade of deepest blue. Soon I had a different kind of headache: one of those behind-the-eyes things that signal physical fatigue rather than mental. Far preferable, in my opinion.

"How about this scenery, bud?" Charlie said to Jonah. "We're lucky to have the whole summer on this mountain."

"And then we go back home?"

"Just until next summer. Don't worry, we have a home here now, too, so we can come back every year!"

"Oh."

Charlie, clearly entranced by the view, hadn't caught the nuance in Jonah's voice, but I had. I gave my son a confident grin in the rear-view mirror. He was nervous, of course. Why wouldn't he be? This was all new to him. Even newer than it was to me.

Finally, the trees began to spread farther apart, and a wooden sign appeared on the side of the road. It depicted a cartoon moon peeking through trees above the caption *Entering the Home of Shy Moon Lake. Visitors Welcome.*

A moment later, the land to the left slanted down to reveal, slightly below us, a wide blue body of water. A lake, all right. *The* lake. Named Shy Moon, for unknown reasons, except maybe the full-moon-like shape of the crater that held it, or the area cleared directly above, as if the trees had simply dropped away to maximize stargazing.

Or maybe the moon's just shy, I thought. I really would have to investigate the name.

Originally, we'd Googled "remote mountain towns," which had led us to the intriguing brochure and the even more intriguing Mrs. Patty Pattick. She had actually sounded surprised when she answered her own phone, as if she weren't used to it working. "Maybe it's the altitude," Charlie had chuckled. And when we went back to the town's website to get more details about the area we had just committed to—mortgaging ourselves for the next 15 years—we couldn't open any of the links. It was weird.

Now, as we turned yet another curve, the lake twisted out of sight again. Half-broken branches reached over the van as if scrabbling for something on the roof.

"This place is scary," Jonah said.

I was about to tell him that the trees were extending their arms in friendly greeting when I caught sight of a pale shape amongst the trees to my side of the road.

A deer?

No, it was a person. A woman, sitting on a big flat rock with her knees drawn up to her chest.

And she was…naked.

I had to focus on the road for a second; when I looked again, turning my head as much as I dared, I saw a blur of moving limbs, and then nothing.

Just the blue-black stripes of trees, and darkened bars of orange-yellow-red light across a flat-topped boulder. No woman, naked or otherwise.

Maybe it really was time for me to stop driving…

"Did you see the naked girl?" I asked Charlie.

He swiveled his head. "What—where?"

"Hey, put your eyeballs back, I must be seeing things."

"What a surprise," he said with a smile.

We passed another, bigger sign, depicting the moon playing hide-and-seek with the lake and the slogan:

WELCOME TO SHY MOON LAKE
Taste the Mystery

A moment later the first buildings appeared, houses half-hidden amongst the trees. Ahead, larger structures faced one another across a grassy square. According to a street sign, the road beneath our minivan was now Main Street.

Our vehicle purred slowly around the picturesque square, past the post office, mom-and-pop stores, and restaurants. The streets were quaintly narrow, the buildings brightly painted, almost whimsical. Funny, though: the businesses' names could only be described as uninspired: "Shy Moon Lake Hardware" and "Shy Moon Lake Produce."

"It's like a theme park, only real," was Charlie's comment.

He was right; everything looked…cute.

Near doorways, fake ducks posed mid-waddle. In windows, fake hawks spread their wings. Even the curbside trashcans looked fetching and gim-micky; festooned with smiling moons as if dressed for a party. "Shy Moon Lake Refuse," the cans read.

On old-fashioned lampposts, large hand-made posters announced in all caps: HISTORICAL RE-ENACTMENT COMING VERY SOON! I wondered what kind of history people would be re-enacting. Garage Sale bartering? Water balloon fights?

In the grassy center of Main Street, a gazebo gleamed. A stone's throw away, a dolphin fountain lifted its spray. Huh, I thought, surprised. Someone's blown the moon motif.

The base of my skull pinged…and I was back to a wintry Saturday, February 15, 1986. My family had almost reached the end of "The Haunted Mansion" ride at the Happiest Place on Earth—Disneyland—when suddenly our cart stopped. We sat there, the four of us stuffed together, me on Daddy's lap, staring at our reflections in a mirrored wall—with a ghost plunked in the middle. I screamed. My father gripped my shoulders and murmured soothing words while my mother told my brother David to stop laughing. *Bru*-ha-ha, *bru*-ha-ha, David cackled as I peed inside the shorts of my brand-new turquoise sailor's suit. The cart still did not move. The ghost didn't either. I stopped crying and looked at the ghost; it looked at me. *I won't let you win*, I thought.

The Happiest Place on Earth had always looked slightly wrong to me after that, and now I had that memory crowding itself into *this* present moment, which might be why the lovely town of Shy Moon Lake—*A Vacation to Live For!*—suddenly looked a little bit off to me, too.

Of course, hallucinating a naked woman on a rock might have had something to do with that.

I won't let you win, I thought—and wondered who I was talking to.

CHAPTER 2

"I'M HOPIN' YOU DON'T SCARE off this new family like you did the Thurstons," declared Mr. Johnston Reed as he stood hunched behind his pharmacy counter. "Mrs. Pattick has succeeded where others failed, you know. We *need* folks coming into town. So, give 'em the chance to stay a minute."

Rikki Finn Stevens ignored him. The shop window overlooked Main Street and beyond that the mossy stone wall that separated the town of Shy Moon Lake from the lake itself. Rikki stared at a deer that was standing just outside the wall as if yearning to go back in.

Or feeling compelled to?

Don't do it, Rikki thought. Just don't.

She watched with satisfaction as the animal finally walked off to the left and vanished into the trees. It could have easily jumped the five-foot wall but had chosen to go elsewhere instead. There had to be a message in that. A personal message. The deer was Rikki's totem. Doc Taylor called "that totem business" nonsense; said the trouble was all in her head. But he was more ignorant than the deer.

It made Rikki want to shriek with frustration—except deer did not shriek. They slipped away if they were to survive at all.

She drew her attention back to the wizened old pharmacist. He looked ridiculous: part stick figure, part lumpy sweater, and part World War II-era pants belted at the armpits. Of course, it was rude *not* to look at him when he spoke to her. Nana would have a fit. But what about when *he* was rude? Why did nothing calamitous ever happen to him? Where was the justice in that?

"I hear it's some rich family from Below," Mr. Reed went on as he bagged Nana's medication. "Another nice couple thrilled to get close to the lake. They don't deserve your shenanigans any more than the Thurstons did."

As if I'm in control of what happens! A knot hardened in Rikki's abdomen. Oh Lord, what now? Indigestion? Appendicitis?

Or worse?

She realized the pharmacist was staring at her, too. His sharp old eyes turned her into a kid again, seven years old and as miserable as a funeral. The problem was that this old man had known her since the day she was born—four weeks early, with no doctor or nurse to attend to her. Thirty years ago! He had given her free candy when she'd been a lonely kindergartner he liked to call "Miz Grit." When she was a grief-stricken second grader, he had gifted her with lollipops. After she entered middle school and became orphaned, he'd slipped her free gum while asking where the hell her grit went.

"Did you hear me? Cat got your tongue?" he said now.

"No, cats have nothing to do with it—and you should know that," she snapped, thinking: *There's some grit for you!*

He only looked annoyed. "What's that?"

"Never mind. You wouldn't understand."

"Mm, maybe not. Fact is, Miz Rikki, you don't seem right. You need to keep your mind clear of those old stories, not like your Nana. How is she faring, by the way?"

"Doc upped the dosage on her medication. But I guess you know that."

"I guess I do."

"She just…sits on the porch. Says she's got time enough for sleep later." *When she's dead.*

"Well, good for her. Fresh air is healthy. How's the blood pressure?"

"Okay."

"Another miracle. Glad to hear it." The pharmacist leaned forward. "*She* should think about going Below, if you ask me."

I didn't, Rikki thought.

"Or at least *Up* onto one of the other mountains. But not for the reasons you think. The problem with Nana is that she believes every story comes her way. And she's raised you just the same."

This was too much. Unfair and…idiotic. Rikki's cheeks felt as hot as a grill. Her words…her *venom*…just flew from her. "You think…we have a *choice?* That we can just *decide* to go Below, or Up—or sideways? For any reason?"

He waved his hand as if to shush her.

"You don't know *anything* about what my family goes through," Rikki cried, her voice breaking. "I wish to God you did."

At the mention of God, Mr. Reed glanced at the pile of Visitors' Center brochures lying face up on the counter. He must know those brochures were misleading. They were dangerous, in fact, worse than trick advertising. *See where star-crossed lovers met their watery fate!*

He cleared his throat. "Lookee here, young lady. I don't like contradicting an elderly lady like your Nana. But now that the Thurston house sold, you need to put things right. You'll be getting a new neighbor, and that's that."

I know. I saw them driving up the mountain while I was trying to do my ritual in the woods. They messed it up.

"So, I'm asking you to be nice," Mr. Reed added. "That's all."

Nice? Elderly? How dare he keep on like this? Johnston Reed was about six days younger than Nana. They had gone to school together a hundred years ago.

"You don't know what you're saying," she practically spat at him. "Because if you did, you would be scared shitless, like I am. We can't just be *nice*. We have to be freakin' perfect!"

He opened his mouth. She cut him off.

"And one of these days 'those old stories' are going to get all of us, *including you*. Which is what you deserve!"

She snatched up the bag of medicine, turned, and stalked out of the pharmacy, slamming the screen door behind her. It shook ominously, like it wasn't stable; like slamming the door would bring down the whole building on top of Mr. Reed's head and kill him; and it would be all her fault.

She tried to tell herself that wouldn't happen. Everything would be fine. Some things needed saying. If enough people *inside* the wall heard the truth often enough to believe it, then maybe folks *outside* could do something to fix it.

She stood on the curb another moment, breathing hard, her neck tingling. Because something right beside her had *moved*.

Something brushed against her skin.

She uttered a small scream and whirled around, looking, listening. But nothing jumped out at her. No buildings or trees fell. No one spoke.

This feeling was not a chill exactly, more like a pocket of air that did not belong. It *could* be caused by a breeze in the trees. She breathed again, slowly, deeply, trying to get her bearings.

Then she heard it. A humming.

It started softly, a distant insect. The insect buzz became…fuller, more liquid, like the trickling vibration of running water.

As she listened, the sound turned into a pattering.

Her ears swelled. She heard the water in her *ears.*

Goddamn you to hell, she thought—and instantly, pain clamped down on the sides of her head. Like fire tongs seizing the temples fast and hard. With a cry, she dropped the pharmacy bag. The sounds were inside her now. She could *taste* the pressure of them.

What was it her doctor had said? "You can't die from a panic attack, Rikki."

But why did she have them? Because she worked so hard to protect everyone? Talk about futile!

Shakily, she managed to pick up the pharmacy bag. She lifted her foot to take another step toward home—and stumbled off the curb.

Her ankle twisted. And she slammed onto the asphalt, her conscience squawking like birds trying to escape from the lake.

Back atcha, Rikki Finn Stevens! Take THAT!

Her ankle throbbed, pain shooting up to her hip. Her foot hurt, too. Great: something was either broken or strained. What would Nana say? Just embody the deer, Rikki thought dully as she lay on the road. That's what.

At that moment, a late-model Caddy—not the car she had seen earlier from the woods—careened around the corner and screeched to a stop. A tourist family piled out: pot-bellied father, mom in basketball shorts, and two kids shaped like M & Ms.

"Oh, my goodness! Are you all right?" cried the woman. "We could have run you over!"

Wish you had, Rikki thought.

The woman came closer. "And your foot is swollen! Look, by the arch…"

"Young lady, let me help you," said the fat guy, with a *puff, puff, puff.*

When he offered his hand, she politely accepted it, cringing inwardly at his moist, bulgy fingers. They felt like latex gloves filled with water. She managed to remain both quiet and wary as she got to her feet, though. *Deer-like.*

The lady tourist said, "Can we call someone?"

"Dial 9-1-1," advised one of the kids. "If they have that around here."

"There's no reception. Unless I run to that pharmacy, use a land-line?" the mama said.

"No," Rikki snapped. Then she caught herself and spoke with saccharine sweetness. "Please. It's not necessary. I live down the street, on the other side of that wall. I'll be fine. Thank you, though. I really appreciate your kindness."

"Well, if you're sure…"

"Wow, you live close to the lake," said the other M&M kid. "*Luuucky!* Mama says we're not allowed to swim."

Rikki replied without looking up. "That's because the shores drop straight down to the bottom as soon as you go in. And it happens really fast. The lake is beautiful, but it's not safe."

And that's about half the truth.

"I wish we'd known about that restriction before we came all the way up here," the woman said. "It's just so hard to get information. The website needs updating or something, it kept freezing my computer. Luckily, we got on that first time, right after we upgraded our Wi-fi. The slower one didn't work at all, not for this town."

"Aggie," said the man.

"Sorry. You said you live on the other side of the wall? We'll go with you, make sure you arrive safe and sound."

The woman sure seemed eager for an expedition past the warning signs. Well, of course she is, Rikki thought bitterly. Why should strangers care about the havoc they rain down on locals?

Still. Even thinking about slapping someone upside the head was *not* nice. Rikki's heart gave another sick little flutter.

Deep down, she did not really mind visitors or newcomers. The town needed them, just like Mr. Reed said. Even if those visitors—all of them, all ages, both genders—kept trying to swim in the lake, boat in the lake, disturb the lake.

Of course, they did.

A pox on all seven houses sitting on the wrong side of this freakin' wall—she fumed as she waved cheerfully to the visitors and headed home, limping, to Nana.

CHAPTER 3

WE WASTED PRECIOUS DAYLIGHT NAVIGATING our way up and down illogical and poorly designed one-way streets that made me feel cross-eyed. "Do they do this on purpose?" I demanded of the universe, while Charlie just looked around, interested in everything he saw or could barely see in the darkening day.

Every house, every tree, every shop. Every *mint green* fire hydrant.

"Is what on purpose?" he said eventually.

"Never mind," I said. "Look at that sign. Doesn't it say Lake End Road?"

"Good job, Jess. You have good eyes. No wonder you're driving."

Turning the correct corner, we passed an old-fashioned pharmacy, the last business in sight. The lake should be at the other end of this road. The asphalt pavement became crunchy gravel as we jostled along like country bumpkins heading for the hills. Except there were no higher peaks than the one we were on: just the ragged rocks of the crater's lip. Because we had gone as high as possible. The crater was at tippy top.

Charlie turned to Jonah. "In a few moments we'll reach the very bashful and elusive Shy Moon Lake. Home of our Summer Home."

Out of the oppressive shadows of the trees, Jonah had apparently found a new attitude. He hollered his approval, and I smiled, braking. An old-world stone wall about five feet high rose before us.

We *had* expected a wall—Mrs. Pattick mentioned it several times. But this one seemed a bit…overwhelming. Not very tall, but with enormous stones. And the mossy barrier meandered to right and left, apparently leaving only one access area to the lake: this gate. Even more mind boggling, on the gate, hung all these hand-scrawled *signs*.

Too many of them. Ridiculous signs. Why hadn't Mrs. Pattick mentioned them?

I sat there, reading.

The Daddy sign at center screamed, "READ THE SIGNS!" Around it jostled a family of smaller ones: Limited Access Only! No Entry! No Swimming! No Boating! Dangerous Beach! Barrier Rocks! Bottomless Lake! And so on.

"What do they say?" Jonah asked with awe in his voice.

"Uh…let's see…" Charlie leaned forward. "They want you to be a good boy and listen to your parents?"

"No, they don't," my son yelled, giggling.

The gate—a massive steel tube attached to the big wall on one side— was kept unlocked, according to Mrs. Pattick. "It's part municipal property, so they can't do that," she had said, never explaining who *they* were. "People are simply discouraged from going too close. Water's deep, you see. The beach is too narrow even where you can access it, and the rocks are sharp. It's for looking, not swimming."

Charlie said now, "Well, I think the signs are a great touch. They're luring tourists by telling them to stay out."

"Mm," I said. "As long as they give us a remote to open the gate each time."

"The whole area is remote," Charlie quipped.

"Oh, Charlie."

"Sorry, I couldn't resist. I'll show penance by opening it for you."

"Yes, please. *If. You. Dare*," I added in my best vampire voice.

He climbed out of the car and showed his muscles, which made Jonah giggle again. Then Charlie lifted the bar with no apparent effort. I drove in, and he lowered the bar again and climbed back into the van. Drama over.

Moving away from the wall, we passed empty docks to our right and a barely used parking lot beyond that. To the left, the lights in a string of white clapboard cottages twinkled like diamonds in a necklace. The lake itself was almost hidden in this premonition of darkness. In Mrs. Pattick's photos, the water had been a clean, smooth bluish green. Now it appeared depthless and perfectly still, more of a mirror.

"It's here, Mommy? Our new house?"

"Yep, I think this is it." I slowed the car by the middle cottage, a confection in white clapboard and blue trim. To my relief, it looked just as charming as it had on the website, except for one thing: a Volkswagen beetle parked in front. "Huh. We've got visitors?"

"One, at least." Charlie looked at me. "You expecting someone?"

"No. I told Mrs. Pattick we'd be coming, but not what time. Remember, she was putting keys under a flowerpot for us?"

"Right, I forgot. How original. Well, maybe she couldn't find a pot."

"Or she wants to welcome us herself."

"That's small-town hospitality for you," Charlie said with no small satisfaction.

"What's 'hospitalatitee'?" asked Jonah.

"It means being friendly to visitors and strangers," Charlie said. "You see, in the city there are lots more people but sometimes less hospitality. We certainly could use more 'hospitali*titty*' in the world." He turned to me, his eyes suddenly wide, astonished, as if he had a revelation. "Maybe that's why there was a naked woman in the woods: to personally give visitors a dose of hospitalitit—*ow*!"

He rubbed his shoulder as if I had really slugged him hard. Laughing, I killed the engine. Jonah undid his own belt and ran out to admire the daisies on the Volkswagen's wheels. The house perched several yards up on a steep slope; breathing deeply, I climbed seven or eight steps to the little front porch. The air smelled so good! Except less humid than I expected: *earthier* for some reason.

The base of my skull gave a sharp twinge…

Lake Ronkonkoma, I thought, seeing it in full relief. Where I spent childhood summers early on. *Here we go…*

The porch at Lake Ronkonkoma was grand like this one: crisply painted, with pine trees on three sides, and all that water a stone's throw away. "Daddy, there are hundreds of mosquitos," I had complained. It was July 4th and I was turning six in two days, and already the bug bites on my body looked like some weird bumpy map. "Well, if you don't want mosquitos, you'd better move to California," Daddy said, which I did much later, long after he was dead…

Charlie appeared next to me. "Uh-oh, you've got that look on your face. That I'm-remembering-a-million-details look."

"I can't help it." I sighed.

"Right. Your 'condition.'"

"Don't say it like that, Charlie. It's a real thing."

"I know it is," he said. "Believe me, I know."

* * *

Hyperthymestic Syndrome—from the Greek word "thymesis" for remembering, and the universal word "hyper"—hits me hardest when I am stressed. So, I guess we could call it "stress-related Hyperthymestic Syndrome."

Take Ronkonkoma (we pronounced it "Ron-CONK-oma") as an example. The lake was bottomless, my brother David and I believed at the time. Of course, we were children, and children believe anything. But for me, now, that water still goes down and down until it spits me out on the other side of the planet. I see the shifting of sun-glossed green water—and fear coils in my belly. I am still drowning. I can hear kids screaming for help, the lifeguard's voice booming. I can smell it too; cold water against my face, with all those lake things growing. Mama grabs my hand to pull me back; the metallic beaded bracelet on my left wrist falls apart. It crumbles into pieces and sinks forever.

"Don't cry, little Jessie, we'll get you another one," Mama says, comforting me on the sand. And Daddy comes running to see what is happening, his rubber flip-flops a-flapping in the sand. "How's my sweetie? Are you all right?"

These are mostly *good* memories, despite how vivid they are and despite the scary parts. Unfortunately, other, completely bad memories *also* assail me at random, and in glorious, mind-numbing detail.

Like the summer day when my father died in a freak accident involving a ladder, a window, a bucket of spackle, and a psychotic cat. Or the other, much-later summer day when my husband abandoned me with a colicky baby and a dying mother.

No one wants the past to linger too much, whether it is good or bad or somewhere in between. The past crowds out the present.

I leaned against Charlie; he put his arm around me. "Love you," I whispered.

"Love you more," he said. "I'm sorry if I made you feel bad."

"No, I'm fine. Really."

"Me too." He inhaled deeply enough for both of us. "I hope we spend a hundred summers here. Let's make so many memories you'll need a lobotomy later."

"Aww, isn't that romantic?"

He laughed. "Well, there *is* enough room for when we expand, right? That's romantic."

Expand…as in more kids. What was that old saying about no matter where you go, there you are?

At age seven years and five months, I had stolen Sandra Kowaski's Slinky. Hidden it in the closet and felt guilty about it. "Where'd you get the Slinky?" David demanded, knowing, because he had been hunting for his blue tow truck. "None of your business," I yelled, and felt bad enough to give the Slinky back to Sandra the next day. Not the same day, but the next. "I don't know how it got in my pocket," I told her.

I should not have lied to Sandra, and I should not have lied to Charlie, not even once. For this most important of lies had only gotten bigger, more complicated, and nefarious, since the day it first popped out of my mouth.

What a tangled web we weave…

Suddenly the blue door of our new cottage swung open and a short, stout lady with perfectly straight hair filled the lighted doorway, at least widthwise. Festive and professional in a Clintonesque pantsuit, she stepped onto the porch, hand outthrust. "Greetings! Mrs. Pattick here! Well! So glad you made it. Welcome to Shy Moon Lake!"

"Thank you," Charlie said.

The three of us shook hands.

"Please forgive my intrusion," said Mrs. Pattick, "but I decided to hand-deliver your keys."

How did you know how to time *this*? I longed to ask. Instead I said, "That's very sweet of you."

She beamed. "Well? What do you think of Shy Moon Lake so far?"

"Pretty as a picture," I said, wincing at my cliché.

"The town is cozy and wholesome. The perfect place in which to expand our family," Charlie added, just like that, *in front of Mrs. Pattick.*

I could not believe my ears. Why was he mentioning our private business?

Mrs. Pattick clasped her hands in obvious delight. "Oh! How nice to hear! Don't you love big families?"

"Yes, ma'am," Charlie said.

No, ma'am, I thought.

At my leg, Jonah asked, "Mommy, why is the moon shy?"

Mrs. Pattick looked down at him. "I assure you," she said in a serious voice, "the moon here is like anywhere else."

Weird. Had she never run into that question, or a curious preschooler, before?

"I know, it's a funny name, bud," I told my son. "You and I will figure it out later, I promise."

And he grinned up at me, dimples flashing, making my heart chirp. I loved his long red eyelashes so much I had the urge to munch on them. Charlie called me a cannibal for notions like that, but what did he know? He wasn't a mother.

Then we entered the house for Mrs. Pattick's official tour, and whatever small bit of nervousness I held in my chest lifted. This place was perfect. Quaintly furnished rooms in cedar and pine. Old-fashioned wallpaper of little kids in pioneer clothing. Roomy cabinets and new windows and an amazing flagstone fireplace. The kitchen was cool and the refrigerator ridiculously huge and state-of-the-art; our whole family could fit inside.

"Wow," I said. "We can definitely do this."

Next, Mrs. Pattick guided Charlie and Jonah outside to show them where the woodpile was while I looked around a bit more. I did the tour again by myself, trying to imagine summers here. Jonah growing, Charlie and I slowing our pace, forgetting how to rush. It would be good for us, for all of us.

Very much in a better mood now, I stepped back onto the front porch—and saw Jonah out here alone, playing.

Something was terribly wrong. Where was Charlie?

Then I realized Jonah was at the railing, *climbing*. Swinging a leg over the top rail, he was about to pitch himself into the shadowy drop-off.

"*Wheeeee!* Mommy, look!"

"Jonah! Stop!" I lurched forward. "Get down! It's not safe!"

I managed to grab onto his shirt, but he let out a startled cry and flopped away from me, boneless as a cat.

For an awful second, I thought I would drop him. Seven feet to the ground.

I pawed at his legs with my free hand. At the same time felt an unwelcome pain in my head, a vision of green water, my bracelet breaking…

No, I thought. No time for that!

And I yanked Jonah back with both hands.

My breath came in short bursts. My hands were shaking. But finally, my baby was safe on his feet. I pulled him around to face him. "I love you, honey, but I'm upset. You could have gotten hurt. You see how high this porch is?"

He nodded, avoiding my eyes.

"It's *not* a jungle gym. I don't want you doing that ever again. Why didn't you stay with daddy?"

He shrugged, tearfully.

At that moment, Charlie rounded the corner from the back of the house, Mrs. Pattick waddling beside him. "Is Jonah here?" he asked. "He slipped away!"

"Because you weren't watching him," I sputtered, still shocked.

Shame-faced, Charlie apologized, and Mrs. Pattick apologized, too. Even Jonah apologized.

Well, I thought. Nothing like a near-catastrophe to start off our summer right.

But I let the subject drop, to everyone's obvious relief. After all, this was not the moment for any more personal comments, not in front of Mrs. Pattick.

Charlie went to the car to unload, Mrs. Pattick on his heels again. Except this time, Jonah clung to my hand.

"Mommy, are you mad at me?"

"No…you just scared me, honey. I'm fine now. Sorry I raised my voice."

He thought about that and smiled. Yeah, he would forgive me. Big of him.

Then he stood on his tippy toes, peering toward the lake. "Who's that?"

"Who's who?"

He pointed. "*There.* In the water."

I squinted at the inky blackness, recalling the town legend about long-ago lovers drowning. "Sorry, honey, it's too dark. You're just seeing tree shadows."

There were indeed tree shadows, thrown by starlight shifting across the dark water like a flutter of insects. Silhouettes of trees appeared suspended between opposing diadems of light—the Milky Way above and its reflection on the waters of Shy Moon Lake below. How thrilling, I thought, to view a night sky containing more than six or seven stars. Against this luminous, scintillating dome, anything seemed possible.

Like…I wondered, what would happen to all this beauty if there were an earthquake?

Violent quakes had no doubt accompanied the birth of the volcano that now cupped the lake. How many points on the Richter scale could these cottages endure before windows shattered, porches toppled: the land crumbling beneath our feet?

Maybe we *will* need to climb inside that refrigerator…

Mrs. Pattick said, "Mrs. McCortney. Are you all right?"

I shook off the unwanted gloom. I might not be as congenitally cheerful as my husband, but I was not usually like this, either. "Yes. Yes, thank you, I'm fine. Just tired. It's been a long day."

As Charlie rose back up the steps, the upper half of his body hidden behind boxes and bags, a door slammed. A porch light flicked on at the cottage next door.

We looked over. A woman with short darkish hair gazed back at us, her expression flash frozen.

"Good evening," I called, waving, happy for the distraction. "We're moving in!"

She did not reply, just stared. She had to have heard me; the cottages were not that far apart.

I stepped to the end of the porch. "My name is Jess. This is my husband Charlie and our son Jonah. We've bought this place, and we're moving in right now."

Still no response from the lady next door. Was she ill? Disabled?

Finally, as if set to a delayed timer, her eyebrows went down, and a smile opened up nice and big. "Well, hello. Welcome!"

"We just arrived. And this is our real estate agent, Mrs.—"

"Pattick," finished the young woman. "Hello, Mrs. Pattick."

"Rikki," said Mrs. Pattick in a flat voice. She rattled her car keys in her hand.

"Would you like to come over for a few minutes, get acquainted?" I asked the neighbor.

There was another long pause. I felt relieved when her smile returned.

"Yes, of course. I'll come welcome you properly," she said.

Then, slowly—with the help of an old-lady cane—the young woman descended her steps, crossed between our cottages, and clumped up our stairs. There *is* something wrong with her, I realized. An injury? And I've made her climb stairs just to meet us?

Mrs. Pattick hardly even cast a look at the neighbor. "I've got to go. Good luck in your new home, Mr. and Mrs. McCortney. And good evening to you, Rikki."

The woman called Rikki said nothing as Mrs. Pattick marched off, her back like the stone wall blocking entrance to Shy Moon Lake.

* * *

"My Nana is waiting. I can't stay much longer, either," Rikki Stevens said a few minutes later.

In those few minutes she had refused to sit, refused a glass of water, refused to step inside our house. Uncomfortable or maybe in pain, she leaned against the railing with her bad foot propped on a bar a little off the ground, her hand playing with her hair.

And despite the amorphous, unsexy nightdress she was wearing, I could not help noticing that she had amazingly long legs. The nightgown made her look a little like a patient from a convalescent hospital. I had to squelch the urge to shove her into a chair to rest.

"Where are you from?" she asked me.

"San Diego. It's pretty, but nothing like this."

"Oh. Well." Said in a monotone. "I've lived here all my life."

"Lucky you," Charlie put in. "My father was a diplomat, so we traveled all over the world."

She shifted her gaze to him. "Really. I've never left Shy Moon Lake."

Charlie said, "It's so beautiful, who would want to leave? Traveling sounds glamorous, but all I've ever wanted was to settle down. A simple life."

"Simple?" A tickle of laughter pulsed at the base of the woman's throat. "Nothing is simple. It only appears that way when you don't know where to look."

An odd comment, I thought. Odd words from an odd duck. *Another odd duck.*

"Do you have kids?" Jonah asked loudly, at my legs again.

The neighbor scowled down at him. "Good God no, I'm not even married."

"Why not?"

I murmured, "*Shh*, honey, that's not polite," but Rikki's scowl vanished again, the smile taking over.

"No worries! It's fine, I understand. You let us know if you need anything. I would be happy to help you in any way I can! My Nana too."

"Is *she* nice?" Jonah wanted to know.

He was obviously trying to get noticed. I grabbed his hand, rubbing his back while Charlie redirected the conversation to the lake. He asked Ms. Stevens if swimming was really taboo, and whether boating was allowed for residents, at least.

The neighbor looked horrified, as if he had suggested setting fire to the trees.

"There. Is. Absolutely. No. Boating. Or Swimming. You saw the signs, right? Didn't Mrs. Pattick tell you how dangerous it is?"

"She mentioned drop-offs and underground caves and insurance," Charlie said. "But we were still hoping to swim. Jonah's been taking lessons since he was two."

"There is no bottom to our lake. He'll drown."

No one knew what to say to that.

Fortunately, the woman excused herself and hobbled off. My little family remained quiet as we watched her go down our stairs, across the patch of land between cottages, and up her own stairs. Her front door slammed. A crotchety old female voice rose from behind a window, words unclear.

Then: more silence.

"Okay*yy*," Charlie said at last. "So, we've moved next door to the Bates Motel?"

"Wow," I said. "Just wow."

"Wow," Jonah repeated, and we began to laugh.

We were laughing about everything, I think; not just the two characters we had met tonight or the magnificent untouched lake with the hysterical signs. We were giddy with the prospect of living at Shy Moon Lake, the whole summer before us like a big blank watery slate.

Odd ducks or no, I would sleep well tonight. With the country air and country sounds and smells, I suspected we'd sleep like the dead.

BACK ATCHA

CHAPTER 4

THAT EVENING, ABEY LEAF STEVENS—KNOWN to so many of the town residents as Nana—turned away from the dark spectacle of a lake. She fixed her gaze on her granddaughter Rikki. "Now. Stop weaseling around and tell me what happened."

"I *did* tell you," Rikki said, eyes downcast.

Nana sniffed. She knew that her granddaughter was only pretending to be nonchalant, bent over her work because she did not feel like talking. Tonight, Rikki was folding laundry: socks meticulously bundled, undies pressed like pages in a book, pillowcases transformed into Origami boxes. Not that Nana could complain. She liked her pillowcases folded like origami boxes. If Rikki didn't do it, who else?

"You can look at me now, little miss," Nana said. "And always remember to look at your elders when they speak. You already broke one foot. Are you looking to break another?"

Rikki shook her head, cheeks flushing.

"Good. It's good sense to be afraid. You hear me?"

"Yes, Nana."

"Now, tell me. What did they say, how did they say it, and what did you do and say back? I need to figure out how big a pain in the ass these new people are going to be and what we're going to do about it."

"It was just a short visit. They didn't say much."

"Oh really. Then what do they want here?"

"Just the usual, I think. Wholesome family time, good prices. The lake."

"Did they say *that* to your face? Gad's sake, girl—stop fiddling!"

Rikki jumped, almost knocking over her cotton treasures. But then she righted the basket and folded her hands in her lap and obediently provided Nana with descriptions of the new family: a red-haired sparrow of a woman married to a big handsome man, and a demanding child. More newcomers from Below, who wanted to swim and generally do as they pleased.

Despite the signs. Again.

Nana's swore lustily. "Damn that Mrs. Pattick! The fool of a woman can't resist making money off our backs."

Rikki just sat there without moving. She looked like a carving of herself.

"Can't let a cottage go empty," Nana went on. "Doesn't affect her enough, nice and dry up where she lives. But that's all right. Because *you* know what to do, don't you?"

That brought the girl back to life. "No. Please, Nana, don't ask me that. This family doesn't know better. They're innocent."

"You think it's *coincidence* that they came here in the first place? You know there's no such thing."

"No. I mean"—biting her lip—"The Thurstons made it Below, and you said they couldn't."

"So, what's your point?"

"Well, no accidents were reported. No bodies found: no fires either. Everyone says they're gone!"

"Oh, and everybody knows more than your Nana?"

"No," Rikki said hoarsely. "Of course not."

"One way or another, these folks are still affected," Nana said.

"But the Thurstons don't live here anymore! *They got away.*"

"At what risk? Have you lost your mind?"

For a long moment, Rikki said nothing. The smudges beneath her eyes gave her an oddly sulky look, like a misfit raccoon. Nana saw that the child's eyebrows had once again been foolishly plucked into two thin upside-down smiles. Why couldn't the girl stop picking at her natural beauty? Nana wished she could wrap her granddaughter in soft blankets and hide her in the closet—not that hiding would do much good.

Goddamn Lake, as mean as a goose.

Rikki sighed, deeply, as if she had layers of lungs. Nana leaned over to pat her hand.

"It's all right, Raquel, meditate on it. And in the meantime, don't forget to mind your p's and q's."

"I know," Rikki whispered. "I…try. But it doesn't *help.*"

"Don't be stupid, of course it does." Nana recalled the Brava family, who used to live two cottages down. There they were, so polite and generous they practically gifted you with casseroles for waving at them—and look what happened to the mother. Forty years old and crushed by a monster-sized branch from a perfectly healthy tree! Everyone knew the cause lay in something Mrs. Brava had said or done, or worse, something one of the *other* families by the lake had done. (The one with the twin boys? Or that naive middle-aged couple still hoping for children of all things? Or the bickering Quiroz family that was gone now, too?)

As old as she was, Nana clearly recalled her own long-ago efforts to leave Shy Moon Lake—and what had come afterward. Extreme vomiting that defied all medical tests. Freak storms, and car trouble, and then a tiny twig that blew into her eyeball and temporarily blinded her.

Let the pompous ass Doc Taylor try to explain—

Nana sat up, inhaling sharply.

The sound had come from this porch. A breath. Or a sigh, mocking her own?

"Nana?" Rikki said in a strangled voice. "Did you hear that?"

Nana put her finger to her lips.

There was no footfall, no creak of the wooden porch. Only the whisper of trees.

But Nana kept listening. Something else was here, too; she would swear it. Something swelling the air like a child's party balloon. Her left ear began to echo.

Water. It was the sound of running water. Of course, it was.

Steadily, the echo in her ear and the whispering of the trees blended into a trickle, and then a rush pulsing into something almost electric…and greedy.

There. *There*! Welcome back, Nana thought viciously. You fucker.

"Is it still here?" Rikki whispered.

Nana said nothing. More suffocating seconds passed. Finally, thank the damn Lake, the sounds faded away.

Tired, she rose to her feet. Tonight, she would go inside the house and sleep in her own bed. And before that, she would light candles, burn incense; say a few prayers. She had not done these small gestures in far too long. Life was like having a really lousy health insurance policy; you couldn't afford to get sick or old. Everything would knock you down if you let it.

"Think of a way to get rid of that woman and her family as fast as you can," she told Rikki. "Certainly, before the reenactment. For our sake as much as theirs."

*   *   *

Alone on the porch, Rikki took her sweet time finishing the sorting and folding of laundry. She was glad Nana had gone inside. Truth was, Rikki relished this kind of housework, especially when no one was watching her. There was something so simple and reassuring in the mindless touch of fresh white cotton; in how neatly life could be laid out and stored.

She finished her tasks, then stood with her back to the lake. She pushed the laundry basket toward the house, making scraping noises against the floor. Her foot still hurt like the dickens, and that was her own fault.

Nana was right; they had to be more diligent, more cautious, more reverent. You could not relax for a minute. Especially at this time of year, as the turning of the cycle approached.

She went to her room, sat on the bed to peel off the bandage and study her bluish-red skin. Ugly punishment, this was. Whether she deserved it or not. Rikki wrapped her foot tightly again before stretching out on the narrow bed of her childhood and closing her eyes. She wished she could vanish. She wished she were one firefly among dozens. Instead, here she was, stuck. On another Saturday night, with another family to warn off.

Not fair.

Why couldn't she just ignore the whole thing? Go to Maria's house and drink her stupid tea? Rikki missed her best friend. Missed talking to someone who approved of her. As young girls they used to enjoy sleepovers. That was a long time ago, before Rikki's mother disappeared and Daddy died.

Pushing her face against the pillowcase, Rikki closed her eyes. *Oh, Daddy. Can you see what this is like? Why did you leave?*

She envisioned his thin face, his hopeless head shake when Nana went on and on about obeying the Lake, manipulating neighbors like puppets, balancing unstable forces with rituals and symbols. Daddy had not believed the Lake could target anyone. But then he had died.

Rikki's limbs grew heavy. On the edge of sleep now, she pictured Shy Moon Lake the way she loved it: early in the morning. At that hour everything seemed brighter: not treacherous and unpredictable but lush with gifts.

Beauty. Nature. Sweet air. Possibility. Fairness. *If this place really has power, why can't it be for good?*

The pain came torpedoing out of the dark.

Rikki bolted upright, gasping. Clawing at her chest.

Can't breathe!

Was this her final punishment for all the doubts and fears? Heart attack? *Death?*

Or was it just a panic attack? Like Doc Taylor said…

She tried to clear her mind; tried to think rationally. This pain…he said it wasn't physical. Which meant she could breathe if she managed to relax.

One-two-three-four-five…hold—release. And again. One-two-three-four. Twice more she did the same thing, until her chest eased. Her breath became less jagged. *So, it's not the heart…*

Encouraged, Rikki focused on her room.

The huddled, purring cats, the fish swimming in their nasty tank, the plants on the windowsill; the shelves full of loved-to-death stuffed cats so old they spewed tiny balls of foam. She meditated on the glowing numerals of her bedside clock. One a.m. And she continued to count.

The attack had taken only a minute: half a minute less than last time. *Progress.*

But why had it happened at all? And sneaking up on her in her sleep this way….

When the monster completely receded—the burning gone and her thoughts no longer thrashing—Rikki stood up. She dislodged two stuffed cats and two real ones from her bed and limped across the house to check on Nana, who snored so loudly she sounded like a boat firing up under cover of night.

Rikki covered the frail old woman with a blanket and headed to the living room. This was the nicest room in the house, if you ignored all the photos propped on pieces of furniture so bulky, they looked like crouching animals. Rikki dusted regularly. She tried to keep their home attractive, though Nana practically lived on the porch. But how do you clean off one hundred and fifty framed photos of mostly dead people? Not to mention all kinds of doohickeys—glass animals, wooden carvings, feathery dream catchers, candles—that cluttered any space escaping the photos. No, this was not an easy house to care for.

Back in her own room, Rikki pulled on a pair of sweatpants under her nightgown. She dug in her closet to locate an old orthopedic boot from a previous injury, along with a single Ugg to balance the boot.

That contained the pain, helped her walk.

Her favorite pet, the mutt named Peaches, whined at the door. Rikki went into the kitchen to open a can. And when the cats heard the noise, they began meowing and hissing and pawing one another out of the way. She refilled their food bowls too, checked their water, and made sure all the burners were off. Finally, she was ready.

She clipped a leash on Peaches and pulled a hooded sweatshirt over her nightgown. At the last moment, she reached inside her closet to grab a symbol of protection and freedom: her father's shoes, the Hush Puppies he had walked in. She stuffed them in her backpack, flung open the front door, and plunged outside.

Trees merged around her. And for a moment—just a brief savory second—their music of frogs and crickets, and the thin soughing of pine needles, comforted her. As a little girl, Rikki had loved this path. She had adored trailing behind her Daddy, absorbing these lovely Earth sounds. She used to run fearlessly to the Indian grinding rocks and handprints. She even dipped her feet in the lake, and nothing happened to her. She splashed and played, exposed to the elements, believing Nature liked her.

Not knowing until she was grown just *how* it liked her.

Overhead, the moon hid behind clouds, obscuring what she would do next. Coincidence? Rikki released Peaches' leash, and he turned in circles and sat, his big tongue hanging stupidly. "Good dog."

Rikki fingered the package in her pocket. When she was ready, she poured the contents into her palm. Tobacco radiated warmth. She would not use too much of it: just a pinch, nothing wasted. Wasted wishes, wasted energy.

Can't just beg for mercy. Gotta sacrifice first.

Bending to sprinkle the fragrant shreds into the waiting mouth of water, she prayed: "Help me do right," though she wasn't exactly sure who she was asking. The Creator? God, or the gods, or her ancestors…or just the Lake?

As a small girl, Rikki had envisioned God as a giant mired in the lakebed. Then Nana explained that in and around Shy Moon Lake, more than any other spot in the world, Spirit dwells in every living and non-living thing. Due to the unique nature of the water and the minerals in the earth here, none of the Ten Commandments could be broken without severe repercussions. Around this one particular crater, divine justice ricochets back from every stone, tree, bird.

Whatever ye reap, ye shall sow—and quickly, as if God is in a hurry.

"It's bad for you and Nana to take this stuff literally," Doc had told Rikki during her last consult about the chest pains. "It isolates you and makes you paranoid. Haven't you ever heard of metaphors?"

Hmmph, she thought now. Metaphors? What did he know? He didn't live within the breath of the Lake.

"*Kwaltup Kwaltup,*" she said, using one of the few Native words her great-grandmother had taught her.

Hopefully, there was no need to get the gulping pronunciation perfect. All that mattered was that tobacco symbolized human effort and earthly enterprise. She did not know the meaning of the words, either, or what language it was; only that Mama had used the same words and performed the same rituals too, a long time ago.

Not that it had helped *her*.

"We're not bad people," Rikki said at the end of her prayer, pleading. "We try to do everything right. Everything you want. Be gentler with us. *Please*."

Peaches growled.

Rikki's head snapped up. She heard no crackling twigs, no shivering leaves: just the same old frogs and crickets and singing pine needles. She looked at the water, studied it hard. Tree shadows appeared to be traveling through it. Not over it; through it. Trees under the water?

She glanced at the dark sky. The moon was still hiding, not bobbing overhead along like a disembodied, half-cut clown face.

Peaches made another noise, more of a whimper this time. Rikki cradled him in the crook of her elbow.

Pulling a pocketknife from her sweatshirt, she swung out the largest blade and pressed its sharp tip into the pad of her left thumb. Her heart skipped and skidded like a flat rock along the surface of the lake. Blood swelled from the cut. It dripped into the water behind the floating tobacco, feeding the Lake with her Life Source.

Would that be enough? Or would she need to keep bleeding?

She held her hand over the water. Viscous fluid, blue-black in the darkness, swam down to feed the greedy Lake. Then, with the ritual finally over, Rikki stood up with the backpack that held her Daddy's shoes.

His precious, precious shoes.

She had not used them like this in a long time. Maybe tonight would help. Certainly, it could not hurt.

And if she had done everything right—if she were blessed for a change—she would not have to scare anybody ever again.

CHAPTER 5

ASSUMING THE DEAD REST IN peace, then we did not sleep like the dead.

At least I didn't.

Charlie curled beside me in his favorite position: a baby with his face mashed against the mattress, bum in the air. Okay, his bum wasn't exactly in the air. But he did exude innocence and bliss. No snoring or thrashing from my love; no muttering or sweating, even in an unfamiliar bed.

I did all of that and more.

Despite the cool night air, with the bedroom window open to night sounds and smells, I couldn't settle. Our high-weave cotton sheets twisted like vines. Luxurious pillows felt more like rocks. The nape of my neck dripped. My eyes burned at the edges, lids itching. And, of course, my head hurt. Images jumped at me like scraps of mismatched wallpaper. Trees and mountain road and immaculate trashcans and signs saying No Boating, No Swimming, No Breathing. Beautiful house, cheap house. Crazy, useless wall.

Should I ask about The Wall at City Hall? Did Shy Moon Lake even *have* a City Hall? Someone had to manufacture those stupid signs…

Of course, I could just live the thug life and tiptoe past the signs. Go swimming anyway. But what kind of role model would I be for Jonah?

To get myself to relax, I pictured the sky with countless stars. The sky leaning low to the ground as if to kiss it. Silhouettes of trees spreading in all directions: a sweet secret net. I almost smelled the lake water.

Then the vision changed.

Big hands rubbing suntan lotion onto my neck. My brother calling, *Last one in is a rotten egg!* The day I turned 13: no party, just the family, but the best birthday gift a water-lover could get—goggles with built-in nose rather than a snorkeling mask.

I hated having my nose covered. I had always feared drowning.

Funny I should end up living by a lake.

Locating a fresh spot on the bed, I curled into a ball, my mind churning out word bubbles.

Charlie, we need to talk.

No. I could do better than that. This summer, I would open up properly to the man I had married.

Charlie, I love you, you are the love of my life. I just have this little confession.

Too dramatic.

Marriage is about forgiveness, right? I don't want to disappoint you; that's the reason I've held back.

In my head, I could hear his response.

"You don't want to disappoint me? Then why not trust me to keep my commitments—for richer, for poorer?"

Because—and here my overdrive memory kicks back in—*because when I was with Jonah's father for three years, five months, three weeks, and four days, I told myself to trust him. Yet on that last day, he went to the pharmacy to buy medicine for Jonah's colic and never came home. Not dead, just free. Free of us. That does things to trust. Try to understand, Charlie.*

"I understand you think I'm like him," Charlie would say. "That shit-for-brains ex-husband of yours. You should know better!"

I do know better, I protest.

It's just that on a random Wednesday, I learned how wrong trust can be. Oh God, how I learned. I was wearing my flannel nightgown with the loose button and Jonah was cocooned in his flannel sack, the blue one with little triangles on it. That night something inside me died: some essential ingredient. Maybe these things do not grow back.

"And you say you love me? You can't have love without trust, Jess. You can't have it both ways. You have to accept what is—or live in the past."

Troubled, I fell asleep. Finally.

*   *   *

A fog lies over the lake. It dangles from trees like the shawl of an old woman.

The signs, I think. I need to obey the signs, or everything will go wrong.

Daylight has not blinked yet. Living things croak and chirp in the dark as I shove my bare feet into warm boots. The boots flap around. Are they Charlie's or my dad's? Why am I wearing them? I check on Jonah, who is sprawled on a stranger's couch, sleeping. The whole living room looks unfamiliar: that couch, a big chair, a desk; someone else's shelves. And boxes galore. The boxes are ours, at least, stacked and waiting for action.

I slip on a jacket, shove my hands deep into the pockets, and step outside.

The scent of pine greets me. My feet sink into the earth. My breath mists. Lake water gloaming from across the lane. I cross the gravel—*flap-crunch, flap-crunch, flap-crunch*—toward a big sign nailed to a tree. It is tilted, written in capital letters.

NO BOATING! NO SWIMMING!
(NO EXPLANATION!)
Ordinance #7-13.

This path crunches like broken shells. No one can see me, but I can see everything, as if I have on night goggles. I will swim if I want to. Why not?

I slip off one of my boots and poke a toe into the water. There is a rush of cold: *ouch!*

I yank out my foot. Press it against the cool ground, huddle deeper inside my coat, and try again.

There. I place one foot in the lake, find smooth stones to rest it on. *Ah, there!*

I feel strangely triumphant—and foolish. Why am I wading in the middle of the night, defying the Powers That Be? Especially when the Powers That Be is probably some old guy with a beard sitting with his shotgun, creating signs just to piss off visitors…

The water grows warmer. My foot tingles. Why did it seem so cold before? How silly. I pull off the other boot.

Warm, silky magic. Why would someone forbid this? Pleasure is a two-edged sword. Yin and Yang. Good and bad. Life and death.

I wonder whether anyone is watching: whether the line of cottages at my back might sequester another insomniac. Maybe the chick with the bad foot?

The water feels like a bath now. I could slip in the rest of the way, rest, sleep for centuries. In the distance, something floats. Someone else sleeping, too—or…?

Don't go, I think, along with its opposite: *Go. It's safe.*

Whatever is floating is not a bird or a log. Could it be a person?

Or two? The drowned lovers…!

The water caresses my knees. It has become opaque, almost brown, the floating thing barely visible. I reach down to savor watery smoothness. *This is what the womb must feel like to an unborn baby…a sack of indescribable comfort, a world within worlds. The brown water reaches for me, too.

It is the yearning of seagrass for wind. I go deeper.

In the water, a clump of dark matter turns. To my surprise, it is oval and knowing. I should dive in and say hello. Ask it what this place, why I have come.

Then:

"Jess, wake up. Do you know where the aspirin is?" says a tired male voice.

The husband.

*   *   *

I am in our new bed again, staring at Charlie's shadowy features. The digital clock shouts 2:12 AM! Charlie was sitting against the headboard, hand on the side of his head.

"Sorry to bother you, hon, but I have this awful headache. Any idea where we put the toiletries?"

"There's Tylenol in my purse," I croak through an impossibly dry mouth.

"Great. I'll go look. You go back to sleep."

I watched him leave the room and listened to myself say: *Stop.*

Except nothing comes out. The word pings uselessly inside my own head. With my skull throbbing, I think of my father's funeral. *He should have told me he was going to spackle the damn ceiling,* my mother screams. *I would have helped him!*

Charlie's footsteps moved down the hallway to the living room and into the kitchen. I listened, still dragged under a kind of muck. He hates women's purses. Maybe he will cart my purse back to me. I can wade through my own junk.

"Charlie?" I had just managed to push myself up to a sitting position when he appeared in the doorway.

"Jess…"

I flicked on the lights. He blinked. In his hand he held a small circular plastic device. "Jess, what is this?"

It was my container of birth control pills.

* * *

For an obscenely long moment, I did not speak. I could not think of a damn thing to say that was both honest and helpful. *I should have told him the truth a long time ago. Why didn't I?*

Meanwhile, Charlie examined the disk more closely. He even turned it upside down—as if there could be any doubt what it was. Then he placed the object on the foot of our bed, next to my real foot. His face had gone as gray as old stone.

"Jess," he repeated. This time his voice sounded both dead and full of wonder. "Why do you carry birth control pills in your purse?"

I almost lied again, almost said: They're just to regulate my period.

I did not, though. It was time to come clean. Way past time. "Charlie, I'm…sorry."

He stared. "Sorry?"

"Oh, Charlie. I wish—"

"You're saying you're on the pill? Why would you be on the pill when we're trying to…?"

"I don't know," I cried, meaning it. Because lying to save myself from the terror of breaking hearts, including my own—well, that was not a reason.

Charlie pushed his hands through his hair. It stuck straight up, making him look a little mad. "What the hell is going on?"

"It's…complicated. I wanted to tell you; I really did. But it was never the right time. And now—"

"—now I had to find *this*." He began to pace, a lion in a cage. "You've been lying to me. For how long? A year? Eighteen months? Our entire god-damn time together?"

My skin felt icy. My limbs were losing circulation. And my heart beat erratically: *thump-thump thumpthumpthump.* I recalled the water of my dream, how warm and comforting.

"Why didn't you just tell me?" Charlie demanded, voice cracking.

"I planned to! I swear it. In a few days I was going to tell you everything."

"A few *days*?"

"I should have done it right away. But I was scared."

"Of what? *Me*?"

Charlie had never been frightening. I couldn't get away with that. "No, I was scared to argue and disappoint you." *Or make you leave…*

He glared at me in a way I had never seen before. In a way I had hoped to never see.

"So, you pretended. Is that it, Jess? You sat around discussing fertility specialists with me if it came to that. Why not just say 'I don't want another kid'"?

"I wasn't thinking, Charlie. Not…at first. You said you wanted kids, lots of them. And I told you I didn't know if I could get pregnant again but would like to and…how do you take that back once you say it?"

"So, why lie in the first place?"

I touched his arm. He flinched away.

"Charlie. Please…listen. You know Jonah was a sickly baby. Mom had her cancer at the same time. Everything was awful. My mother dying…and raising a child without his father or grandparents. Jonah kept screaming for his daddy. He was only six months old when Mike left, but it tore him up."

"And *that's* your reason?" Charlie's normally merry eyes had gone so flat—oddly like the eyes of Mike Benson, the father Jonah didn't know; the ex-husband I was conjuring into this room with my words. "Sorry, but that's not good enough. You'd better tell me the whole damn story. And start at the beginning."

*   *   *

The beginning had, in fact, been Jonah's colic, which was so intense and relentless that even his pediatrician looked like he wanted to jump out of his high-rise window to escape my child's screaming.

From the moment Jonah was born—five weeks too early—he seemed to thrash and burn inside his own velvety skin. The poor baby could not rest in a car seat or sling, on my lap, or at my breast. He could not sleep other than passing out from exhaustion for a few minutes at a time. The doctor had no idea what to do. So, I turned to baby books for guidance. I researched colic until I could recite verbatim all the theories, about baby gas and bloating and connecting brain neurons. I discussed colic *ad nauseum* with my sick mother, my long-suffering friends, and even half-willing neighbors. I would have discussed it with the mail carrier if he had stayed still long enough.

In my distorted mind, mom's vomiting from chemo seemed related to my ineptitude. I could not leave her or my baby with a stranger even if we could afford the help. Mike was working late, and shoving ear plugs into his ears at night. My big brother David never showed up to change a diaper or empty a bedpan. He was too busy eating mushrooms for his vision quest in the far-off jungles of Brazil. In some of my least charitable moments, I hoped that *he* would be the one vomiting and screaming next, and that there would be no family around to help him.

Bit by bit I devolved into a disorganized, weeping mess. I began dropping things, as if my fingers were made of rubber bands. I made embarrassing, confusing mistakes like pulling down my pants to pee while lowering myself onto a dining room chair instead of the toilet. My back and neck ached from carrying Jonah, the writhing sausage, as I walked the floor—or washed and fetched for mom, who was mortified at her grandbaby's wailing. My ears rang; my nose ran. I had aged overnight, from the unattractive flap of belly, to the growing sense that life with all its rich possibilities already short-circuited.

"Your baby has a temporary nervous system problem," the doctor tried to reassure me. "Think of it this way. Jonah was premature. He is not quite ready for this world. A little raw, you could say. But don't worry; it will pass."

I did not mention the shameful, sick fantasies I had of shutting my son inside a dresser drawer. But *I* knew I had those fantasies, and I hated myself for them. I felt sure I would be punished.

Then, somewhere in the middle of all this pain, fatigue, and guilt, Mike left us. He said he was going to the pharmacy to fetch another bottle of Mylicon for the baby's tummy—though no medicine had ever helped before—and simply did not return.

He never even phoned.

For a long time, I could not believe my husband was missing. I refused to believe that new fathers could disappear in route from the local Walgreen's. Instead, I imagined him stumbling lost inside the store, desperately snatching little bottles of infant antacid.

Or maybe he had dropped dead...?

Sometimes I found myself wondering if I had died, too, and didn't know it. Wasn't there a Dante's Inferno for new mothers? I suspected I had postpartum psychosis. Scariest of all, I believed that both my baby and my mother really would die, which was what I deserved for getting so maudlin about caring for them.

These were terrible weeks, worse months. In the end, though, the doctor was right. Jonah turned six months old and stopped caterwauling. He started smiling and cooing, bringing joy to family, friends, neighbors, and mailman. Mom finally healed enough to go on disability and live with her sister. I went back to teaching halftime. I still had not heard from my estranged husband but thankfully had stopped wanting to.

By the time I divorced the missing Mike—who'd finally sent a postcard from Maui saying, "*Hey Jess, hope you two are well, sorry I had to leave to concentrate on myself...*"—I met a lean and happy Charlie McCortney eating sushi at a local restaurant. Jonah had just turned a healthy, inquisitive two. I had a job I liked, some money in the bank, and a perfect little family, though it came with a price.

I had become emotionally insular, like a neighborhood no outsider can enter because of its walls.

Despite that, I fell for Charlie in a big way. I never believed he might become another Mike. The only problem was his desire to have more children. Lots of them. I simply could not fathom bringing another child into this world, unless I had enough strength to raise two kids alone. In difficult times, one child poses a challenge. The idea of two made me want to lose myself at the local Walgreen's.

None of this was a reason to lie, though. Or keep the lie going.

Finished with my story, I squeezed Charlie's hand. "Do you understand…just a little?"

His fingers lay dead in mine. "I don't know. You should have trusted me. I'm not Mike."

"I know you're not, and I do trust you. That's not it."

"Then none of this makes sense." He pulled his hand free. "It's crap."

I agreed. Crap. The very same crap I had planned to shed in Shy Moon Lake. But we had not even been here a whole day…

"So, what happens now?" Charlie asked, his eyes averted. "Do you go off the pill and pretend you want more kids? Or am I supposed to forget everything and not mind that you lied?"

"Oh, Charlie." It hurt to speak his name. "I don't know. But I love you. And I'm sorry. I just wish—"

"Don't bother wishing. It's too late for that."

He turned and stalked out of the room, leaving me alone with my guilt.

As I deserved to be.

CHAPTER 6

CHARLES BARRON MCCORTNEY DID NOT consider himself a naïve kind of guy. Nor did he believe he was an idiot. He had instincts—good ones—and he knew his wife. Or thought he knew her.

Yet here he was, storming away from their new cottage in the middle of the night, his head as hard and heavy as a bowling ball. How could she do this to him? How could she lie about something so big and important, something that *mattered*?

Charlie could not remember the last time he'd been this angry. Normally he had miles of patience. Growing up in a family as big as his (seven kids!) had taught him some vital lessons about life. Back then, throwing a tantrum had been as pointless as reaching for a third helping of food; if he grabbed too eagerly or out of turn, either a parent or an older sibling would clobber him with the serving spoon.

So, his philosophy had always been simple. Never sweat the small stuff. Be polite, don't ruffle feathers, don't be greedy, and don't hold a grudge.

"Jess," he remembered saying when they first fell in love. "After we get married let's have a baby together. In fact, let's have lots of them." And she had said: "I don't know if I can get pregnant again because of what happened last time—but yes, let's try."

Why shouldn't he believe her? He had trusted Jess implicitly—and they had made love again and again, trying for just one of those future babies.

"Wouldn't it be something if this was the lucky time?" he had said just the other day. He remembered her mouth tasting a little sour, her carrot-y hair smelling of jasmine. As always, her body felt luscious to touch. He loved the freckles on her chest; savored gazing at her slim, muscular limbs, heart-shaped face, and cleft chin, all the while thinking of millions of microscopic sperm cells breast-stroking frantically toward the great yellow sun. *And number four million six hundred and fifty-four pulling ahead by one hundredth of a millimeter…*

Was it all a joke? If so, the joke was on him.

Turning away from the lake, Charlie began to sprint. He went past the stupid wall and up the slope toward the picture-perfect town with its old-fashioned streetlights and shops in Lego colors. And he was instantly out of breath. Due to the altitude? He didn't care.

Maybe I'll just keep running. Run right out of here. Out of this town, and out of her life.

He imagined Jess finding his footprints in the dirt. Let *her* feel discounted and betrayed.

Of course, she has already been betrayed, he told himself. The thought gave him pause, more than he wanted. So, he was paying the price for her ~~shit for brains ex husband~~? He was no Mike, goddamn it. That was the rub: *Because* he was no Mike, Charlie would end up facing his wife. He would find a way to forgive her. For God's sake, they had Jonah. Love did not just quit.

Did it?

Circling around the square, he glanced indifferently at the tidy streets, the charming lampposts, the hand-scrawled posters of some re-enactment festival. Then he glanced over at the anomalous dolphin fountain—and halted.

A floaty-looking figure hovered near the edge of the fountain. He reached for his glasses.

Yes…a tall, long-legged woman wearing jeans and nightgown and hooded sweatshirt, stood by the fountain, looking down into it as if making a wish.

He moved a step closer. She had a dog alongside her, and a boot on her foot. One orthopedic boot.

Ah. The neighbor from the Bates Motel…

He felt sleazy spying on her. But he could not resist easing closer; she seemed so—

His thoughts slammed to a halt again. The woman was not looking into the fountain, she was staring at a pair of shoes perched on the fountain's ledge. Big male shoes, oxfords. Beige. Mourning her injured foot? The lady's expression was rapturous as she bent down and lifted the shoes in both hands, as if transporting gold to a king.

Okay…so the new neighbor with the bad foot was wandering around town in the middle of the night to worship a pair of shoes on the ledge of a public fountain? That could happen.

He snorted. Go with it. *Fodder for poetry.*

"Excuse me," he called. "Miss Stevens?"

She turned in his direction, expression blank.

"I'm your neighbor. The new one, remember, from next door? Charlie McCortney. Are you, uh, all right?"

She smiled at him—more of a grimace—before doing an abrupt-face and hobbling away toward the wall and gate, the shoes still displayed before her.

Wow, he thought.

He sat down on the edge of that incongruous fountain and felt utterly unbalanced.

WHAT HAPPENED TO THE BIRDS?

CHAPTER 7

A LOON WOKE ME AT daybreak with its lonely laugh. *Wa-hahahahaha. Wa-haaaaaaa.*

Struggling to open my eyes, I thought: No, not lonely. Not laughter. This lamenting outside—from near the lake—is a wail from the damned.

I burrowed back under the covers. Truth is, I felt like never coming out. I hated the empty spaces all over the bed, for Charlie was not here with me. Hadn't been since he had charged out of the house during the night.

Well, of course he wasn't here. He was probably in Florida by now, having a beer with Mike, sharing war stories about me.

Wa-haaaaaaa.

Go ahead and wail, I silently told one of the most eerie birds in existence. I had once read about the history of loons stretching back more than 50 million years. *Wa-heeeeeel. Wa-hearme.*

Wa-Hear. Me.

I stumbled into the living room and found Jonah asleep on the couch, Charlie snoring on the easy chair by the fireplace. And I moved closer, with my heart weighing heavy in my chest.

Charlie's face showed that dark stubble he always got overnight. His long legs, clad in rumpled jeans, dangled carelessly over the arm of the chair. His left hand, the ringed one, had settled under his chin. Shadows showed under closed eyes. Even in sleep, a sour expression worried his brow.

My husband's spirit was crushed—and I had done the crushing.

Not a nice thing to live with.

Then I glanced at the living room windows, distracted by another thought. They were bare. Anyone could see in here. Miss Rikki Stevens might be down by the lake right now, focusing her binoculars. The idea turned my stomach. Why hadn't we realized this about the windows last night?

Need air.

Suddenly queasy, I flung myself outside.

If only I could shake off this awful thing I had done, lying to Charlie. I had damaged our marriage, perhaps forever. For the first time, we had not entangled our legs throughout the night, had not sighed dreams into each other's hair. At dawn we had not shared each other's lovely and unlovely features: the murmurs, the sweaty snuggles; the sour morning breath.

I missed all of it already—and deserved to miss it. No wonder the loon keened so plaintively. *Wa-ha.ha.ha.*

Looking up, I spotted the noisy creature. It was flying from treetop to treetop, around the periphery of the morning-gray water, showing striped black and white scarf, and black wings with white underneath. And I found myself envying it. Yes, envying a *loon*. It was graceful and free. What was I?

As I watched, the bird dipped lower. It touched the lake's shimmery surface, settled its weight—and started flapping wildly.

Uh-oh, I thought. What now?

This was not normal flapping. The wings spun ferociously, like gears stuck in neutral when they needed to go in reverse. *Whop-p-p-p!*

Was it trying to swim with its *wings…?*

Waves sloshed, and the *whopp, whopp, whopp* kept going. I thought of the "helicoptering" noise of a car racing on the freeway with windows cracked. Except this poor creature was not getting anywhere, not really. For an absurdly long time, it hovered on the lake's surface, thrashing. Until at last it accelerated, rose into the air, and vanished amongst the trees.

I slammed my bottom hard on the step of our porch. Okay, I told myself. Don't freak out here. So, what if a loon acts…loony?

Because birds do not do that, I thought. Not loons, anyway. They are water animals, unafraid of swimming.

Unless they're not allowed to swim here, either?

Now I was being ridiculous. I laughed aloud, sounding raucous and crazier than normal.

But afterward, I felt better. I really did. Having lost my mind a little, the air seemed to settle around me like an old coat. I sunk down a bit and let myself be comforted.

I was fussing too much.

Whatever the birds did or did not do, this place was tantalizing. Much better than the photos on the website. And right now, I had it all to myself. No one else witnessed the drowning-loon thing, far as I could tell. No man or woman happened to be outside enjoying a morning run or walking a dog. No visitors wandered about disobeying signs. At this moment, no waterfowl were out either, no critters flying. No sound of stirring from inside the cottage behind me.

All mine.

Slowly, I began to feel less like laughing or crying. I kind of liked the idea of going over to that forbidden lake, just to touch its surface. No harm in that, I thought. If Shy Moon Lake was a precious, unsullied jewel, weren't we meant to savor its beauty?

This amazing volcanic crater was like…like the source of everything: the bellybutton of the world.

All that vivid, untouched, inviting water…and trees and mountains and shrubbery and boulders rising boldly and nimbly onto neighboring crags, so people could look jealously down. Those houses perched up there were too far away, big homes with large windows offering faraway views. Those people did not live here.

But I was lucky. *I* did.

My head throbbed for a second—a pressure in the ears. Not at the base of the skull or behind my eyes, not my normal headaches at all. More like a sinus infection.

I rubbed the left ear and stood and stretched. All seven houses on this road were unmistakably charming: wooden and fresh and beribboned with heart-warming raised porches. Who could ask for anything more?

Except these homes, these cottages, should be almost impossible to afford. Why weren't they? The highest point of land on the adjacent mountain reached a jagged peak above town, looking for all the world like the back of a Therapod dinosaur. Definitely impressive.

Still rubbing my ear, I skipped down the steps to the narrow lane that connected the houses. But I did not cross over it to make the final descent to the lake. Instead I turned right and wandered toward the wall, deep in thought. If this fairy cluster of homes had taken advantage of erosion to get close to beauty, then why complicate access to it with a wall covered with useless signs…and a gate nobody bothered to lock?

What Mrs. Pattack had said about private property and municipal land—well, that didn't make much sense either.

The private areas could be cordoned off and leave the public part alone. And those signs could not be official; why didn't anyone take them down?

The lake drew my gaze back in that direction, almost against my will: colors shifting nimbly in the early-morning light. Under diminishing fingers of mist, shadow and light oscillated across it like sprites.

You would think the water-birds would love it here. You'd think—

I stopped, squinted.

Something appeared to be floating out there on the lake. Not a bird. Bigger, and quite a distance off. An illicit boater? Fisherman?

No, the shape was larger still, and farther away.

I realized I was looking at an island.

Rocky, crowned in evergreens, perched right there in the center of the lake. How had I missed it before? And why hadn't Charlie and I noticed a freaking *island* in any of the photos online?

My eyes felt itchy, as if sand had scraped under the eyelids. I rubbed my face and looked again.

Not an island.

A fallen tree, maybe; floating, dying boughs upraised? Or I was seeing things, maybe because of—

A shrill voice rang out in the morning air, killing my thought.

"Hellooooo, good *moooooorning!*"

I whirled around, half-expecting to see the loon again, flapping.

Instead, a human female in her 60s walked briskly in my direction along the drive—also waving her arms as if she, too, really wanted to fly.

* * *

She wore a crisp sweat-suit, bright green, with a fluttering green and gold scarf that transformed her into the Jolly Green Giant at a garden party. And her fine aristocratic features did not go well with that sweat-suit, either. Nor did her delicately sculpted nose, high cheekbones, and sharp hazel eyes.

"So! You must be the new neighbor. I'm Mrs. Spiro!" she said, flashing a set of even, overly white teeth that screamed "dentures."

I smiled back and shook one of her rather large hands. She must have been over six feet tall, almost as big as Charlie. Her hand felt warm and dry.

"You look a bit cold, my dear," she said, eyeing my nightgown.

I laughed, embarrassed. "Oh, that's right. Excuse me, it's our first morning here, so I couldn't resist wandering outside. Everything is so beautiful."

"Yes, isn't it? I operate an inn, behind those trees on the other side of the wall."

She did not live in the cottages, then. Which meant she hadn't obeyed the KEEP OUT signs on the wall.

Amused, I looked where she pointed. The rooftop of a handsome large house peeked over the wall between swelling greenery.

"Shy Moon Lake Inn," Mrs. Spiro said proudly, as if the name were somehow more original than all the other "Shy Moon Lake" emporia we had seen. "My house was the second built in this area by the Europeans, burnt down once, and renovated five times. We have lived here for generations. Perfect location, too. Closest to the lake without being"—a delicate pause—"too close."

Too close?

"Did you come here alone?" she asked.

This was a small town all right. I said, "No, my husband and son are in the house sleeping."

She asked where we had come from, how we had heard of Shy Moon Lake; and what had made us choose a lakeside cottage over one of the more valuable homes at higher elevations. And when I mentioned Mrs. Pattick, she nodded with satisfaction, as if she had suspected as much.

Then she reached into the pocket of her sweatshirt and withdrew a square of cloth.

"I brought a gift," she said almost shyly. "For our new arrivals, to welcome you and ease the way."

Ease the way? I stifled an urge to giggle.

She handed me a…potholder. It was colorful and handmade and embroidered with intricate Gothic script. "Go on, read the inscription."

"*Whatsoever a man soweth, that shall he also reap,*" I read aloud. "Oh, how…thoughtful. Thank you. Did you make this yourself?"

"Yes, indeed. There's more writing on the other side."

I turned over the potholder to silently read the second aphorism: *I am a sorcerer. I have created and will continue to create my own world.*

"That's…lovely, too. But…" A chill at my neck made me trail off. Why this quote, for me and my family? Unless the potholder meant to call a cook a sorcerer? Which made sense, sort of…

"The first quote is from the Bible, as I'm sure you know," Mrs. Spiro said conspiratorially, as if we were two girls at school sharing delicious gossip about the top quarterback. "The other comes from the Jewish Kabbalah. Though they both could have originated here in Shy Moon Lake if you ask me."

"Oh. Well, this is a beautiful piece of work. And an…interesting blend of ideas. Are there a lot of churches in Shy Moon Lake? Or synagogues?"

"Not even a Hindu temple." She emitted a surprisingly delicate giggle. "Perhaps I should stop now. I usually don't care to squelch myself, but some things do need time."

"We're going to be here all summer," I said, thinking for the first time: *just* for the summer. "Is there something we should know?"

"Only that this is a place of legends, Mrs. McCortney."

"Please, call me Jess."

"Jess. You may think me a bit forward, but you should know that there are stories. You will hear things. Maybe even see things. And you will have questions."

"Ah," I said, glancing toward the lake. I did not see the floating log anymore and did not want to be caught searching for it.

"Remember, when you need to talk, I'm right on the other side of the wall," Mrs. Spiro said. "Practically a neighbor!"

"Thanks. I do have one question, if you don't mind. These stories… do they have to do with the, ah, lovers who drowned in the lake? I read about them."

"Oh, yes, in those silly brochures." She touched an orange-painted nail to her chin. "The truth is always more complicated than any bit of propaganda, don't you think? Mistakes may not be forgiven here, but it's not always as dire as all that."

Was this a joke? This nice lady was turning out to be as batshit crazy as Mrs. Pattick and Rikki Stevens of the Bates Hotel.

Mrs. Spiro's voice turned bright again.

"Oh, just listen to me go on! Please excuse an old hen for liking to talk. I suggest you hang my gift in your kitchen where you can see it, and we will visit another time, after you are more settled. I do love to babysit youngsters, by the way, if you and your husband have need. You may ask around town for a reference. Everyone can vouch for my character."

"That's very nice of you." *Over my dead body.*

After we said goodbye, I made a beeline for home and shoved the potholder in a kitchen drawer.

Then I sat, numb, in the living room. Charlie and Jonah were still sound asleep. I spent a long moment watching them, thinking about the innkeeper and the loon—and my marriage. Would Charlie forgive me? Good God, we were still newlyweds! I had to make it up to him. But how? I had already apologized. And I couldn't change the past.

The future, then. Only…did that mean having a pack of kids I did not want?

These boys might sleep all morning, I decided, and with some effort, shook off my gloom. We had moved here for the summer to create good family memories. *So, create them!* There must be other, more normal people with children around here… playmates for Jonah.

I just needed to find them.

With that fixed in mind, I got dressed, and scribbled a note for Charlie, and left the house again. And this time I carried with me a tray of neatly wrapped loaves of homemade banana bread that I had brought to Shy Moon Lake for exactly such a purpose.

*   *   *

I started at the end of our road—a cul-de-sac, really—farthest from the gate. The first two houses appeared abandoned. I knocked anyway while another loon—or maybe the same—complained overhead. I waited awhile, then left those porches, taking my loaves with me.

The third cottage hid its windows behind thick shutters like eyes screwed shut against the light. I figured no one would be home there either. I felt a prickling on the back of my neck, as if someone were watching from a gap in the shutters. But I saw no one.

A few people did emerge down the road through the pointless gate: a middle-aged couple heading toward the boat-less docks, and behind them, a kid riding his bike.

If I could not find anyone at home, I decided, I would offer that kid a loaf, and maybe the couple too.

The fourth cottage had a fresh lick of paint. Up close, though, the surface appeared thin and bumpy and a little discolored, as if new paint had been slapped over the old without scraping or priming. A garden, penned in with a short white fence, boasted two bright tomato plants.

Someone definitely lives here, I thought. Sweet eyelet curtains stirred behind the front window. But glancing into the glass, I saw only my own face looking and my own arms carrying the tray.

Then the door swung open.

I nearly dropped the bread.

"Hello," said a high-pitched female voice.

The woman—if you could call her that—was sort of a waif, surprisingly middle-aged in face, old in hair, and pre-pubescent in body. She wore a modest cotton dress from a different decade, her small white hands clutched the edge of the door as I introduced myself. Then she offered me a soft, limp handshake with a whispered name: Hannah Mason.

Was she ill? Another member of the Bates family?

Already wary, I explained that I lived two doors down and offered her a loaf of bread. To my surprise, she accepted it. Keeping my voice upbeat and friendly, I added something about arriving last night with my husband and preschool-age son.

That was when Hannah's expression changed, flourishing into something warm and bright. It made her much prettier and more normal looking than she had been a minute ago.

"Oh, I do love children, especially young ones!" she enthused.

"Yes, they're so fresh and honest," I said.

"Will he attend…school?"

"In the fall, yes, but not here."

"Yes. Oh, that's good." Did she seem relieved? She added, "Your family *bought* the Thurston place?"

"Thurston?"

"The family that used to live there."

"Oh right, Mrs. Pattick mentioned them. Yes, we did."

"And you…like it?"

"Sure. Everything is beautiful." Our conversation seemed to stall out, so I returned to the topic of children. "My little boy adores all the trees."

"Of course, he does! Who doesn't love a tree? I adore watching children play outdoors. I don't have any of my own, you see."

"Well, you're welcome to entertain my little monster any time," I said lightly.

Hannah nudged the door a fraction toward closing. "I should go now. Thank you for the bread."

"Wait." I suppressed an impulse to block the door with my foot. "I was wondering, do you know if there are any kids in these cottages? I knocked on a few doors, but no one answered."

"No. No little ones here."

"Ah, too bad."

"Yes," she said, door closing another inch.

"People do *live* here, though. Right? The cottages aren't empty?"

"No, not for long. They never stay empty long."

From somewhere behind me, I could hear the kid on the bike. He was singing loudly and painfully out of tune: about worms going in and going out.

"I'm sorry, I can't talk," Hannah whispered, eyes tilted toward the singing. "Goodbye."

And she shut the door in my face.

*   *   *

Walking toward Cottage Number Five, I had to dodge the bike. It swerved up and down the street as if its rider, a thin boy of about ten with shaggy hair, was shit-faced drunk.

"Hey, careful," I called out.

The boy waved back enthusiastically, like he appreciated the feedback.

Glad I made your day, I thought.

The front door of the next cottage was wedged open, Mozart's *Requiem* playing within. When I rapped on the doorjamb, a lanky teenager with pimples peeked out (a teenager listening to *Requiem*?). He had short, heavily moussed hair, bleached blond stubble, a bumpy nose, and intelligent eyes. His voice was the familiar adolescent monotone.

"Good morning. Help you?"

I introduced myself and asked if his parents were in. When he said no, I offered him a loaf of banana bread anyway. He declined politely, saying thank you about three times, and disappeared back inside, shutting the door in my face.

Again.

Confused more than disappointed, I had just returned to the road when a voice said, "Excuse me?"

Whirling around, I saw the teenager again—or a facsimile. This version had the same nose, the keen eyes and thin face, but with better skin. He was wearing shorts, a tee shirt, and white socks, no shoes.

"You're a twin," I said. "I just met your brother."

"I know." Grown-up-like, the boy thrust out his hand. "Name's Steve. Pleasure to meet you. I don't know if my brother was polite enough, so I wanted to thank you for coming. Thanks for being friendly and introducing yourself and offering him"—a glance at my tray—"*that*."

"Oh, your brother did thank me. Three times, in fact. No worries."

"Good. He sometimes forgets. Uh, I'll be seeing you. *Ma'am*," he added, with a furtive glance at the lake, as if it might be listening.

"You can call me Jess."

"'Kay. Miz Jess. Nice to meet you."

I smiled. "Is everyone around here so polite?"

"We try." He did not smile back.

"That's…nice. Refreshing. Would you like a loaf of bread, too? I have plenty."

He squinted at the tray. "What kind?"

"Banana. Here, take one."

I pressed a loaf into his hand—and jumped back as this perfectly composed boy cried out and swung his arm around, smacking the loaf away, sending it soaring like a culinary baseball.

It landed on the lane with a small *plthh*. I gaped at him, speechless.

He glared, with his eyes bright, angry; even terrified. All serenity and manners gone. "Shit! Are you crazy? I'm fucking allergic! If that thing—that *bread*—has *nuts* and touches me, I'm fucking dead!"

Before I could respond, someone else spoke. *You freak of nature, you betrayed me!*

What?

No one was with us, just me and the kid.

Must be another memory, I thought.

Except there was no pain in the base of my skull, no further minutiae leaping out at me. No recollection of where, when, and what I was reliving, which day of the week or the time or what I was wearing or eating and why.

Besides, no one in my life had ever called me *freak of nature*. I felt sure of it.

In sixth grade, Dimples Denise had called me "batty" because I feared getting clobbered during softball practice. I had been called "dufus" and "space cadet" and "brainiac." But never *freak of nature*.

The teenager with the nut allergy still clutched the sides of his head.

"Are you okay?" I asked, stepping forward to help him.

At that moment, out of the corner of my eye, I glimpsed the bicyclist careening at us—and I dropped the tray. I plowed my shoulder against the nut allergy twin, pushing him backward.

The bike swerved; brakes screeched.

In absurd, slow-motion ballet movements, we all toppled down. The bike wobbled and fell in the other direction, one wheel spinning madly. Lumps of banana bread lay ruined under my hips.

Slowly, the scene settled into place. Country sounds descended: buzzing insects, a bird cawing, some dog yipping from far away. My sanity also returned, replacing that awful voice in my head.

That *other* voice. Whoever it was.

The kid with the bike extricated himself. "Wow," he said disgustedly, brushing himself off. "Just wow. That coulda been bad."

"It *was* bad, asshole," spat the teenager. He stood, too, and looked like he was going to lunge at the kid.

Then, to my surprise, he glanced at the lake and hesitated. His jaw tightened and a smile spread over his face.

"Please be more careful," he said to the boy with the bike. And to me: "We are both very sorry, Ma'am, to cause you any problems. Forgive our rudeness."

By the time I found my voice, the biker had peddled off and the twin was striding up the steps to his cottage.

"It wasn't your fault," I called after him. "It was an accident!"

"Maybe," he said over his shoulder, voice loud and clear. "But I do apologize. For my language and for everything else I, uh, did."

"That's okay," I said. "Really! And…have a…uh, nice day!"

Suddenly I felt very, very homesick.

CHAPTER 8

"MR. REED DOESN'T CALL ME Miz Grit anymore," Rikki said glumly.

She and Nana sat on the porch with their morning tea, Earl Gray with just a touch of milk. Not really enjoying each other's company but as used to each other as fleas on a dog.

"What?" Nana said, watching the lake, as usual.

Rikki sighed. The day had grown uncomfortably warm already. For the next two months the weather would only become hotter and drier, until it was like kindling begging for a match. A storm might offer occasional relief. But their cottage did not have air conditioning. Even if one day they could afford a cooling system. they would never get one; too many opportunities for the equipment to whir and knock and drip and leak and who knew what else.

Instead, they sweated here on the porch, along with whatever flies sneaked in and then flung themselves at the screen trying to get back out.

"Mr. Reed," Rikki repeated. "When I went to get your prescriptions yesterday, we talked a bit. He used to be so nice, he gave me things. Now it's 'Miz Rikki this, Miz Rikki that,' with this tone, like he expected more of us. I think he's disappointed."

"I don't give a fig what he is," Nana said, still glaring at the lake. "When I was a girl, we called him 'Lil Jon. Little runt of a thing, when his brothers were so tall and twice as bright. Yet they dropped dead a decade ago and here he is still wasting his breath."

"He was nice to me…after Daddy died."

"Is that a fact."

Rikki looked at the lake, too, and stepped hard on her resentment. Nana always went on about rectitude and balance and harmony, yet never did she hesitate to snipe or complain when it suited her. "Do *you* think I've lost my grit?"

No response.

"Nana?"

The old woman finally turned away from the water to reach into her craft basket. Her current "project" was to become a scarf, apparently, if she finished it, if she didn't die first. The scarf, a mean-looking brown, sagged and stretched and grew little unexplained bumps, not unlike Nana's skin.

"Grit for what?" she said at last.

"I think he means doing something with my life. Like I'm a coward for staying home with you," Rikki said.

"Where else would you go?"

"I don't know. But…I'm not a coward. Am I?"

"I told you, don't listen to gossip. No one understands what you go through except me."

"But do you think he's right?"

"About what?"

"That I'm a *coward*."

"How would I know? What you are is unemployed," Nana said. "Every summer it's the same thing. You work some before that excuse of a school closes and money stops rollin' in. Maybe that's what he means by losing your grit."

Rikki slapped her hand down on the table. The cups jumped.

"No, he doesn't mean that! And no one else will *hire* me, you know that. Especially now, with my foot. I can't even wait tables!"

"That does put a crimp on things," Nana said, smiling a little at her awful joke.

Rikki tried not to cry. "Anyway: if I worked more, who would take care of *you*?"

"No one. It's your job."

That was when Rikki realized what her grandmother had wanted all along. *Go get work* meant: *Tell me again that you won't leave me.*

Nana needed her as much as she needed Nana. They were family. It was perfectly normal for Rikki to wake up every morning wondering whether today would be The Day, when Nana would not awaken, leaving Rikki officially alone with the Lake. Anyone would feel this way, in the same circumstances. She and her only relative worth a damn were bound together in history, destiny, and purpose.

"Mr. Reed says we're superstitious," Rikki said.

"Oh, did he?" Nana shot back. "Yet he isn't foolish enough to come on this side of the wall, is he? Just stays over there, nice and safe in his castle on the hill."

A fly was scuttling on the screen door now, searching for freedom. In fact, Rikki could reach over and pluck off its puny legs if she wanted to—or release the poor thing outside.

The choice was hers.

Was that crazy? To feel powerful because she could manipulate a *fly*?

God manipulated things all the time, didn't he? Or *She*...

"If I had grit, I *would* go Below," Rikki burst out—and watched Nana's expression crumple.

"You listen to me, child, and listen good. We can't leave the Lake. You and I live here, and we will die here. The only question is *how* and *when*—and that's up to you."

Suddenly, a scream pierced the air.

Heart pounding, Rikki scrambled to her feet.

The scream was followed by a clang of metal like garbage cans falling over.

"Oh no," she murmured, for she knew instantly what it was.

For only *one* new family had moved into the cottages.

Only *one* family had recently added to the legacy that stretched back so many generations.

Only one new woman by the lake was of child-bearing age and was already as manipulated as these flies on the porch.

"You see, it's getting time," Nana said, also knowing. "No time like the present to get it done."

CHAPTER 9

THE LAST TIME I GOT knocked down by a bicycle was on August 4, two days after my seventh birthday—and Gunnar Von dem Knesebeck had done it on purpose.

After running me down, he sat on his bike smirking for all the world to see. His Levi's were dirty at the knees, his Yankees ball-cap shadowing green eyes that managed to reflect no evil at all. He was an ash-blond kid, tall for his age; already a known sadist who plucked the legs off spiders and then raced over their circular remains. Gunnar's bike—a battered blue Schwinn with a banana seat his little sister had peppered with girly stickers—was his weapon of choice. One time he had run over a black kid's toes simply because they got in the way. Gunnar also liked to torment cats by banging his bike into fences wherever they lay purring in the sun.

So, when he hit me with his bike on the sidewalk in front of my driveway, I wasn't particularly surprised.

Nor did I expect him to be sorry. Maybe If I had cracked my head open, he would feel a twinge of guilt. Or if I died. Then maybe the adult Von dem Knesebeck would find God *before* prison rather than after.

He knocked me down on purpose, I thought on that long-ago sidewalk. And I thought the same thing now in Shy Moon Lake: *That kid knocked me down on purpose.*

Why?

I looked up the lane, to where the kid was straddling his bike, talking to his parents. They scowled at me, then hustled their progeny toward the gateway in the wall. I touched my forehead, came away with a dot of blood on my fingertips. No brain fluid, though. I was not going to die. I just needed a Band-Aid.

"Are you all right?" called a female voice, from the cottage next door.

She of the purplish hair and injured foot stood on her porch step, staring blankly at me. Did she cultivate that expression?

"Yes, I'm just dandy. Had a little bike accident, that's all." I nodded at the tray lying on the roadside. One or two of the loaves looked more-or-less intact. "Would you like some banana bread? I was going to bring you a loaf anyway. Oh—and it has nuts in it."

To my surprise, Rikki Stevens smiled: the first genuine smile I had seen on that woman.

"I love nuts," she said, before hobbling down to get her loaf.

*   *   *

Inside the house, Charlie and Jonah were awake, watching TV. Both looked up in alarm at the mess of my face.

Jonah jumped to his feet and threw both skinny arms around my waist. "Mommy, you're bleeding!"

"Hey pal, take it easy, let me see," Charlie said, pushing back my hair to study my scalp. "Mm, not too bad. Better come into the kitchen—I found the first aid kit."

The kitchen was stuffy, as if the windows had been shut for years. Of course, the shade from an oak tree outside kept this room closed and shadowed, nothing like the rest of the cottage. The ceiling light blinked once, then steadied.

Charlie began cleaning my cut while I recited a much doctored and purposely vague story about bikes colliding. My husband unwrapped a SpongeBob Band-Aid and stuck it on my forehead.

There was a *tick-tick-tick* sound overhead. The kitchen light went out.

"Oh, what now," he muttered.

Behind us, the refrigerator vibrated with a throbbing rattle. I turned to look at it—and gasped.

For in the wall next to the refrigerator was an ugly hole the size and shape of a serving bowl. I stared at it in shock. This hole in the wall was new. It had not been there yesterday. I tried to imagine Charlie venting his anger—his anger at *me*—on the kitchen wall.

Impossible.

"That's a big hole," enthused Jonah. "Daddy made it!"

"Oh really. Well, tell me about it. I'm all ears," I managed to say in a reasonable sort of way.

Shamefaced, Charlie said, "I'm really sorry, Jess, I was about to tell you."

"I'm sure you were."

"It's kind of hard to explain. But when Jonah and I woke up this morning, there were noises coming from that wall. All this knocking and thumping, even a gushing sound. I was afraid a pipe had broken. So, I tried to figure it out."

"With what? A sledgehammer?"

He winced. "No. More of a...kitchen tool. A meat tenderizer, I think."

"You beat a hole in the wall with a *meat tenderizer*?"

"I really am sorry. I don't know what I was thinking. I'll plaster the wall, promise. I just wanted to"—glancing again at Jonah—"stop the noise."

"He said it was making him crazy," Jonah said helpfully.

I had the absurd impulse to laugh. It's all of us, I thought. We are untethered. What do we do next?

"Well," I said. "Did you…learn anything? About the leak?"

"No. There aren't even any pipes back there. Of course, it could be *under* the house. If it is a leak."

"What else could it be?"

"Who knows. Hopefully, a plumber can figure it out."

"I just can't believe we didn't check everything out before we put down money."

"Jess, we had an assessment."

"No, that Pattick lady had an assessment done, or did it herself. We just trusted her pictures. How sick is that?"

Jonah blurted, "Mommy, do you want me to use my doctor's kit, too? To help you feel better?"

I smiled at him, and he ran out of the room to fetch his blue plastic kit. Then, whooping with excitement, he hauled it onto the kitchen table and peered inside. "Mm, maybe this will help." He withdrew a yellow hammer. "These." Gray and blue stethoscope. Popsicle stick. Plastic thermometer. "And *this*." More SpongeBob bandages.

When Jonah stuck the thermometer between my lips, it tasted like sawdust. "Thank you so much," I said.

"I think you need a hospital," he announced to the room, and wandered away, either searching for a hospital or losing interest in his patient.

At least I won't have to pay the medical bills, I thought with another urge to giggle. Then I looked at Charlie's face. He wore an expression I didn't quite recognize: part exasperation, part embarrassment, part…fear?

He said, "I'm going to get a little air, if you don't mind. Clear my head. Maybe I'll go into town, ask about a plumber."

"Charlie, wait." When I touched his arm, it felt as stiff as a bannister. "Where did you go last night? To town?"

He nodded.

"Oh. You were gone a long time."

Another nod.

"Is it as nice as we thought?" I asked in a lighter tone.

"Sure. As far as I could tell at night," Charlie said.

"Before you go out, there's something else I have to tell you. About the accident I had today."

Charlie waited. I forced myself to continue.

"I heard something out there, like one of my memories…but different. I mean, normally, when I get a 'memory' I know exactly *who* and *what* I'm thinking about. You know, like in a YouTube video. It gets switched on and I see everything, usually mundane stuff that doesn't mean much."

"Okay."

"But this morning…it was detached. Loud and clear, but not… well, *mine*."

Charlie said nothing.

"The voice came from inside my head, of course, but it wasn't anybody I ever knew. Not like one of my memories at all."

"Ah…okay," he said, sounding only slightly okay himself.

Sometimes my syndrome did make me feel a little nuts, as if I were dragging all of my memorabilia around in a suitcase without wheels. But I had never felt *this* nuts…and Charlie wasn't helping.

I slumped back on the kitchen chair, recalling how Shy Moon Lake had appeared at dawn. The pure, unsullied beauty of it…

"Don't cry," Charlie said, stepping closer. "Come on, honey. It'll be okay."

* * *

I looked up at him gratefully, at his dear troubled face with the poet's scar. "Oh, Charlie. I feel awful about everything that's happened. I'm so sorry I hurt you. Do you think you'll ever forgive me?"

He took a long time in answering. "I think so. I want to forgive you. I just can't turn it on and off like a faucet."

"That's okay," I said. "You need time. Time is good."

He leaned in to kiss me, and his lips were warm, hinting at the loving man I had married.

"Hey," I said. "If Jonah takes a nap later, maybe we can spend a little quality time together. Just the two of us?"

He said nothing…and that seemed wrong, too.

"Remember before we got married?" I said, over-bright and trying too hard. "How we used to…*indulge* while Jonah was watching cartoons? And we knew it was okay because he never came into a room without screaming for us first. Everything was okay as long as we worked fast. Fast and furious…"

When Charlie still did not speak, I thought: *Stupid. Why do I sound stupid?*

We had always enjoyed silliness together, even celebrated it. Like last year when Jonah's daycare program did a skit on playground safety, Charlie made a costume of boards and buckets to transform himself into a seesaw, while I fashioned a hat out of a basketball hoop and threw Styrofoam balls at my own forehead. Later—with Jonah fast asleep—basketball and free play found mutual ecstatic expression, and I loved every moment of it.

This was *Charlie* with me. No need to feel foolish!

"You look cute all scruffy like this," I said, still trying despite myself, running my hand across his chest, down his faded work shirt to the bulge in his pants. A nice thing, that bulge. For a moment, I was so relieved I wanted to sing.

Then the bulge deflated under my hand.

Charlie gently disentangled himself from me. "Sorry, Jess, now's not the time or place. And I really do need that walk."

As if on cue, Jonah ran back into the kitchen, wearing his Superman cape and proving Charlie's point about times and places. Having dressed himself, my son also wore his sweatshirt backwards and his shorts inside out. Across the bridge of his nose he balanced Charlie's designer sunglasses, which were new and tinted and cost about eight hundred bucks. My purse dangled over Jonah's shoulder, completing the picture. Hermaphroditic and very, very busy.

Caught between a laugh and a sob, I said, "Nice outfit, buddy," just as Charlie said, "Nice cape," and left the room without retrieving his glasses.

He jogged down the steps and away from us and the cottage.

WHOSE VOICE IS THIS?

CHAPTER 10

AS SOON AS HE WAS free of the cottage, Charlie began to run.

Normally he welcomed the burn and cramp of sprinting, which signaled life and vitality and change. He liked fatigue and sweat: the triumph of converting simple mobility into sport.

But today was different. Today he just felt old.

Crossing through the wall's gate into town, Charlie took random turns, his thoughts sticky and grim. A single question snarled in there like used packing tape: *How did my marriage get so screwed up?* He had no answer to that, doubted if anyone did.

And now the street abruptly ended in a cul-de-sac, providing the perfect metaphor for his life. The sweet little houses looked a little wrong, a little crooked, as if a God-like pinball wizard had tilted the table, throwing askew houses, cars, trees.

Must be the altitude, Charlie thought. I need oxygen.

He turned around and found his way to a different street, not jogging anymore but taking firm, fake-it-till-you-make-it steps. One street led to another. At long last he reached the rear entrance of a hardware store on the back side of Main Street. A sign read: *Shy Moon Lake Hardware.*

He snorted. The mountains around this town were so very dramatic, yet the stores had the blandest names—as if their owners had become overwhelmed by all the beauty outside and could not conjure up even the smallest bit of their own from within.

Like me?

He continued down Main Street, following the perimeter of the square until he crossed over to the fountain. This thing is also strange, he thought. Dolphins happened to be his favorite critter. If he had not gone into law like his father, he might be a marine biologist by now. He'd be working with dolphins; studying them, playing with them rather than living off the ol' family trust fund.

But I don't practice law, and I don't work with dolphins. I'm a spoiled wannabe poet trying to find myself. Jess isn't the only one with issues.

He was part of the problem, then. It took two people to make a marriage—and destroy one.

"Hey, darlin', you dozed off," he remembered saying to her just the previous weekend. "Come on, Jesse James; time to get rollin' before the little one rouses himself." Classic Jess, she had groaned and burrowed into the pillow. You *worry about the kid today, Romeo,* her body seemed to say. *It's your turn…* So he nudged her. Blew on her hair, tasted her skin, and savored the salt. She opened one eye then the other: dark green eyes hinting of mischief even if the mischief hadn't quite woken up yet. Had she been thinking about it then: thinking about *not* making babies?

Charlie shook away the memory, left the fountain, and headed home without stopping to ask about plumbers. When his eye caught the glitter of lake-water spangling like cut glass, he looked away. He walked mechanically, to the gateway, and from there to the middle cottage and up the porch steps—and then stopped.

From the corner of his eye he spied movement in a window next door. A figure twisting furtively. Was Rikki Stevens watching *him*?

He fumbled in his pockets for his prescription sunglasses before remembering that Jonah had them. He squinted at the neighbor's house. Even without his glasses, half-blinded by the glare of sunlight on siding, he could see a shape standing at the side window. Probably *her* shape: the lady with the purple hair and bad foot. Rikki. He was about to look away when another thought hit him.

I shouldn't be able to see inside that window with the sun the way it is.

But he could see her, quite clearly. See that strange young woman standing directly in front of the window, staring pensively toward the lake. Despite the pallor and purplish hair, she had a pretty face. He fancied he could make out her eyes: eyes like black raisins.

Oh, so now you're a Peeping Tom?

This was wrong, like everything else. Watching that woman was not something he would normally do. Still. *How come I can see so well without my glasses?*

Then, to his astonishment, she lifted her arms and shrugged out of her sweatshirt. Did she not realize he was there? By all the laws of physics, she should be able to see him much more plainly than he saw her. She tossed the sweatshirt aside, revealing a second garment: a cropped tee shirt probably two sizes too small. And a line of pure man-poetry rattled through Charlie's head: *Whoa, nice knockers.*

Thoroughly disgusted with himself, he turned away.

As soon as he got in the house, he would do something useful, like really search for a plumber. In a damn phone book if he could find one.

CHAPTER 11

AS SOON AS WE REACHED the lake, Jonah turned into his version of an Indian, and time soared and drifted like—forgive the pun—a stream of feathers.

He ran along the pebbly shore, whooping and hollering for all he was worth while wearing a headdress of twigs and leaves. The enactment was not very PC of him, I know. But hey, a four-year-old knows nothing of that. Kids are natural profilers. "Oh look, a fat lady from the circus," they say. Or: "Mommy: that man looks like a bad guy!" At least Jonah did not attempt to scalp me; I'd trained him well. Instead, he divided his pies (rocks) with the white dude (me) and made up his own language. "*Kwaltup Kwaltup*, Mommy. It's lake language. It means 'peace.'"

"Peace to you, too," I said happily. "I mean, uh, *kwaltup*."

Playing is not just for kids; I have always believed that. They only need it to grow up. We need play to remember why we bothered to grow up in the first place.

The air smelled intoxicating, of honeysuckle, pine, eucalyptus, and every mountain lake that has ever existed. The cottages skirting the water had paths connecting them like umbilical cords, as if we residents shared the same placenta. When Jonah and I left the shoreline, venturing into the woods, the trees thickened, then thinned again at a collection of huge white boulders jutting up in a circle.

"Jonah, look!"

He darted forward, climbed onto one of the rocks, and tumbled. "Ow! *Mommmmy!*"

Bending to kiss his knee, I noticed the hollows on top of the boulder. "Honey, these are grinding rocks. Native women used to come here to crush and grind acorns for cooking. And look over there! Handprints. These must be very old." I pressed my palms against the cool stone. "And must have belonged to a child." *Or a very small woman.*

"The hands are *red*," Jonah said with awe. "Mommy, they fit me!"

It occurred to me that there was something strange about the red hands. The redness, for one thing, but that wasn't all of it...and then I realized the prints were reversed. When I put my hands against them, our thumbs were on opposite sides. Almost as if the prints had been produced...well, from *inside* the stone.

"She was finger-painting," Jonah said.

She? "Yeah. That's as good as explanation as any, sweet-pea." Better than mine, at least. For it became obvious that whoever had made these prints had simply crossed her arms before pressing the paint, or whatever it was against the stone.

Jonah reached down to place his own palms over the prints, and I had the impulse to yank him away. But he stopped all by himself. He turned his head and looked at me.

"Is it blood, Mommy? Is that why the hands are red?"

"Oh, no. I'm sure it's not blood." The skin of my arms tingled with goosebumps. Don't be ridiculous, I told myself. This was a lovely spot. I could easily imagine women squatting in their calf-hide skirts, pulverizing acorns into flour. History coming alive. Nothing to feel scared of.

Then I felt a pang in my head.

Not the usual pain, though. This was duller, more like radiating nerves.

I closed my eyes and waited for uber-vivid memories to drift like snow in a snow-globe. Instead, I heard a voice.

Save me, Great Spirit.

I looked up sharply. What—?

Save me. Save me. Save me.

"Jonah, did you hear that?"

"Hear what?"

I grabbed his arm. "That voice. Didn't you hear it?"

He stared at me with wide eyes.

I let go of him and stood up. "We should go back now."

"Why? Is something wrong?"

"Of course not. Don't be silly. It's just time."

"But…can we go swimming?"

"No." My voice sounded sharp. I shook my head. "You saw the signs, honey. And there are all those rocks by the water."

"I'm not scared of rocks!"

"Of course not. But the lake is deep. It's not safe."

"Can't we just touch it?" he asked, wiggling his fingers.

"I'm not sure," I said, thinking: *Of* course, *we can touch it!* How could touching water be unsafe?

"Maybe. But let's get closer to the house first," I said.

⋆　⋆　⋆

The best spot seemed to be near the gate: a wide area of shore featuring not only uncomfortable pebbles and rocks but a few drifts of actual soft sand. It looked as if someone had begun to build a real beach here, then stopped.

Perhaps the same someone who had also built the dock that extended half-heartedly into the water a little farther down the shoreline?

As Jonah and I laid down our towel, I wondered about Charlie. How long could it take to walk into town and get the name of a plumber? I thought of returning to the cottage to check on him…but realized I didn't want to, not yet. I felt a bit possessive of my time alone with Jonah. Especially in the presence of so much beauty.

"Don't forget, I'm an Indian," my son said, "and we need to build my castle."

I didn't correct his revisionist architectural history as he distributed plastic shovels, rake, and bucket. Rocks and sand would form the ramparts… but we would need water, too. I cast another admiring look at the lake. Sun pennies skittered harmlessly in every direction, a glittering, expanding cascade. And my little boy smiled up at me so brightly, my heart swung free.

I will hold his hand every second, I told myself.

So, bucket in hand, we approached the water's edge. Jonah put down the bucket and reached for the water with one small finger…and I held my breath. His finger slid into the water.

It got…well, wet.

Jonah's face lit up; I giggled.

What had I expected? That the water would *bite*?

"How does it feel?" I asked.

"Nice!" he said and stuck in his whole hand.

I almost jumped to snatch it out…and thankfully resisted. That silly stone wall back there behind us—that wall with its ladder of overblown signs screaming danger—was not going to ruin our fun. Those signs had nothing to do with me, with us.

The sunlit water slid neatly over my toes, too, and it was cool, yes, not too cold. Silky and secret and marvelous. I waded to my ankles and felt around amongst the rocks with my toes.

They rattled and shifted forward a bit, as if yearning to slide off into unseen depths.

"This is far enough," I told Jonah. "Stay next to me."

With water up to his knees, he said, "Mommy, it bumps me!" and laughed; and the sound seemed to fly up and whirl through the air like a thousand memories, all good.

Then he asked, "Why do people get drownded here?"

"I don't know," I said. "Maybe they're just not good swimmers."

"Do they sink? Is there a bottom?"

"Everything has a bottom." *Except Lake Ronkonkoma.*

"Are there monsters?"

"No, sweetie. No monsters. Just, uh, regular critters. Like birds." *One bird, anyway.*

"*They* swim."

"Of course. Hey, why don't we go back? It's getting late." I squatted and put my arms around his narrow shoulders.

Suddenly, there was a loud bang. A scream split the air.

A woman.

I jumped around and saw her slim figure running wildly in our direction. She had popped out from one of the last cottages; one of the places where I had failed to find someone home earlier today. The woman's face twisted in a grimace.

"Stop!" she shrieked, waving her arms. "What are you doing? *Get out of the water*! Ou*uuuuu*t!"

She was talking to *us?* I stared back at her, shocked.

Jonah's grip on my legs tightened. "Mommy, what's she saying?"

"I have no idea, honey. Just stay close."

Another woman slammed out of a different cottage, another figure running right at us yelling and waving with both arms. "Hey! You! Get out of the water! Now! *Please!*"

Before I think what to do, *another* door opened, and a big-bellied guy in a muscle shirt emerged, hammering after the women. "Get out! Get out! Get out!"

I scooped Jonah up in both arms, kicking the plastic bucket, and began yelling, too. "Stop! It's okay! Okay? We are not swimming! Just wading!"

But the people kept coming. They did not listen.

I glanced around for a place to go…a way to slip past and get home. And then I realized that more people—*for God's sake, where had they all come from?*—had emerged from other doors, other cottages. They, too, were barreling in our direction. I thought of a magician's hat of rabbits and began to shake.

Charlie, where are you?

Thank God, the first woman abruptly stopped about ten feet from us. Her mouth opened again, and she began yelping like a dog in a trap: *Oh! Oh! Oh!*

The guy behind her also halted. He pointed an accusing finger. "You don't know what you're doing!"

I heard a metallic crash in the distance—another bike? I couldn't tell. My mind was stuck on the whites of the eyes, the open mouths, the harsh high-toned voices. What was *wrong* with these people? And I had thought Rikki Stevens strange. She was the only one not here!

"Never go in!" a guy in a robe shouted, his face—jowly, red, and enraged—hovered over sleeves that looked more like bat wings.

Then there was someone else, moaning and pleading. "My God. It's not just you…not just you…"

Not just you, *what?* I wanted to scream.

They had converged in a group now, staring bug-eyed, as if Jonah and I teetered on the ledge of a skyscraper. "…Mommy…?" he whimpered, still in my arms.

Do something! I thought—and surprising even myself, burst out of the water.

I sprinted away at an obtuse angle, up the embankment and toward the gate, while Jonah sobbed into my skin.

As we approached the gap in the wall, a slightly built woman stepped into the space. I swerved away and then looked again.

Wasn't she the pleasant, middle-aged waif who loved children? Our eyes met. And hers appeared ineffably sad as she mouthed at me, like a human guppy *Stay away. Stay away!*

Stay away from *what*?

I didn't know, but I was turning anyway, heading down the lane toward the public parking and the dock. The parking area was surrounded by boulders and densities of trees; the dock a miserable structure that looked like it was about to collapse into the dreaded waters of the lake. So, that was a certain dead end.

My heart hammering, I focused on the large wooden shed next to the dock. It wasn't in particularly good shape, but it had walls and a roof and a door—and as far as I could see, no crazy people lurking.

By now, Jonah felt as heavy in my arms as a full-grown man. I staggered to the door, slipped my son onto his feet, and grabbed the doorknob.

It did not turn.

The door was locked, or rusted, or broken…and I was certainly not strong enough to break it down.

Still clutching Jonah, I wheeled around to see what was coming next… but nothing was coming next. Everyone but us had gone.

The lane stretched before us, deserted, dappled in sunlight, as lovely and peaceful as a painting.

My breath fled in a whoosh. No.

It wasn't possible.

Only seconds ago, eight or ten people had been chasing us, shrieking in terror, shouting nonsensical warnings. Where had they all gone?

Back inside their hidey-holes?

"Where are they, Mama?" Jonah whimpered, looking over his shoulder. "Why did they chase us?"

"I don't know, sweetheart. I'm sorry, I really don't."

"But…they scared me."

"I know. I know. Maybe they had a…reason. Like they seemed really bothered that we…went into the water." I glanced around again, trying to figure it all out. "Let's just go home."

"Okay, but *which* home?" he said in his baby voice. "I wanna go to our other house."

"I know you do." I looked over my shoulder at the door of the shed, for the first time wondering what the building had been used for.

The glass was filthy, so I cleaned a spot with some spit and my fist.

Then I peered inside…at rows of rowboats, neatly stacked and covered in cobwebs.

TOO MUCH STRESS

CHAPTER 12

I SHOULD HAVE TOLD CHARLIE about it in the first moment I saw him. I should have told him about the weird red handprints and the weird, scary neighbors, and about the harrowing chase to that abandoned boat shed by the docks.

But as soon as Jonah and I entered the cottage, my son started shivering and crying about a headache. A quick check with a thermometer showed he had a fever of over one hundred. I put off explaining anything to Charlie.

An hour later, I had a temperature, too. I could not help wondering if *I* had been feverish all morning long. Perhaps I had hallucinated the whole don't-go-in-the-water episode. Was that possible?

I thought about asking Jonah exactly what he remembered, but he was too sick. Part of me also dreaded what my little boy might say: that he might ask, "Remember about what?"

Then Charlie staggered into the kitchen to get the thermometer, and the first thing he said to me was "I feel like...um, poop."

So, yes, we were good and sick, all three of us. Which is why for the next two weeks, my family stayed inside our cottage like opossums hiding from a fox. If I even thought about my marriage or my son or this town that we had bought ourselves into—well, would lose it altogether and my mouth would gape like a frightened opossum, drooling or leaking green fluid.

And so, I did not think.

During our convalescence, Charlie did manage to collect a short list of recommended plumbers. Despite interrupting himself with groaning and sneezing, he also managed to call them. None of them answered their phones or responded to messages, though. This meant that the hole in the kitchen wall remained, as did the whooshing and knocking sounds occasionally emanating from that general area.

On the brighter side, the hole did not seem so important to me anymore. It had become just one more family member coughing up phlegm.

Meanwhile, outside, it rained. Hard.

I would say it rained "cats and dogs" but the image that came to mind was "branches and rocks." A bad summer storm, the news called it.

Jonah seemed happy enough to stay inside, and I didn't question it. Then, by the end of the second week, our colds were mostly better, the weather had cleared, and we were down to eating Cheerios three meals a day.

Time to do something else.

Uneasy, I peeked out the front window at the lake. Of course, there was no sign of the mysterious guy with the black flapping bathrobe, or the woman shouting "Out! Out! Out!" or the worried middle-aged waif named Hannah. Did they, like me, hide behind their couches peeking out the window, preferring to come out when no one expected it…?

Slowly, I was developing a new theory, one involving well-water contamination. Something like that could also explain why we had fallen so sick. And if the water in Shy Moon Lake *was* contaminated, or we were ingesting lead through old pipes, how long before Jonah, Charlie, and I started shouting and chasing people around, too?

Outside, life appeared as bucolic as wallpaper.

A couple of touristy-looking people walked down the sunny lane. No one tried to stop them. Someone in a hoodie slouched along unmolested. No bikes attempted to run anybody down. The only familiar figure I saw all morning was Rikki, limping down her front steps in an orthopedic boot. She looked over at me and waved.

I waved back, resentfully. There she was, leggy and pretty in a Country Goth sort of way, with her punkish hair and empty eyes. They were more like pinpoints, older than the trees.

I did not know her, but I didn't trust her, any more than I trusted anyone else.

Then Charlie came upon me venturing onto the porch. He had shaven, put on clean jeans and a crisp white tee shirt. In our previous life, I would have told him how yummy he looked—and attacked.

Now I just smiled weakly.

"Hey, babe," he said. "Good to see you getting out. But staying in your PJ's?"

"I'll get dressed tomorrow, if everything is okay."

"You mean us, or out there?"

"Both," I said.

He laughed. "Ah, the neighborhood watch. I forgot that this town is so much like South Central L.A."

"Charlie," I said. "Can you sit with me a second? I need to tell you something."

Immediately, his expression darkened. I could almost read his mind: *What shocking news have you got for me now?* But we settled on the porch swing, the front door left open so we could hear Jonah play in the living room. And I took a deep breath and plunged in with my story, describing everything I had avoided thinking about for the past fourteen days.

The wild-eyed strangers running and reaching.

The screaming, nonsensical pleas—and our terror.

The unused shack filled with old rowboats.

One thing I left out of my story was how abruptly our pursuers had disappeared, like rabbits out of a hat. I did not want to push my luck with Charlie.

It was a long monologue, and he listened like a hero. His bewildered expression slipped only a little, showing the alarm underneath. "That's quite a story," he said at last.

"I know. That's why I didn't tell you sooner," I admitted. "Plus, we were sick, and I didn't want to upset Jonah."

"But he was there with you. He saw…this behavior?"

"Of course. I told you. How could he not?"

Charlie paused, looking down at his hands. He steepled his fingers like a professor of some heavy topic like "Abnormal Psychology." "Okay. Then why hasn't he mentioned it to me? Did you tell him not to?"

"I wouldn't ask him to keep a secret like that. I don't know, maybe he blocked it out."

"Well, that's possible. I guess."

"I think it…scared him. He's a kid. He just wants to play. Plus, he's been sick. But *I* want to find out what's going on. We *have* to if we're going to live in this place, even for the summer. I can't just spend all my time hiding."

Charlie reared his head back. "You want to find out more about what, exactly? The neighbors? Or the lake?"

"I think it's tied together. The neighbors were genuinely warning us. There is something dangerous in that water."

There, the truth was out. I had said it, no matter how ridiculous sounding.

Charlie turned his eyes in my direction—and I saw *pity*.

"Jess. Do you hear yourself? What do you think is in there? Too much fluoride?"

"Come on, Charlie. Don't be sarcastic. It doesn't help."

"It doesn't?" He looked like he was about to either laugh or cry; I couldn't tell which. "Look. Honey. If the neighbors *were* trying to warn you, why all the shouting and chasing? Why not just talk to you like normal human beings?"

Good question. And one I could not answer—especially with my head still hurting.

Charlie said, "Instead of being suspicious of who knows what, you could just go and ask them directly. Knock on doors like you did with the banana bread, and—"

Suddenly I bolted up, an acrid taste in my mouth.

"Nauseous," I said, and ran for the bathroom.

*   *   *

While I retched into the maw of the cottage's porcelain god, memories flew at me like gnats.

At 23, puking in the ER with a case of food poisoning. A rainy Thursday, the last day in April. The nurse who helped me had rolls of fat on her ankles. And a bout of the stomach flu three years ago, with Mom suffering similarly in the other bathroom. I wore a pink shirt that would forever remind me of Pepto Bismol, which I had not been able to take ever since. My kindergarten graduation, too, flew past my tired mind: vivid upchucking all over my lavender plaid frou-frou dress and white patent-leather shoes. The fear. The smell. *Mommy, I'm sick.*

I want to live, not die….

I lifted my head.

It was that voice again. Not a memory. It couldn't be. *I would remember.*

"No," I said aloud, and listened for a response.

Nothing.

I stood up, rinsed my mouth, and left the bathroom.

* * *

"Are you okay?" Charlie asked worriedly. I managed a nod, and he placed a hand on my forehead. "Mm. Nope, no fever."

"Maybe I need to eat something besides Cheerios," I said. "That might help."

We went into the kitchen where he fixed me a cup of hot tea and the last piece of toast. And I picked at it, brooding. "Charlie…I need you to believe me. About everything I told you before I went into the bathroom. I will never lie to you again. You know that, right? All that stuff I said—it really happened."

He nodded, and I reached for him. We held on for a long time.

Then I looked up. "Where's Jonah?"

"Oh, he got tired of TV, which I'll take as a good sign," Charlie said. "I didn't want him to hear you get sick, so I sent him to the porch."

"Alone? He's on the porch *alone*?" I scrambled up and bolted from the kitchen.

"Wait! Jess? He's just playing with his truck," Charlie called after me.

No, no, not outside, I thought as I raced through the hallway and the living room toward the front door. Don't trust him playing on the porch. Don't trust him near the lake. Not *this* lake.

But Jonah was sitting peacefully on the porch floor, playing with his big truck, just as Charlie had said.

I skidded to a halt, relieved and embarrassed. When had I become such a fussy mother hen? As if to mock my histrionics, the lake looked as bland as a mirror. Just reflecting back whatever was already there.

Charlie came up behind me. "Jesus. You okay?"

"Yes—and please don't sound like that."

"Okay," he said.

I told him that I was going to get dressed after all. I had decided to take a walk alone to clear my head. I would also pick up some food and maybe check out the library.

"You don't want us to go with you?" Charlie asked, his voice suspicious.

"No," I said. "It's easier without Jonah. Just watch him, okay? With both eyes."

He agreed, and I agreed, and then I did just that: threw on some clothes, kissed my son goodbye, grabbed my purse, and fled the cottage into the wild wilderness of this stupid little town.

Charlie and I did not kiss before I left. He didn't seem to want to, and the truth was: for some reason I couldn't understand, I didn't want to either.

*   *   *

The Shy Moon Lake Library, an edifice of brown and white stucco, had been built charmingly into the side of an enormous boulder like an animal burrowing into its lair.

In fact, the whole town looked exceedingly disarming today, as if it knew I was mad at it. Visitors window-shopped, merchants arranged displays, sweeping out non-existent trash, innocently stacking goods. A group of kids hauled backpacks down sidewalks, chattering in happy voices, searching for good clean fun. Where did they camp? Were they tourists or locals?

Or did they, too, know secrets no one was telling?

The library smelled deliciously of books. In the main room, a young mother read to her toddler while an old man dozed in a chair. Two computers predating my mother's flip phone hulked in the corner, and tastefully framed photos in black and white drew the eye to every wall.

In these photos the town appeared smaller, emptier: unfinished. In one of the Main Street photos, a building leaned over to one side as if taking a nap. Then I noticed branches scattered over the ground, shards of glass littering the sidewalk. In the next picture, women in long dresses and men in old-fashioned hats stared at a huge conflagration—a building? Several buildings? In other photos the square had been damaged badly, though not by fire; houses were flattened, early model cars stalled in debris.

"That was after 'the big one,' over seventy-five years ago," said a mellifluous female voice.

I whirled around to find an attractive old lady wearing a wristband of keys. Her long-sleeved dress emphasized a narrow waist. Her smile flashed curiosity, as if she already knew I was the new lakeside resident.

Or was that more paranoia?

"You must be the librarian," I said warmly.

"Yes, Mrs. Collins, Head Librarian. I see you are interested in our history."

"Very much so. My name is Jess McCortney. My family moved here for the summer."

I held out my hand, and she nodded, smile still there, more neutral than knowing. But she didn't take my hand. *Worried about contamination?* I wondered.

I said, "I've learned bits and pieces about this town, but not enough to give me…perspective."

"And one needs perspective in Shy Moon Lake, doesn't one?" she said.

That kind of threw me, too.

"Mm, let's see," she went on. "Half our buildings were damaged or destroyed in this shaker right here—the biggest earthquake in living memory. I was ten at the time. I'm eighty-five now."

Her age was offered with jaunty pride, something I rarely witnessed in women.

"It must have been terrifying," I said, referring to the earthquake, not her age.

"Oh, I don't worry too much about earthquakes. When it's your time, it's your time."

I didn't worry too much about earthquakes, either. Apparently, I worried about everything else.

"My daughter ducks under tables whenever the earth shakes," she said. "I just put my robe on as calm as can be and stand in a doorway when I get to one. Why rush around or race outside and catch cold? That would kill me faster than any earthquake."

"Good point. Too bad no one can predict them."

"Unless you have a dog that howls in advance, or cats that climb walls straight up, because they feel it coming. Animals do that, you know. At least *our* animals."

"Oh. They do?" *Oh boy, here we go…*

"They sense floods and volcanic activity, too."

"What floods?" I asked, thinking: The Lake! The Lake!

"I'm afraid that's a conversation for another day," she said, turning away.

I stopped her, saying, "Mrs. Collins, I'd like to use a computer, please. Is there a password?"

She hesitated, then led me to the two little workstations. She turned on a computer that did not require a password and stood waiting for it to wake up. "So…you said it's Mrs. McCortney?"

"Yes, but please call me Jess."

"Of course. And…I hope you are staying where you can see the best views?"

"We're in one of the lakeshore cottages. So yes, we see the lake up close and personal."

Her smile faded. "How nice. Well, I hope you like it. Many people do prefer to settle on Mount Dragon, the adjacent mountain at higher elevation. In fact, there are quite a few rentals and homes where you can really see the crater shape of Shy Moon Lake. You might want to check what is available up there, too."

I stared at her in confusion. "But we bought our place. And like I said, it's close to the water."

"Oh, right, my apologies. I must have forgotten. Did you say the middle cottage?"

No, I had not said that. So, she had known all along, pretending not to know. Goosebumps prickled along my arms again.

"Yes, it's the middle cottage," I said.

"Right. That would be the Thurston's old place. They did go Below, or so I heard."

"We bought it long distance, sight unseen. Through a Realtor named Patty Pattick."

"Ah, yes. She is known for doing that sort of thing."

What sort of thing? Selling real estate that everybody should want? Or selling it long distance? More baffled than ever, I settled myself in front of the computer.

"As I said, the Internet is dicey," Mrs. Collins said from behind me. "If you have difficulty getting online, you can always try another day. I...wish you luck, Mrs. McCortney. Jess."

"Wait. Mrs. Collins? Can I ask one more thing? Do you know why the Internet is dicey? My cell phone doesn't work either on this mountain. I've given up on social media. And everyone seems to accept it, though no one can explain why."

"I'm afraid I can't help you, either. During the school year the Internet here *is* used despite its limitations. Some people have luck with it. Like your Mrs. Pattick."

My Mrs. Pattick?

"The problem may be timing or the altitude, or…isolation," the librarian added.

Toxins in the water or birds in the sky?

I pushed away from the gut-wrenchingly slow computer. "May I look at some print materials instead? Books or local newspapers?"

"Yes…yes. Of course. They are in the periodical section, in a special room. You'll find back copies of *The Shy Moon Eclipse.*"

"That would be perfect, thank you."

"I will need to get you the key, though," she added, looking as pained as if she had actually swallowed one.

CHAPTER 13

"**IT'S TOO CALM OUTSIDE. I** don't trust it," Hannah Mason remarked to her husband at home in Cottage Number Four. A few minutes earlier she had been standing at the window in their living room and had *watched* it happen.

The sudden release of skittish wind. An un-ruffling of leaves.

The uncanny quiet that settled like dust on her skin…

Now she waited at his armchair, hand on sloping shoulder, silently imploring this dear, decent man to listen. He was forty-eight years old and rapidly graying. He did not like to think about the old stories. But she was about to turn forty and no doubt infertile, at least in Shy Moon Lake. If she couldn't confide all that she knew with her woman's fully honed instincts, she could surely share *something*.

"Stansey? Did you hear what I said?"

When he looked up, his glasses—square and intellectual-looking—slid down his nose. He pushed them back into place. "Yes, sweetheart, I heard you. I was just reading."

"I know you were, and I'm sorry to interrupt. I know you like to unwind after"—after what? Unpacking cartons and approving re-dos at the register was a simple job he enjoyed. And she would gladly unpack cartons and approve re-do's rather than remain a stay-at-home mom with no children—"after all your diligent work. But Stansey, I was looking outside and saw everything *stop*. As if someone had flicked a switch."

"Oh, Hannah."

"No, listen. Earlier there was all that wind blowing. Remember?"

He nodded.

"Well, I was watching when all the branches *stopped moving*. All the leaves. The surface of the water, too. As if something *left*."

Stan shook his scraggly head. He needed a haircut again. Quickly she smoothed his grays. His body shifted in her direction as he peered up at her with sad brown eyes.

"Hannah, honey. You said you weren't going to fret anymore. We agreed."

He was right. They *had* agreed.

But they had agreed to lots of things. To get pregnant in their first year of marriage ten years ago. To carry that pregnancy to term and conceive baby number two only six months after baby number one. To spring onward to babies three and four, thriving inside their bubble of un-breached love within this claustrophobic place called Shy Moon Lake.

Of course, they had tried leaving. After losing pregnancy after pregnancy, it had seemed wiser to attempt to go elsewhere: meaning *Below*. But the first time they had tried, their car engine died. Then their rental's engine died. The second rental barely escaped getting smashed by a falling tree, which slammed onto the road right in front of them, blocking access down the mountain.

How could it be coincidence? In Hannah's opinion, it could not.

Whether she suffered more miscarriages or never felt a growing belly again, the outcome was the same. She and Stan were not permitted to become parents. They had been found wanting; had failed a test she never understood or asked for.

It's because I am not vulnerable enough, she thought suddenly. *We* are not. Stan and I cannot be divided.

He was still reading the paper, if you wanted to call *The Shy Moon Eclipse* a newspaper. Once upon a time Hannah had looked forward to reading the editor's wit, his frankness, and intelligence. Carl Roberson's writing had been…brave. Hannah wished she had known him better; her husband used to meet him for drinks. But Stan no longer mentioned his unfortunate friend. He avoided discussing Carl's unsolved disappearance in the same way that he avoided discussing Hannah's observations and theories about the lake. Stan disliked hearing her fret over the wind, shadows, light, moon, trees, and handprints at the grinding rocks. Most importantly, he refused to risk trying to leave here again on another day, in another car.

Instead, they had abandoned the idea. He stayed in a job he liked; they chose to stay in the cottage she knew they could not leave. Stan said he felt fine with the only investment they had, but she needed more. She needed, at times, to talk.

"I think this calm means something, Stan. Something significant. I know you don't like to hear it. But if you come to the window, you'll notice a—"

He kindly waited for her to finish.

"—*lifting*, as if a vacuum's been released."

"Hannah—"

"Please believe me."

He put aside the paper, got up, and walked with her to the open window. Once there, he placed his dear pudgy hand on her shoulder, and cocked his head. "It *is* quiet," he said softly.

"And…*unoccupied*. Empty. So you do hear it?"

Stan caressed her cheek so gently it made her want to cry. "Hannah, Hannah, you can't go on like this. *We* feel empty because of all we've lost." He flashed her those puppy dog eyes of love and regret. "There may still be hope in that department, though. You know what the doctor said. You're healthy, I'm healthy. We're not that old. It might happen if we relax."

He kissed her hand and held it against his cheek. And she stayed there, inhaling his scents of musky cologne and old-fashioned pomade. She couldn't think of pulling away from her husband even when he was flat-out wrong.

Then he patted her hand and returned to his chair and his paper, and she took the opportunity to slip outside.

*   *   *

We feel empty because of all that we've lost.

Hannah paused on their porch, studying the lovely, undamaged day. Each leaf rested gently against the sky. The air smelled rich with peace. Sunlight streamed straight and true. The lake sparkled so sweetly it made her want to cry. It was perfect, and yet…*wrong*. She wasn't sure whether she envisioned a malevolent spirit changing its mind and moving away or gathering its forces for the future—and that made all the difference in the world.

Where have you gone to? And for how long…?

Still hugging her empty womb, she descended the stairs and walked twenty-five feet or so away from the cottage.

Maybe there *is* hope, she thought. Could it be?

CHAPTER 14

THE LIBRARIAN LED ME TO a side room with tall cabinets. After another turn of a key, she stepped aside, and lopsided towers of *The Shy Moon Eclipse* appeared.

As excited as an archeologist removing artifacts from a tomb, I thanked her again. She left, and I dug in.

The newspapers dated from different months and different years, in no particular order. I transferred small sections at a time and patted them into piles. The paper's format was distinctive, kind of like the town's trash cans. Each edition opened into two main sections that were unashamedly tongue-in-cheek: "Shy Moon Lake News" and "News from the Rest of the World." And the editorial pages displayed a map of the entire world with Shy Moon Lake center stage.

I liked any publication that could laugh at itself. I felt less sure about the editorials, though. They tried to be unbiased about whatever they were discussing, with one "Pro" and one "Against" section. But the subjects came across as silly because of all the exclamation points. "Dolphin Fountain Refurbishing Hotly Debated!" and "The Wall at Shy Moon Lake Should Be Modernized!" and "Hospitality Avoids Potlucks!" and "Trumpet Player Saves Puppy!" and "Lost Wallet Delivered to Woman's Doorstep!"

Ha. *Well, screw the wall.* It hadn't been modernized, had it?

Not surprisingly, *The Shy Moon Eclipse* sported a tiny graphic moon ducking behind a lake. As I flipped pages, the graphic began reappearing in different places, left margin or right, up or down, with the lake and moon teeter-tottering to one side or the other. Until on one page there was a lake but no moon; that stumped me until I spotted it on the facing page.

I kept scanning for references to the lake, handprints, cottages, warning signs, zombie neighbors, or shacks filled with unused boats. Nothing.

The editor-in-chief, a guy named Carl Roberson, used a catchy phrase to support certain social issues—*Carl Commends*—and a similar phrase to decry them—*Carl Condemns*. He did try to be fair, though none of his work displayed what you'd call "sterling journalism."

My nose began to twitch, and my stomach turned queasy again. I withdrew a package of Saltines from my bag and moved onto the next pile of papers. Three years earlier, one of the two mechanic shops in town was going belly-up. I yawned.

Then I sat still, my heart thumping.

In this edition of *Carl Condemns*, Carl Roberson stated that he had been ill and spent time re-evaluating the town of Shy Moon Lake along with this small newspaper business he'd inherited from his uncle. With uncharacteristic bluntness, the editor-in-chief wrote that he was tired of what went on "close to the lake." He asked families to refrain from gossiping; from relying on superstition and fantasy to explain away coincidences. Carl Roberson especially derided the local assertions of "Tit-for-Tat." Apparently, he was referring to the speculation by local residents that "another" cottage family had fallen victim to the "old pattern" of Shy Moon Lake.

Fascinated, I raced through the details.

A resident had fallen in her bathtub, and after tragically becoming paralyzed, she did manage to move "Below" to a proper facility. Yet folks "close to the situation" referred to her accident as a "closing of the karmic circle caused by the woman trying to leave her husband of 50 years."

Really? Were they serious?

Carl did not approve of this kind of foolishness. He called it bad for business, bad for morale, and bad for the spirit of Shy Moon Lake. He said he refused to believe that Eleanor McGrath, the woman in the wheelchair, could be "punished" by some unseen power for behaving badly. He decried all and any mean-spirited rumors that this poor woman had gotten her Just Desserts—or "tit-for-*splat*," as he put it.

I thought that Eleanor McGrath—whoever she was—did not deserve to be the brunt of such a nasty pun. And I found it ludicrous and insulting for anyone to believe that just because a woman abandoned her husband, she merited a broken neck.

Carl Roberson doubted whether the authorities had investigated anything having to do with this woman's misfortune. Does anybody in this town deal with facts? he demanded. Someone could have pushed the lady, or maybe she had stepped on a bar of soap. We need to stop blaming the boogey-man for acts of violence and foolishness. "Maybe," he wrote, "we should take those old legends and shove them into the lake itself."

Lastly, he referred to a particularly absurd case of superstition run wild. This story involved a man who had disobeyed the signs (horrors!), waded his feet into the lake—and choked on his own saliva (or on lake water?). "Yes, he broke the rules and drowned, and it is a shame CPR did not work," Carl Roberson wrote. "Does that have to mean that a *curse* killed him? Why? Why do the perfectly intelligent residents of Shy Moon Lake insist on explaining every mishap with something more sinister than water going down the wrong pipe, or even a heart attack?"

Accidents happen, the editorial concluded. Get a clue, people. Get educated, for God's sake. Stop believing whatever you hear. This area has the best views in the state. Do you really want to scare people away? *Shy Moon Lake will become a ghost town if we're not careful.*

The editorial against Carl's viewpoint was written by a woman named Martha Divers. It insisted that the warning signs on the wall were there for a reason; to protect people. Come on, Carl. Open *your* eyes. This place is not as benevolent as you think. One day you'll see. Oh, yes you will…

I threw away the empty saltine wrapper and kept going. Another Carl Roberson editorial poked holes in a story about an old couple who sworn they had seen a ghost. Imagine that! Carl said with obvious sarcasm. Aging, gullible tourists witnessing a phantom Indian woman near the grinding rocks!

Residents, too, ask if the red handprints belong to our ghostly visitor. They ask: Is this woman our Juliet of the lake? If so, what does she want of us? What are she and Romeo trying to tell us? Please listen, fellow residents: this is more superstitious nonsense, unwise and unhelpful to whoever cares about our beautiful town. We have a fascinating history and natural beauty, including an amazing crater lake. Why tell camp stories to make ourselves special? Why not get rid of the "drowned couple" brochures and attract visitors some other way?

At the end of that same issue, a headline read: SHY MOON LAKE RE-ENACTMENT CLUB ACTS BADLY. Beneath the headline, a cartoon male Indian clutched a pile of torn clothing, his feathered headdress rumpled and askew. According to the article, the town's Re-enactment Club planned to celebrate its half-century of existence by borrowing authentic costumes from the town's Historical Society. Except this year the new president of the club, Miss Rikki Finn Stevens, was proposing something scandalous: that the members portraying Indians at the festival rip and otherwise damage the borrowed costumes, in order for everyone to "fully experience the trauma of the original events that took place here." Fortunately, in the end, the costumes were not ripped or damaged. They were returned intact, against the will of Miss Stevens.

I snorted. *That woman's more psycho than I thought.*

Then, in the last pile, I noticed another article. This one favored over-zealous alliteration: "Temblor Threatens to Tumble the Moon from Shy Moon Lake."

Earthquakes again.

Here the moon graphic rolled down the tiny mountain because a 6.5 quake had startled residents at 4:00 in the afternoon—apparently *the* typical time for earthquakes in Shy Moon Lake. Larger than any other in twenty years, this earthquake clearly foretold more quakes to come. Of course, Carl Roberson, opining on the subject, doubted that earthquakes cared about the time of day. He did not believe the town's cats had cried and hissed beforehand. Nor did he give credence to the common knowledge that local dogs howled, chased empty air, or barked at shadows. He particularly scoffed at the notion of dead catfish turning up at the lakeshore. Catfish had been unheard of in Shy Moon Lake for a hundred years. What did it matter if people submitted photos of fish floating on the lake after the earthquake? Those pictures were clearly photoshopped....

"One day I am going to get to the bottom of all these stories, even if I have to put on scuba gear to do it," Carl Roberson wrote.

Poor guy, I thought, and glanced at the last paper. It had a much more recent date—and a different name on the editorial page: James Zimmerman.

To my surprise, Zimmerman appeared on the staff listing too, as Editor-in-Chief.

Carl Roberson had disappeared from *The Shy Moon Eclipse.*

CHAPTER 15

CHARLIE HATED TO THINK OF Jonah as dependent on those old *Shrek* movies.

Sure, when there's no babysitter to hire, no grandparents present to share the load, and the kid's parents keep going off on solo walks or sitting around the house having intense discussions or hammering walls or vomiting in the bathroom—well, *Shrek* fills the gaps.

But so many times in a row? Charlie grabbed the TV remote.

"No*ooo*, don't shut it," Jonah cried. "I wanna watch it again!"

"Aw, come on, bud. How many times can you see this? Don't you get tired of it?"

"No!"

Charlie knew he should not cave. But he was exhausted, and what harm in cartoons? At least Jonah was occupied. The boy did not seem upset that his mom had gone off without him. "Okay, go nuts," Charlie said, and went into the kitchen.

Unpacked boxes still waited on counters for someone to care. Why hadn't he and Jess unpacked already? At least a plumber had finally returned his calls. The man had come and gone again in one hour: a guy who wheezed while he worked and never found a damn thing wrong except that the floors were lopsided, the molding cracked, and the refrigerator's light bulb would not go on even after he changed it three times. Why make comments like that and say nothing conclusive about the pipes? Yes, forty bucks was cheap for a plumber. Still, it was forty bucks wasted.

Is this house a waste, too?

Charlie refused to become paranoid about it like Jess. His fiery, adorable, gutsy; impulsive bride—paranoid! She also happened to be secretive. "What's happened to you?" he whispered aloud.

Jonah had fallen asleep on the rug in front of *Shrek*. Charlie kissed the boy's forehead and covered him in a fresh cool sheet. He was about to shut the TV, too, but hesitated. It won't hurt, he told himself, to walk outside a few hundred feet, look at the lake. Jonah would yell if he woke up. There was no way Charlie would not hear that from a few feet away, through open windows.

That was part of Jess's paranoia too: *Don't leave Jonah alone for ten seconds.* She used to be different.

After another moment of indecision, Charlie left the TV on and stepped out into the flawless day. *Ahhh.* How sweet and placid the air seemed! And nobody out, not one freaking neighbor. What was Jess so worried about?

Then he noticed a thin girl—no, a woman—standing a-ways down the lane. She was hugging herself, staring at the lake, and her head bobbed as if she could hear an orchestra playing inside her head.

Another unstable female, then? Unless she was wearing earbuds.

A couple of birds squawked overhead. He shielded his eyes to watch them for a moment, and when he turned back to the road, the woman was gone.

He shook his head. Let it pass.

He crossed the lane to the pebbly shore, admiring the charming scene before him. The water looked unreal, a painting of itself. Shades of blue and green shone like intricately cut glass. What color *was* that? Indigo? Teal? Beryl?

As he continued to look, the colors seemed to disconnect and dissolve. Yet he thought the crater shape of the lake itself marvelously defined. A unique place, he told himself for the hundredth time.

Then he noticed another bird, this one sliding down the sky to land on the water, smooth as glass.

And this time he laughed with pleasure.

Well, how about that? So much for Jess's theory about birds fearing the lake!

CHAPTER 16

"**EXCUSE ME, IS EVERYTHING ALL** right?" the librarian asked.

At the sound of her voice, I jerked, dropped a paper, and bonked my knee. *Stupid table.* "Oh, hi, Mrs. Collins. You startled me."

"I did knock. Didn't you hear?"

"No, sorry, I'm lost in all this"—my hand encompassed the mess in front of me.

Which was not exactly true. For the last ten minutes or so I had been distracted, leapfrogging over memories more than newspaper articles. Like the time when I was nine and won a six-foot salami in a spelling bee and got my picture on the front cover of a local rag called *The Bonita Bee*. A funny word trick, everybody said, and I thought they were saying that I was dishonest and had tricked my way to winning.

"I see. Very good, then," Mrs. Collins said now. "I was just checking." And she quickly left again.

I grabbed the next newspaper, from only a year earlier, and tried to concentrate. This edition showed no more Carl Roberson material. No more talk of "stupid superstitions" and "gossip" and "dumb club rituals." For some reason, the paper itself had become dumb, and superstitious. And silly.

Where was its previous Editor-in-Chief? Had he moved "Below"?

Or drowned?

On the back page, I stumbled upon a small article with no byline. "Local Schoolteachers Attempt Symbolic End in Shy Moon Lake." At least it's not Schoolteacher and *Poet*, I thought uncomfortably.

This article told the story of a pair of teachers—live-in lovers—who had settled into a lakeside cottage, started fighting, and ended up trying to drown each other in the lake. They were rescued at the last minute and moved to the top of Mount Dragon—separately.

Why hadn't they left the area completely? I certainly would if Charlie and I went temporarily berserk and tried to murder each other.

Not that that will ever happen.

✳ ✳ ✳

The girl working alone in the Visitors' Center struck me as too young to have a driver's permit, much less run a business by herself. When the door tinkled, she shoved aside her *Stars* magazine, tossed her glistening shoulder-length locks, and offered me a bland blue-eyed smile. "Hi," she said.

"Hi," I said back, with as much cheerfulness as I could muster. I was feeling even worse than in the library, like maybe I was relapsing. "I'm Jess McCortney, a new resident."

"Oh. Great. Can I help you?" Her nametag advertised her name well enough. Kayla.

There had been a Kayla in camp, age 11. *That* Kayla lost an eye from an accident during archery lessons. I had witnessed the whole thing; the arrow going in the wrong direction and stabbing her in the face. And because Kayla had been the meanest kid at camp, it had been hard to feel too sorry for her. Some of the kids said she even deserved a bad eye, that it was her "karma" for being a snot.

THE SPIRIT OF SHY MOON LAKE

"I sure hope you can," I said to this Kayla. "I was passing by and thought you might have information on the lake."

The girl gestured at a meager-looking display against the far wall: one lake-view poster thumbtacked crookedly above a plastic stand with rental and real estate brochures. Not what I wanted.

Then I noticed another pile on Kayla's counter. These brochures were slick and colorful—identical to the one that Charlie and I had downloaded from the Internet before buying the cottage.

"Wow, this is the one we found online," I said.

She shrugged without interest.

"We started by Googling mountain towns and got to Shy Moon Lake, but after a while we couldn't get back to the site. Like it was under construction. There *is* still a website, right?"

"Of course." She sounded offended.

"I ask because I can't use my phone or laptop here to get online, so I can't recheck. Which is also strange."

Kayla said nothing. Her computer wasn't working, I noticed…or it wasn't on. And she did not have a cell phone connected to her via intravenous line, like kids her age did back home. *Curious and curiouser.*

"I mean, my cell has data, and the house is *supposed* to have wireless," I said. "The computer even says I'm connected. But it doesn't work, and I can't get tech support. This whole mountain is like one big black hole." The girl glanced anxiously at her unread magazine, but I refused to stop mid-stream. "*And* the library's Internet doesn't work, or only works now and again. When it feels like it, I guess. None of it makes sense."

She nodded. "Some town, huh?"

"Well, it is beautiful. Do you happen to know who makes the brochures?"

"We do. I mean the Center makes them, and the newspaper helps with printing. We don't have a very big budget." Again, her eyes yearned toward the magazine.

"I'm sorry, Kayla, I don't mean to be rude. I'm just…frustrated. Would you mind a few more questions?"

"No, go ahead."

"Is the, ah, Romeo and Juliet story in the brochure true?"

"Sure. Why not?" She reached into a drawer and un-wrapped a stick of gum—and I shook away memories of a necklace made of bubble gum wrappers, age nine, Stephanie Caprese's house…

"I read that there was another couple that almost died in the lake," I said. "Not the original couple, one much more recent. And another man who died while just wading. Are *those* stories real?"

"I guess so."

I waggled the brochure. "This thing talks about 'two colliding cultures.' I assume that means Native American and European?"

She pointed a finger toward the wall clock. "I'm going on break in five minutes."

"Sorry to keep you…but what about the red handprints? You know: on those boulders near the lake? And something about a club. Keepers of the Lake or something? I saw a sign about a re-enactment."

Kayla reached into a different drawer and tossed down a blue half-sheet. "Here's a list of activities, including the historical society. Not anything to write home about. But you might ask these folks, if they're still alive."

I tried not to laugh. "Why wouldn't they be?"

"Oh, they're old. I mean Ebenezer Scrooge-old. Only kids and Grandmas have activities in Shy Moon Lake. Believe me: I've lived here my whole life. If you graduate from high school without dying of boredom first, you win a prize."

Gotta be boring to get bored, retorted my teacher's mind. But I also laughed, which felt good. "Kayla, I think you're perfect for the Visitors' Center."

"Oh really? Thanks." She paused. "There *is* a re-enactment festival happening soon."

"Great. What do they re-enact?"

"They pick variations of the same thing every year. There used to be Indians living around the crater. I can't pronounce their name or tell you *when*. But they ate acorns mashed on rocks and used weeds or reeds or whatever they're called to make baskets. These Indians were peaceful, I think, not like the Aztecs or any of those dudes."

Dudes. Right. "And the handprints?"

"They have to do with these raunchy dances some people say were done for entertainment, or maybe religion. It was, like, a million years ago. The women did this imitation of childbirth, and the white folks hated it. They were hung up. So, the two groups had a lot of problems getting along." Kayla paused. "You really should ask the club. They also talk about a massacre. But that might be just talk. That's all anyone does around here. Talk."

"You're really not a small-town person, are you?"

"God, no. This place is practically, like, stone-age. I'm surprised our cars even work. First thing I'm gonna do when I graduate is try to go Below."

"'Try?' Is it hard to go, um, Below?"

"Guess I'll find out."

I cleared my throat. "So, club members re-enact sexual themes? Do they try to show the drowning, too? Or the massacre?"

"Kinda-sorta. There are these two sections of the club—my mom calls them 'factions'—and they're always fighting over which legends to do. Like one group wants to show the couple drowning, but they can't because they're not allowed to go in the water. Then the other group is trying to get the history right except no one can agree what the real history is. I mean: the handprints are cool, but *that* story keeps changing, too. Some club members

117

are so ancient I don't know how they can stand up, much less re-enact any-thing at all. You're better off just enjoying the views if you want my opinion."

Wow, what an ambassador! "Well, Kayla, I appreciate your advice. And I sure hope you get to move on to bigger and better things."

"Me too." She shot another look at the clock. "I don't wanna be rude, but…is there anything else?"

"Just another quick question if you don't mind. Do you know where the name 'Shy Moon Lake' comes from?"

"Not a clue. I don't ask. It's like Shakespeare said: 'Who the hell cares about names?'"

"Hey," I said, "you really are funny. Maybe I'll come back some time and we can chat again. My family is living next to the lake, in one of the cottages."

"The Thurston place," she said. Eyes suddenly big. Her cheeks flushed pink.

I moved closer. "What is it? What's wrong?"

She shook her head.

"Come on, tell me. Is it something about my cottage? Did you know the Thurstons?"

Still the girl did not respond.

"Don't you think I have a right to know?" I added a bit heatedly—and that seemed to penetrate her fog.

She blurted, "It's just that…well, *they* almost drowned, too! They shouldn't have been there in the first place…"

I waited, holding my breath…and hearing voices from the past shout-ing as I floundered in Lake Ronkonkoma, trying to swim, trying to breathe…

"Their kid ran *into* the lake," Kayla said. "He had to be rescued and it took so long that he has brain damage. But at least they made it Below. My uncle says that's all that matters."

I had no response this time. Nothing coherent.

"Not that your house is jinxed or anything," Kayla added hastily. "It's just another sad story. See why I want to leave?"

Needing to do something with my hands, I picked up the whole pile of pretty brochures. They still looked sleek and colorful, but they *felt* wrong, almost slimy against my fingers. I fumbled, and the brochures slipped from my hands to flutter onto the floor.

"Oh! Sorry. Let me get that." When I stood back up, strangely winded, I glanced at my hand in surprise. The brochure on top was different. Made of cheap paper; homemade, amateurish, with wording that seemed the same… and then didn't.

"*Come to Shy Moon Lake*," read the caption at bottom. "*A Vacation to Die For.*"

Who had done this? A comedian?

"Look, Kayla," I said, holding it up. "What's this?"

She stared without blinking. "I've got to go."

"No, wait. Look at this brochure! It says 'die,' not 'live.' Why? Do you know who made it?"

"It's time for my break. You can come back later!"

"*Please.* Just another minute. Tell me about the wall around the lake. All those signs saying how dangerous it is. *Why* is the lake so dangerous?"

Kayla shook her head—back and forth; back and forth—as if she were losing an argument with someone I could not see. And she was still backing away, inching her escape from me and my questions.

I swallowed the urge to grab her by the arm. "Kayla…I'm sorry. I really don't mean to harass you. But I need to figure things out. Do you know Rikki Stevens?"

"Yes. A little." She took two giant steps in reverse.

Then she disappeared through the back door, leaving me alone in the Visitors' Center to take care of myself.

I grabbed the oddball brochure on my way out.

CHAPTER 17

FUNNY HOW JESS FREAKED OUT *because birds don't land on this lake,* Charlie thought as he watched the black bird float happily along. *Wait till I tell her!*

The one loon that she claimed had briefly touched the water—and then fought to get off as if escaping electrocution—had no doubt been sick. Unless *Jess* is the sick one, Charlie couldn't help thinking. Not the bird.

As he continued to watch, another loon appeared.

It landed in the water near a stand of cattails. Then a couple of ducks glided into view, paddling contentedly. Moments later, two geese emerged from behind a boulder.

Getting busy around here.

He began walking along the lane toward the forest…but the splashing and quacks and chips and bird calls were turning into a goddamn party. Charlie stopped walking and stared at the lake. A stubby-winged, snake-necked cormorant appeared, followed by another weird-looking bird—a grebe?—whose legs stuck straight back like an arrow. Next, a bunch of coots schmoozed and strutted onto the stage like stuffed shirts at a cocktail party. *Pip-pip-pip*! Meanwhile, a single egret, tall and elegant, stood off a little, weighing its options.

Charlie reached into his pocket for the cell phone that was useless except as a camera. *Gotta show Jess...*

Then he heard something human. A small cough.

At the end of the lane, several yards away, a figure sat on the rocky shore beside a big boulder. He recognized the neighbor, Miss Rikki Stevens. She of the punk hair, long legs, big bust, and injured foot. Rikki was hugging her knees, head bent forward, orthopedic boot tossed aside like the shed skin of a snake. He had no idea what she was doing here alone behind a rock, but it couldn't be good. Her shoulders shook.

"Excuse me, Miss?" he called, moving closer. "It's Rikki Stevens, right? Are you okay?"

She gazed up at him, face very white. In contrast, her hair was the color of an eggplant. Her eyes looked feverish. "Oh," she said. "Oh*h*!"

He was careful not to move too quickly, not to scare her. "I don't want to intrude...but do you need help?"

"No," she said—and let out a strange noise: a whimper or snort. Her lips curled upward slightly. Her mouth widened.

He saw teeth. And all at once he realized she wasn't sad or in pain. She was *happy*.

"It left," she whispered. "Can you believe it? It *left*!"

"What left?"

"I never thought...I didn't expect...oh, never mind. I can't explain. But it doesn't matter. It finally happened!"

Her smile became broader. Charlie found it surprisingly warm and pretty, *Too bad she's insane.*

"Well, I'm glad you're all right," he said, starting to back away. "I just wanted to check."

Then he heard his name called from the other direction. "*Charlie!*"

Jess.

He whirled around. To his surprise, his wife ran down the path toward him with great exuberance, as if they were long-lost lovers in a film. Her hair flew in clouds of red. Her cheeks glowed pink, her smile iridescent. He spread his arms to greet her. How could he resist? And she threw herself into his arms, panting and laughing. They hugged so tightly he could feel the rapid flutter of her heart inside her ribcage.

"Hey, hey, what's this?" he whispered into her neck.

She pulled back to look at him, and her eyes *glittered*. "Charlie, did you *see* those birds? They're on the lake!"

Oh. That was it? The birds.

Charlie looked again at her eyes. Was she on drugs or something? "Yeah, I know. I was about to take a picture for you."

"I can't believe it. I can't believe how wonderful I feel! Like a new person. Like I've been *reborn*. Hey, Charlie? Where's Jonah?" she said, then noticed Rikki sitting against the curve of rock. Jess's whole body stiffened. "Oh. Hi. I didn't see you."

"Hello," said Rikki absently. She was staring in the other direction, toward the lake. "Look," she said.

Something was happening on the surface of the water. A stirring followed the beat of silence, then wild flapping began...

"Oh no," Jess moaned.

Charlie instinctively grasped her hand as the lovely collection of birds—ducks and loons and cormorants and coots and even egret—rose screaming skyward. In a cacophony of sound and motion, the critters struggled to go up, up, up from the shimmering water.

For no good reason that he could see.

Feathers flew. And after several ear-splitting seconds of zigzag flying—no GPS built into these birds—the cyclone of critters whooped their success. They were completely off the lake now except for a single loon, which inched upward...and then faltered and splashed down, down, down.

The bird tried again: its wings desperate.

Then Charlie saw—he actually *saw with his own eyes*—a swell of water ballooning under the bird.

The water folded over the bird like a hand, and the hand yanked the bird down into the lake.

Jess screamed.

Did that really happen? Had the water actually *pulled* the loon in?

Charlie rubbed his eyes and looked again.

The bird bobbed back to the surface, seemingly okay. It stirred, wings flap-flap-flapping—and then keeled over.

Rings of water expanded away. Everything grew still: air, water, bird.

Charlie felt himself breathing heavily. Jess's face was a mask of horror.

"My God, what was *that*? Charlie, did you *see* that? What the fuck was *that*?"

"Honey, it's okay. Calm down."

"No!" She yanked her hand away and plunged past him.

She ran past the trees, stumbling along the shore in the direction of the dead bird.

Good lord, what now? "Jess," he shouted at her retreating back. "Wait! Where are you going?"

"You'd better go get her," said Rikki Finn Stevens in a tired voice. She was standing right behind him, the boot back on and ready to go. "Because *it's* back too," she added before limping away.

*   *   *

Charlie had long legs, and he used them to sprint across mean, rocky ground, dodging boulders until he was able to reach out and grab his wife's slim shoulder.

She staggered, losing her balance while managing to kick off her shoes.

"For God's sake! Hold on, Jess. Where are you going? Stop fighting me!"

She squirmed out from under him and kept running, shoes left on the dirt behind her. Charlie looked down, flashing upon the memory of Rikki Stevens by the dolphin fountain late at night, holding a pair of shoes.

Maybe we've all lost our freaking minds, he thought. And especially Jess.

She was going to jump into the *lake*? To give CPR to a dead bird? Where were the groceries she'd supposedly been out buying? Or the library books?

He began running again and grabbed her arm. She fought him off, pummeling him with small but mean fists.

"I want to see that bird," she cried in full voice: a tormented child.

"Come on. *Stop.* You hear me?"

She whimpered.

"Snap out of it now. Okay? Just put your shoes back on. Everything's fine."

"No! No, it's not fine! I-I-saw that poor thing! It just—dropped dead. Probably because it's on that…that…"

In his arms, *she* felt like a bird. Small, slim, fragile bones. Heart still fluttering rapidly. "Shhh, take it easy. That's my gallant Jess, wanting to avenge dead birds."

"Don't say that! It's not funny!"

"Okay! Okay. Maybe it's not funny, but it *is* dead. Come on, honey. You're not going to jump into a bottomless lake to save a bird, right? Remember the signs. We're not allowed in the water. You want to get fined?"

She finally stopped fighting.

She gazed up at him, tears streaking her freckled cheeks. "But you *saw* it, right? How scared they were?"

Reluctantly, he nodded. "I saw the birds fly away. We don't really know how scared they were, or of what. This is nature, Jessie. Unpredictable and violent. Death happens."

She glared at him, eyes with that over-bright wet look. "Except there was nothing there to kill it. All the birds were happy. They were moseying along, acting like fucking birds. Then...*bam!*" Suddenly she stopped, as if struck by a thought. "Wait. Charlie, where the hell is Jonah?"

Oh, shit.

Charlie had the awful sinking realization that he had really blown it this time. He had left their child alone for more than a few minutes.

Not that it should be such a big deal, right? Jonah was sound asleep, and they were so close...

"He's fine, Jess. Don't worry about—"

"I can't believe you left him alone. *Again*?"

"Stop screaming. We can get there in two minutes."

"So that makes it okay? To abandon him? Like...like that poor bird?"

Whimpering again, she ran barefooted toward home.

Charlie cursed and grabbed her damn shoes and jogged behind her up the stairway to the porch, and into the living room—where the TV was still droning and Jonah still snoring.

Thank God, Charlie thought.

But Jess turned on him anyway, her expression a ball of fury. "Don't you *ever* do that to us again, Charlie McCortney, do you hear me?"

He held up his hands. "I'm sorry, okay? I didn't think a few minutes would hurt. But I shouldn't have ignored your instructions."

"*Anything* can happen in a few minutes. Especially here!"

"He wouldn't wake up and go to the lake by himself. You know that. He'd call for us, and I was right in front of the house."

"No, you were down at the end of the lane talking to *her*. What if Jonah had gone out then? What if the lake—"

"What? If the lake *what*?"

"What if it…called to him?"

Charlie's heart gave a sick little flip. "What does that mean?"

"Never mind, I can't talk now. Nauseous," Jess said abruptly, and bolted toward the bathroom.

PLEASING
THE LAKE

CHAPTER 18

"RAQUEL," NANA CRIED FAINTLY. "HELP!"

Rikki, who had just clumped onto the porch from outside, saw her grandmother thrashing in her chair and ran, sprained foot be damned.

"Oh God, Nana, what is it? Wake up! Are you okay?"

"The air," Nana gasped. "What happened?"

At least she could speak, so she couldn't have an obstruction. Rikki placed a palm on the old woman's forehead. Cool but clammy. The wrinkled features—usually arranged into a sourness that indicated decent-enough health—looked pinched.

"Can you breathe? Where does it hurt?"

Nana only shook her head.

"Then I'm calling someone. Wait here," Rikki said.

"*No.*"

The word came out as a bark. Rikki stopped in her tracks. That was a healthy set of lungs she'd just heard, no doubt about it.

"No calls, Rikki," Nana said. "It takes forever for anyone to show up. And what are they going to do when they get here?"

"They'll check your vitals, maybe take you to—"

"To where? That crappy medical center? Or maybe Below. Ha."

"They could at least check your heart."

"My ticker is still ticking, and it will stop when it stops. I'm asking you here and now: *What's happened to the goddamn air?*"

Rikki collapsed on the chair across from Nana. "So, you know. You felt it, too."

"Of course, I did, even in my sleep."

"I thought it was...a miracle. The birds were landing on the water, Nana. I *saw* them. A cloud of birds, all different kinds. They were swimming and playing, and the air felt light, like there had never been smoke, never a fire or earthquake, never anything bad. Then...it was over. All the birds panicked and tried to leave, and they did it...except for one."

"What happened to that one?" demanded Nana, eyes suddenly sharp.

"Dead."

"Dead how?"

"Why does it *matter*?"

"Because it does. I need to know everything. Tell me," Nana said.

"Well, it was struggling to get out of the water, to fly away with the others, when this...this wave appeared and *dragged* the bird down. We saw the whole thing."

"*We?*"

"The new neighbors were there. We watched it together."

Nana's voice turned strangely gentle. "One day we will stand before the gods, and we will know we've done the right thing."

"But...why did the air change? What does it mean?"

"Only the lake knows," Nana said.

"And why did it get better only to go back again? Just to tease us?" Rikki wiped her nose with the edge of her long-sleeved shirt. "I hate this," she said, talking to the cotton sleeve—and so finally telling Nana, too, how bad it was for her, how much she worried about losing the last of her family and ending up alone *because of that lake.* "Can't we hide, Nana? Just stay inside and lock all the windows and doors?"

"Windows and doors only work against those on *this* side of the earthly journey. We can't hide from the other side. Raquel, look at me."

She looked.

"You need to be as brave as the ancestors that came before you. Listen, my child. We come from a long line of warriors. Are you going to fight or give up?"

"Fight," Rikki said.

"Are you going to listen to my advice or to people who don't know the spirit of Shy Moon Lake?"

"Your advice."

"Are you going to fear life, or fight to the death?"

"Fight," Rikki said again. "I just wish I could see what we're fighting exactly. Our ancestors didn't go to battle without weapons, blind and dumb and smelling things that aren't there and hearing things that aren't right… and trying to figure the whole thing out with no one around to help them."

"Oh yes they did," Nana said. "Anyway, "*I'm* around to help you. Who else do you need?"

Who else, indeed.

CHAPTER 19

"HOW DO YOU FEEL NOW?" Charlie asked anxiously from the bedroom doorway.

It was early evening, and I lay in bed resting. One small light glowed with the window wide open to cool air. I was watching the lake, though not quite able to see it. And that gave me an excited feeling I could not begin to explain, either to my husband or myself.

Everything seemed a-jumble—though not in a bad way. This place, this lake, could be *any* lake, in any time period. Lake Ronkonkoma went so far down that bodies rarely washed ashore, yet on the 7th of August in my 10th year, I found a small bone on the beach, as if a dog had drowned and decayed and then been coughed up. My brother said it was disgusting finding a bone, but I thought the dog had found a nice resting place in the lake. *There are worse ways to die...*

Or not. That bird, the loon, had not been happy.

Charlie came to sit on the edge of the mattress, as worried as a grandma. He had aged five years in less than three weeks.

"Don't fret so much, I'm better now," I said to cheer him. And in a way it was true. "The fresh air settles my stomach. Maybe I'll get up with you guys for dinner and Family Game Night."

"Really? That would be great," said Charlie. "If you're sure."

"Sure, I'm sure."

"You're hungry?"

"Not yet. I had crackers a little earlier."

"That's it? Funny how you keep getting sick." He looked down at his fingernails for a moment, then up. "I can't help wondering"—he paused—"have you thought that you could possibly be…pregnant?"

I froze. "No, that's impossible. I never went off the pill, remember?"

"Maybe you missed one."

"I wouldn't do that. I'm not pregnant. I *can't* be."

He stiffened.

"Sorry," I said. "I don't mean to sound so negative."

To my surprise he accepted my apology right away. He slid down next to me and slipped an arm around my shoulders. "Okay. Let me ask you this. Aren't you…a little late?"

"No." I thought about it. "Well, maybe. Only two days. That's noth—"

"Except you're rarely late. Right? When did you know with Jonah?"

"I don't remember." I slumped against the headboard; his arm slid off me. "Maybe it *was* only a couple of days. Oh God."

He said mildly, too mildly: "Would it really be so bad?"

I shook my head. Didn't speak.

He said, "I love you and Jonah. We'd make it work, no matter what."

At that, I smiled. Sort of. "I love you, too, Charlie. And no, it wouldn't be so bad. I love babies."

Then I burst into tears.

*   *   *

True to my word, I did get out of bed to eat whatever we had left from the city—the last giant can of ravioli and a smaller can of green beans—and I did not get sick.

I *can't* be pregnant, I kept thinking.

If I were, canned ravioli and green beans should have sent me running back to the bathroom. Anyway, my pills were all accounted for. I had not missed even one. Which meant that being pregnant right now was statistically improbable, if not impossible.

After dinner, we washed up, unpacked the game box, and took out "Chutes and Ladders." If I climb up a ladder, I'm not pregnant, I thought. But if I slide down the chute, maybe I am.

I lost spectacularly, multiple times. And when my game piece arrived at the top chute only to be immediately tossed down like so much trash, an image of the afternoon's dead bird swiped at the back of my eyeballs.

All the other birds had gotten away; why not that one?

Bad behavior? Bad karma?

Maybe "Chutes and Ladders" really was trying to tell me something, like a Ouija Board.

I decided that rest might bring on reluctant periods. So, I said an early goodnight to both boys and turned in.

My muscles twitched, for some reason. I just could not get comfortable: first my back, then my knees, and then a little lump of something poking at me from under the sheets. I reached down and found a hair-tie. After that, I looked out the window again.

I wished I could talk to Charlie, have a heart to heart. But what would I say? *Am I sick or pregnant or crazy? Charlie, pick one.*

What irony a second baby would be! To lose Charlie's trust over my desperation to not get pregnant…and then end up raising another child anyway?

Or was I having another baby *because* of what I'd done to Charlie? Like it was my punishment…

Now that *is* crazy, I thought.

I was not a religious person, but I sure wished I could pray. I had not been able to since that long-ago day when Dad died. I guess I believed that any Being who refused to help a man like him would feel uninspired to help a kid like me. Tonight, though, I yearned for faith.

I started by thinking about a nice vague "Higher Power": someone beneficent and not frightening to beseech, kind of like Mother Teresa. I conjured her up, complete with the blue and white head-cover thing I'd seen in *Time* magazine. She'd been visiting a refugee camp, unconditionally loving the sick and forlorn, feeding the hungry, assisting the parched to sip life-saving water.

Water. The word caught my mind.

Ah, yes. Water is one of the most basic elements. Water, Earth, Fire, Air.

Water waits in lakes and rivers and oceans, and fountains, and sweat, and tears. Water inside our bodies and if we are lucky, soothing dry throats.

It changes faces, fluid or solid. Water gifts and destroys. It combines the comfort of a Mother Teresa, the viciousness of a tsunami, the potential for the first primitive life forms in an unforgiving universe…

I punched my pillow and turned again.

A vision of Shy Moon Lake came to me, its glorious crater shape encircling my being.

Water.

Suddenly I shivered, feeling the enormity of it. Of losing my mind…

Hell no! No lake that scares the shit out of birds is going to get me, too!

Unless…unless, of course, that poor bird *needed* to die? Or it was destined to die for the benefit of someone else.

Could that be?

We all die, I thought. **It's just a matter of when and how. More important is how we** *live.*

Miraculously, my limbs now sunk into the coolness of those bedsheets, and I began to drift. Thoughts and feelings spoke dimly and without meaning, like words in a foreign film.

I felt myself cleansed…swept along a shoreline so pristine it could only be called one thing:

Sacred.

⋆　⋆　⋆

The trees here are implausibly thick: the original anchors of the world.

And the air smells rich and heady, of unsullied growth and viability. Even the shine and cast of the sand…and rocks…seem primordial: the first trees, the first waters.

Is this Atlantis, then? The beginning of all things…?

Or we can call it Heaven.

A slim brown canoe appears on the far side of those gray-blue waters. And people are paddling oars: maybe two or three; faces indistinct. The canoe glides toward…an island.

Not Heaven.

The tiny lump of land looks rounded, like the back of a whale. What am I supposed to do? Why don't I know?

I turn and gaze up and down the shore. Everything is familiar and not. No wall; no dock; no town. No cottages. Only lines of smoke rising gently above the distant trees. Campfires.

Go that way.

⋆　⋆　⋆

The trees glisten with raindrops so fine they shimmer. But I don't remember it raining.

Drumbeats sound from the direction of the campfires as I walk over roots, pinecones and needles and rocks, on a path that winds this way and that, rising and descending again.

The drumbeat stops.

Peering through a grove of trees, I glimpse a hut made of sticks and reeds. Someone is sitting in front of it. A woman.

Her shoulders are straight back, her long shiny hair cascading to a bare waist. No drum in sight.

I inhale quietly, so as not to disturb her.

The woman is combing her hair, luxuriating in its texture. I wish I could touch and groom it myself. She lays down the comb and begins plaiting those long tresses, twirling the hair, clipping it atop her head with small sticks. She shrugs on a shirt made of animal skin, dangling fringes. Her breasts are bare for only a moment before she places on top of her head a large headdress made of feathers and bone.

Then she stands. I draw in my breath.

She is naked below the waist, and I see folds and skin and hair that confuse me. A heartbeat later she is wearing pants, loose, masculine looking. Not a skirt.

I must be dreaming. All I need to do is open my eyes.

The woman turns and looks directly at me. She—or *he*—has a painted face; the markings similar to what I've seen in museums of Native American chiefs. I hear the voice again—*that same voice*—except not inside my head.

It is in my chest this time, resonating and pulsating like a second heart.

Now you see me.

Now you know.

Now we are One.

CHAPTER 20

CHARLIE HAD BEEN AWAKE IN the living room half the night, creating pro and con lists and convincing arguments in his head. Finally, over-tired and irritable, he went to bed, crawling under the sheets next to Jess, yet hesitant to touch her. He fell instantly asleep—and awoke with a decision on his lips.

The choice seemed so obvious. Why had he even vacillated? His irritability lifted like a sweaty nightshirt.

Buying a summer cottage, sight unseen, in a remote corner of the mountains had originally been a lark, a spontaneous grab for the Good Life with his new family. Jess, too, had indulged in summer-lake fantasies. These were such simple dreams, easy to achieve if you have money, which Charlie did, no big thanks to his own endeavors. What was the point of a trust fund if you didn't use it to bring joy to your wife's face? To watch your son skipping rocks and exploring? In Shy Moon Lake, Jonah could have old-fashioned summers. They all could.

That was what Charlie had paid for. But it was not happening.

For one reason or another, this place unsettled them. It had rattled and cowed, maybe even ruined, their marriage. In a short time, so many disappointments and worries had accumulated that he could not see past the pile. It was bigger than the fucking wall around this lake.

Okay, so buying the cottage was a mistake—*but not an irreparable one.* Charlie refused to let any place get the best of them. As soon as Jess woke up, they would turn back the clock.

Dawn tinted the sky through the bedroom window. Jess smiled in her sleep. Eventually, she opened her eyes.

"Morning, darlin," he said. "Can we talk?"

She blinked. Nodded.

"I've been thinking. I guess I thought so much I barely slept. But that's okay, because I've had a revelation." He picked up her left hand, cradling it. "Jessie, I know you're not happy here. It's too stressful. *We're* not happy. I'm not sure why…it all changed so fast. Nothing is what we expected. It just feels wrong, like skin that doesn't fit."

She opened her mouth. He held up a hand.

"Wait, let me finish. I don't want you to feel bad. Please. *I* don't. I mean, it's a letdown. But some things are not meant to be. You and I have been through a tough patch, and we can recover at home. Where we belong."

She stared at him with wide eyes.

He added hastily, "Of course we can *visit* Shy Moon Lake if we want. That's always an option. Let's just not live here. We'll go home and pick up where we left off. A clean slate for both of us."

There, he was also telling her that he forgave her for everything. That they would be okay. She inclined her head, moved by his speech.

Then she looked up at him, and he realized she was not feeling moved in the way he had thought. Again.

"Oh no, Charlie, that's not what I want at all! How could you suggest leaving? I *love* it here."

"You—what?"

She plucked at the covers. "I love this place." Ever more quickly her fingers moved in a nervous tic. "I *belong* here, don't you know?"

A CALMNESS
IN THE AIR

CHAPTER 21

I STARED AT CHARLIE, WILLING him to understand, my heart thudding so hard I could hear it echo. Pure adrenalin washed through my veins. Yet at the same time, everything around and within me felt…quiet and clean. *Revealed.* It was like stepping out of a hot shower and opening the bathroom window and watching swirls of steam dissipate.

In this unspoiled Garden of Eden called Shy Moon Lake, my family had *space*. Space, air, and water. What could be better than that?

Except Charlie stared back at me as if trying to figure out which spaceship I had dropped in from. His voice sounded childishly frightened. "What in the world are you talking about? Since when do you belong *here*?"

"I don't know," I admitted. "I just feel…different. Maybe it's the nature. And no traffic. Isn't it nice to live in a town where we don't need a car?"

"Sure, but…Jesus."

I could not help giggling. "Maybe it *is* a spiritual thing. Kind of hard to describe. Like we just have to have faith."

He drew back, mouth open.

"Come on, Charlie. Close your mouth; you look like a fish."

He closed his mouth.

"You think I sound crazy," I said, feeling generous. Poor Charlie, he needed me to explain. All of this wasn't natural for him. "I get that. With my memory, I sometimes feel crazy. But not now. Oh, honey, not anymore."

"What—"

"The memories come less here! And I think it's because I feel…rooted."

"Rooted?"

"Small towns do that, you said so yourself. They open you up and calm you down. Living here, I intuit things."

At that last bit, he looked as horrified as if I'd suddenly confessed to murdering small children. "You *intuit* things?"

"I feel spiritually connected to nature: to the lake, trees, wildlife." On the periphery of my mind, I recalled foraging, gathering herbs and plants for ceremonies…

What? What ceremonies?

Suddenly I was not sure of the difference between what I intuited from others, and what I remembered for myself. Why didn't I know?

"Holy shit, Jess, do you hear yourself?" Charlie just about yelped.

"Oh honey. Don't get upset. I feel comfortable here—and it's turned into *this*." I patted my flat stomach. "It can't be coincidence, right?"

He looked at my stomach, too.

"The truth about the pills was *supposed* to come out in Shy Moon Lake," I went on, explaining, explaining the unexplainable. "We reap what we sow. Remember the potholder?"

He shook his head.

"On our first day, the innkeeper? She gave me that potholder with all the wisdom on it. I showed you. It's in the kitchen, in a drawer. Come to think of it, I should hang it over the sink."

"Really. So, now you're going all on me woo-woo, too?"

"It's not woo-woo that I can sense the spirit of this place. It's destiny." I touched my middle again.

"Jesus, I . . ." He broke off. "Wait a minute. Now you *want* to be pregnant?"

I nodded.

There was a long silence.

Then: "Well. Good," he said. "Except we, uh, haven't confirmed it. Should I run to the pharmacy, pick up a test?"

"Okay," I said.

"Okay," he said.

I leaned forward for a kiss. After a beat, he met me halfway. Our arms encircled one another in what must have been an intimate embrace.

Yet I had the strangest impression that Charlie was hugging a wire dummy.

The bird—my *soul*—had flown.

CHAPTER 22

THE SCREEN DOOR TO THE pharmacy squeaked.

Waving hello to the old man behind the counter, Charlie followed signs to Health and Wellness. Old wooden floors squeaked as he walked. He felt conspicuous perusing the shelves for pregnancy tests though this aisle also contained novelty soap, freshly cut wood, and coffee. Over-the-counter medications had been stored up high, where small children could not reach; the Sudafed was practically nailed down. To the right of that, pregnancy tests hid on the uppermost shelf. He grabbed the second to last box and brought it to the register.

"Beautiful day, young man," said the pharmacist, hunting around for his glasses. "You visiting our little town?"

"Yes and no," Charlie said. "We bought a summer home."

"That's wonderful. Up mountain then, catching the views?"

"No, I guess we've got the best view of all: the lake at our front door."

"Ah, the cottages. Seven dollars, twenty-five cents, please."

"You have no more of these on the shelf, Mr. Reed," said a woman from behind Charlie.

A feminine hand placed a "1 Minute Response" box on the counter next to Charlie's. Three pairs of eyes took a moment to sum up the coincidence: two pregnancy tests on the shelf; two pregnancy tests purchased at the same time by two different customers from two different couples.

The old man smiled, gums flashing. "Well, well. Thank you for letting me know how popular these are. I'll have to stock up."

Charlie grinned, and the woman buying the other test giggled appealingly. She was slender, bird bones at the neck and shoulders, making her appear younger than she probably was.

"You're in good form today," she told the pharmacist. "That's nice to see. Are you feeling better?"

"Fit as a fiddle." The old guy stuck out a blue-veined hand toward Charlie. "Let me back up and introduce myself. Name's Johnston Reed. Pharmacist, clerk, sometimes stock-boy, and once or twice, midwife."

"Pleased to meet you, sir. I'm Charlie McCortney."

The woman shook Charlie's hand, too. Hers felt small and soft, like a balled-up hankie. "I'm Hannah Mason. It's always nice to meet new people in a small town."

"How's Stan doing?" Mr. Reed asked her. "Stayin' off the sweets, I hope?"

"Yes, he certainly is. I make sure that he has all the sugar he needs already."

That got another laugh.

The lady's eager to be pregnant, Charlie thought with a pang. Truly eager, not woo-woo eager. *Don't think about it.*

The two customers said goodbye to Mr. Reed and walked into the sunshine. "We may have shocked him," the woman said with that same charming giggle. "He's such a kind man. He's worked in that pharmacy my whole life."

"Nice."

"I believe I've met your wife," she said, turning to face him. "Red hair, right?"

"Yep, that's Jess."

"She seems like such a sparkly person. I'd love to get to know her."

"I'm sure that can be arranged. Where do you live?"

"Didn't I mention that? We're in the cottages, like you." There was an awkward pause. Then Hannah said, "You moved into the Thurston place, which is three houses away, on the left."

"Great," Charlie said. "We're practically next-door neighbors. When did you meet Jess?"

"The first time was when she was kind enough to gift me with home-made banana bread. The second time she was"—a glance at the warning signs they were passing as they went through the gate—"she was with your son."

"Well, we'd be happy to have you over some time. You and your husband."

"We would love that, too. Stan—my hubby—is shy, but he comes around."

Charlie nodded at the pharmacy bag. "And who knows; we might be celebrating at the same time."

She laughed and they walked silently onto a tree-lined path toward the row of cottages.

"May I ask you a personal question?" she asked suddenly. Her gaze was focused on the lake.

"Sure," he said, though he didn't like the sound of it.

"Excuse me if this seems a bit forward," Hannah Mason said. "But does your wife have twins in the family?"

CHAPTER 23

CHARLIE WAS SO SURPRISED, HIS feet stopped moving. "No," he said. "I don't think so. Why?"

Then he caught himself.

"Wait, she does have an Aunt Jeannie with a twin sister. I forgot about them. But why did you happen to ask that?" *And how did you know?*

The neighbor bit her lip. "I shouldn't have said anything. I apologize. I'm usually more discrete."

"Discrete?"

"It was just a hunch. I usually resist those. Please forgive my intrusion." She began to move away from him, head bent.

"Wait." Charlie hurried forward, caught up with her. "What's wrong? Are you all right?"

"Yes, fine. I'm fine. Really." But she leaned away from him, kept going.

Charlie was flummoxed. He had no idea what that business of twins meant or what had scared her. Plus, he was suddenly out breath. They weren't running. He should be used to the altitude. What the hell was going on?

The sky above them was rapidly changing; the sun had ducked behind a bank of darkening clouds. Walking quickly to catch up to her again, he gestured at the flat green water. "Can I ask *you* a question? You've lived here a long time. What is it about this lake? Why does it seem so…different?"

"Oh, I'm sure I don't know—"

"Please, I want your perspective."

"I don't have—"

"And your question about twins. Why did you ask that?"

She shook her head, avoiding his eyes.

"Mrs. Mason. I don't mean to be rude. You seem like a wonderful person, and I'm glad to meet you. But my family hasn't been here long. There's no one for me to ask these things."

She did not say *What things?*

"My wife has been, well, I guess you could say *changed.* Now we're buying a pregnancy test." He rattled the bag in his hand. "*So, what do twins have to do with Shy Moon Lake?*"

She took a deep breath and paused there on the path. "You have to be careful, that's all. *If* the stories are true. *If* your wife is pregnant. I haven't been able to keep a pregnancy going. So, *if* she is expecting twins…if the stories are *true*…then she may be in trouble. Maybe all of us are."

Good lord, she *was* crazy, just like Rikki Stevens. He didn't know whether to laugh or cry.

Rain began to fall; big fat drops that dropped onto their heads like water balloons. *Plop! Plop! Plop!* Charlie wiped his hair out of his eyes and ducked under a tree. Hannah followed. They huddled there together as a keening noise rose from their right—from the lake.

"What," Charlie asked loudly, "is *that*?"

She didn't answer.

The noise grew. Trees began to stir. He watched, dumbfounded, as their leaves blew in odd circular motions. Branches bent, screeching, at the uptick in wind. What had happened to the beautiful summer day? No reason to feel panicky…but what *was* this?

A cyclone in the mountains?

A hurricane?

Typhoon?

The rain had become a deluge. He heard it roar, felt it slap him. In no time he was soaked, water pouring over them from all directions, like a monster sprinkler run amok. He tried to block his face from the needles of rain; tried to protect the neighbor too. And peering half-blind at the lake, he thought he saw the surface turning into *swirls*.

How could that be? This lake had no currents, no tides….

Yet the shapes swelled, forming a single enormous vortex centered on a…gray hump?

An *island* had appeared. In the middle of the lake.

Jess had mentioned an island. He had not believed her.

"What's happening?" he screamed over the gale, pointing. "What *is* that?"

Hannah yelled something incomprehensible. Then she bolted away from their shelter into the muscle of the storm. She was running and tripping away from him again as if *he* were the danger.

Exasperated, Charlie called, "Hey! Come back!"

The wind was now shrieking like a thing in pain. Cottage shutters banged in the distance. Bowing tree branches felt like claws against his skin. Charlie found that his feet wouldn't move. He was in a Carnival Fun House, stuck to the ground, getting hammered with water and wind. He closed his eyes and made up his mind. Then he *pushed*, using his old football shoulder to plow back onto the lane, against those hoses of pressure…toward Hannah.

Something big and awkward banged toward him. Cardboard? An old signpost? And Hannah screamed. She seemed to smash against the debris—and went down.

Fast. Like the dead bird.

Charlie leaped over something else, probably a branch. He banged his ankle, lurched forward, and dropped into the madly running water that used to be a street.

Hannah was ahead, low down, unmoving. It's killed her, he thought savagely.

But no, here she was, rising out of the swirling mess, wild and unsteady. She emitted another sound, maybe a shriek, maybe a laugh—and ran off crookedly in the other direction.

Toward the lake.

"Stop!" Charlie shouted. "Come back, you're hurt!"

"No," she screamed as she ran. "*Noooooo!*"

As he stood there in the maelstrom, he saw—he actually *witnessed*, five yards in front of her—the wall of wind and rain change shape.

Before his eyes it became a rolling series of gusts…fingers of a hand inside some weird glove. And it pointed to the lake, as if the storm *wanted* her to go in that direction.

As if it were *directing* her.

"Jesus!" Charlie ran forward blindly, groping for something to grasp, to guide him.

Then everything stopped.

The wind.

The rain.

The freakish, furious sounds.

Even the island in the middle of the lake vanished. The surface of the lake reflected placid blue sky.

The neighbor stood hunched over in the middle of the road sobbing, hands over her face. "*Please,*" she shouted in Charlie's direction, as if it were *his* fault, as if he had done all this. "Never ask me anything again!"

He tried to speak. But she kept going, crying as she splashed across puddles toward her cottage. She staggered upstairs; opened the front door. The door slammed, and then she was gone.

Squeezing the soaking wet bag miraculously still in his hand, Charlie had no choice. He went home too.

CHAPTER 24

"HEY," I SAID WHEN CHARLIE stumbled in the front door. "Did you get the test?"

Automatically, I held out my hand to take the pharmacy bag—and drew back. The bag was dripping wet, drops splashing onto our hardwood floor. "Jeez. This thing is soaked! What happened?" I peered into his face, at his wet hair. "And so are you. My God. Did you fall into a sprinkler?"

"Very funny, Jess. Just hilarious." He grabbed a sweater off a nearby hook to use as a towel across his face. Then he stalked over to the TV and lowered the volume. Jonah mumbled, "Hi, Daddy," without looking up. My husband just turned to me and chin-gestured toward the kitchen. "Please," he added.

We went to our usual spot, the kitchen table, where I asked him again what had happened, and he started ranting about a storm. Not a sprinkler but a goddamn storm. Had I not noticed the driving rain and hurricane winds that had almost ripped out the trees by their roots just a few minutes earlier?

No, I had not. I kept waiting for him to break out laughing, to say he was just poking fun…but there was none of that to be had.

I said, "Well…I didn't notice anything."

Our eyes met. His looked wild, angry. And I felt a little afraid. I had seen that dark a fury once before…but could not call up the memory. Did not know the month or the year or exactly who, or why. **He wants to kill me**, I thought—and didn't know who I meant. Not Charlie!

"For God's sake," he sputtered. "How could you not notice! Are you deaf? Blind? Didn't Jonah notice?"

"I don't think so. Sorry, Charlie."

"'Sorry Charlie?' Did you really just say that?"

"Okay. I'm *not* sorry, Charlie? Is that what you want me to say?'"

"Come on, Jess. It was…like a flash hurricane or something. That's why I'm so surprised. And I was there, in the middle of it. Getting pummeled along with one of our neighbors."

"One of our neighbors?"

"Hannah Mason. You've met her. I ran into her at the pharmacy and we were walking back when the thing hit. Ask *her* if you don't believe me."

"I didn't say I don't believe you. I said I didn't notice a storm."

"But that's impossible! It was like a *freight train*. How could you not notice a freight train?"

I didn't answer. Didn't tell him the TV was on.

"And I saw an *island* in the middle of the lake," Charlie added.

I nodded, comforted somehow. The island was there. I had known in my gut that it would be. And that made me wish I *had* experienced the storm; had felt it move against my own skin….

Charlie was still talking, his voice still slightly out of control. "Then this…this branch came diving out of nowhere and *nailed* that poor woman on the head, like it was trying to kill her or something."

"Oh my God. Is she okay?"

"I think so. But that's not the point. The wind was *after* her. It was like a fucking cartoon glove, *pointing* and *dragging* her toward the—"

"Charlie, you're shouting again. Jonah will hear you."

Behind him, the wall behind the refrigerator began to knock. *Hey, I'm here. Don't forget me.*

"I hate this house," he spat.

"Charlie. Honey. It's okay, really. Whatever happened, it's over now. You're home, safe and sound." I gestured at the kitchen window to prove my point. Because the sun was shining. Anybody could see that. "By the way, thanks for going to the pharmacy for me." I opened the wet pharmacy bag. A small pool of water had collected under it on the kitchen table. "How about we move on to a more important question?"

"Right. Let's just change the subject," Charlie said without smiling. Then his shoulders seemed to relax. "Okay, open the box. Are you ready to pee on a stick?"

"I love it when you talk dirty," I said, and trotted off to the bathroom with all the anticipation of opening gifts on Christmas morning.

CHAPTER 25

"TWO LINES," SHE ANNOUNCED FIVE minutes later, wonder in her voice. "I am, as they used to say, *with child*."

And you have never looked more beautiful, Charlie thought.

Faint rosy light from the bedroom window tinged her cheeks. She was smiling reverently at the stick; at the two red lines that told them she held two heartbeats within one body; two futures with two souls. Hers and their child's.

"Jessie," he said, reaching out to gather her into his arms.

Smelling the scent of lemons from her shampoo, he wanted more than anything to carry her away from this place. To a castle maybe. A fortress of health, wealth, safety, and joy. *Like our condo back in the city...*

"You're a great mother," he whispered. "Jonah will love having a sibling."

"Yes, he will," she agreed, without any of the regret or fear in her voice that he fully expected. "And you'll be a great father. You already are."

"I love him."

"I know. He loves you, too."

They held each other silently for a moment. Then Charlie asked, "Are you nervous?"

"No." But she nodded. "Yeah, I guess I am. A little."

"Me too."

Inside this room, no walls were knocking. We are in a bubble, not a vortex, he thought. Jess and I with Jonah and Baby-To-Be. Will it be a freckled, redheaded, green-eyed girl? Or a tall, slouchy little boy I can call Chaz? If they had a girl, they would call her Lina, after his own mother. Or Kaj, which meant "gust of wind" in Hawaiian. That seemed fitting.

Excitement began to spread through his veins. Why brood about unlikely tempests, vengeful tree branches, and islands rising out of forbidden lakes? He was going to be a *Dad*.

Gratefully, he kissed his wife's lips. She opened her mouth.

"Mm," he said. "Time to put Jonah to bed?"

"Nice idea, Romeo, but he needs a bath first."

One more kiss and reluctantly they disentangled themselves.

"Just think," Charlie said as they left the bedroom. "When we get home, we'll get us some yellow and green paint and do up a nice, politically correct and gender-neutral nursery. What say you?"

She stopped mid-hallway, frowning. "But *this* is home now. I told you."

"Jess," he said, the tightness in his chest returning. "Not now. That's not what—"

"I know the house was meant for summers. But Charlie, I can't leave while I'm pregnant! We have to stay. I have to have the baby *here*."

LATE NIGHT CALLING

CHAPTER 26

WHY IS IT PEOPLE SAY they want you to be happy and then protest when you actually are?

Even people who love you do this, I realized that night while getting Jonah ready for bed. *Especially* people who love you. Pondering the irony of that distracted me so much, I had trouble with the most normal of tasks. Where were his jammies? Did we remember to floss? My mind felt slippery yet hyper-focused.

Most puzzling of all was this longing that grew inside me, nestled in my chest like a wish I'd never known I had. How amazing, I thought, would it feel to be *free*? To run outside as I want, breathing this air of the gods until I'd drunk my fill. Even the screens on the windows of the cottage were starting to annoy me. I had the impulse to rip them off and stick my whole head out of doors. Because *freedom* was out there.

Freedom from what, I didn't know. Not my family. Why would I want that?

Not everything can be named, I decided. Do birds yearn for the sky because of some intellectual equation? Of course not. Instinct is a real thing. Maybe Charlie *thinks* he wants me to be happy, but he doesn't understand. Poor guy lacks the instinct.

All will be well. Stay, and there will be renewal.

That voice. By now I recognized it.

The Unnamed One.

Was my future child talking to me? *Hello there*, I whispered inside my mind.

No one answered, and soon enough, my other child was in bed, sleeping like an angel. Little kids always do, don't they? Innocence radiated from Jonah's freckled face; eyelashes resting on cheeks, hands holding each other like old friends. I rested my lips against his pure, scented skin and inhaled. *Here. Mommy is here. Don't worry; that hasn't changed.*

Then I left him without a second glance. I entered the living room and stood there, momentarily stymied.

I'm Wifey, too. Don't forget that.

Charlie slouched in the big chair, reading, his long legs dangling awkwardly. He was immersed in a tome by Stephen King, *11-22-63*. I took in the scene: a fat book, the braided rug, and gleam of wooden floors—all spelling *cozy*. Except in one great sense this scene was not quite cozy. Something did not fit, like in one of those children's books whose pages were cluttered with objects. *What's wrong with this picture?*

I cleared my throat. Charlie looked up.

"How's the novel?" I asked.

He paused, as if searching for a trick behind the question. Then his expression settled. "It's good. The Kennedy assassination and time travel, a perfect combination."

"Sounds like fun."

"It is. The guy tries to change the past, but it doesn't want to be changed."

"Doesn't sound very realistic, then. Sometimes the past is begging to be changed."

"Oh. You referring to anything in particular?"

"I don't think so."

He put down the book. "Look, Jess. If Jonah's asleep, we need to finish our conversation. Okay?"

"Okay." I came around and sat at his feet, warming his toes.

He straightened his position, moving those toes away from me. "I admit I'm completely baffled about what you said earlier."

"Sorry."

"I mean: you suddenly want to stay here for *nine months*? I still can't believe it."

"I know," I said simply. I did know.

"And you were serious?"

"Oh, Charlie, don't sound like that. It's not so bad. *This*"—I touched my flat belly—"happened here. Like I said, the past *wanting* to be changed."

"What does Stephen King and 'the past' have to do with it?"

"Why do you sound so angry?"

"And how can *you* go from not wanting to stay here to, what the hell, let's just camp through the winter instead of going home?"

"I don't know. I feel...animated here."

He gaped, visibly appalled. "*Animated*?"

You can do better than that, I told myself—and my head flashed with pain; it even radiated into my ears. I recalled a sweater I had worn in November 1985. Thanksgiving Day. The sweater had pretty snowflakes on it, midnight blue on white, but made me itch. *Take it off*, I screamed to my mother. *I don't like it!* Mom tried not to smile; I had seen the curve at the corners of her mouth. *Shhh, I'm taking it off.* She lifted the hated wool off me...lifted the skirt made of bark...and the basket cap protecting my tender face from the hot sun.

There, see how Mama takes care of you?

I shook away the intrusion—literally tossed away the knowledge that *this* voice was not my mother's.

Or was it? Was I trying to disown my own past?

"Charlie, listen," I said through dry lips. "Shy Moon Lake is beautiful. We're lucky to have financial security, to own this house. So why not have the baby here and then decide if we want to go back?"

"*If*? So now it's '*if*'?" He rose from the chair like the Incredible Hulk. His eyes were raging. "Are you freaking kidding me?"

"Shh, Jonah will wake up."

"Give me a break! He could sleep through an earthquake."

I giggled for some reason, which seemed to horrify Charlie even more.

"What are you laughing at?"

"Sorry. I didn't mean it."

He nodded, no longer the Incredible Hulk; just a man who felt awful.

"Please try to understand," I said gently. "That's all I'm asking."

"Right. Duly noted."

"It's like…a complete circle. Like the shape of the crater. For nine months I can walk along this lake every day and swim—"

"*Swim?* Like the loon?"

"Okay, not swim. But you wanted me to like it here, and I do. So, what's the problem?"

He did not say what I knew he was thinking: *Be careful what you wish for.*

Shakily, I stood. My back hurt and my ears were still ringing.

"I need a walk," I said, not adding the last part: *alone.*

But Charlie seemed to hear it anyway.

"I don't want you going anywhere alone. Not again."

"This is a safe place, and I'm a big girl."

"Come on, Jess, it's dark. We'll all go tomorrow."

"Oh, for crying out loud," I said, already halfway to the door. "Don't be silly. It'll be a short walk in a small town. What can happen?"

*   *   *

I was right to insist; my walk alone both invigorated and soothed me.

I simply followed the shore into the woods. In the moonlight, I climbed freely over rocks and bramble, unafraid and unencumbered. My tennis shoes turned all squishy before I realized how much time had passed. I had gotten a dozen scratches on my arms and legs, and a few of them were bleeding: faint thin red lines, like a hidden map rising to the surface.

I didn't even think about town.

When I returned home, Charlie was conked out in the big chair. I checked on Jonah then went to bed alone, cuts unwashed. I did not bother to undress except to remove the shoes, just tumbled in, fuzzy teeth and all. And the blessed night enveloped me, the covers of our bed as warm and nurturing as hot washcloths.

Odd how sated I felt lying here without Charlie. My insides glowed with the intimate scent of the lake.

Sacred.

CHAPTER 27

AS SOON AS JESS LEFT, Charlie rushed out to the porch.

He ached to follow her, to find out what she was up to, if anything. Not that he could imagine what she might be up to. But he had to make sure she was safe.

Why does she have to walk alone at night?

This is what distrust feels like, he thought miserably. Like spoiled milk.

A figure, faintly visible, moved along the lake's edge as if gliding on water. Jess? Charlie wanted to call her back, to invent some excuse like Jonah crying for her. Or Charlie could follow her for real. Why not?

Because he would be leaving Jonah alone again. And now that thought scared Charlie, too.

The night air cooled the sweat on his face. As he waited, trying to decide what to do, the figure fully merged with darkness. Too late, he thought. Country sounds took over: an owl's plaintive hoot, the secret rustling of leaves, a creaking undertone to the wooden planks under his feet. Eventually, his heartbeat eased.

Shouldn't be following her anyway.

He went back inside to Jonah.

∗   ∗   ∗

Sometime later, Charlie awoke with a start. He sat up.

Where am I?

Then he remembered. Oh, the living room chair. He had nodded off after coming in from the porch. So, was Jess still…?

He nearly tripped over a side-table in his rush to the bedroom. Be here, he prayed, squinting at his watch. Three o'clock! She *had* to be safely in bed. What would he do if she wasn't?

He reached the doorway and slumped in relief. She *was* here. Thank God.

Jess always slept like some small burrowing animal, with pillows piled around her. He yanked off his jeans, pulled away the covers—and stopped.

The pillows were there. But Jess was not.

∗   ∗   ∗

He ran out of the cottage without pants. *Christ! Can't search for her in my underwear!*

He whirled around and raced back in, dread twisting his gut. A minute later he was outside again, shoving his legs in jeans, panting like he was having a coronary. He forced himself to wait a few more seconds, to zip up the pants and catch his breath.

The night grew quiet. No owls, no leaves rustling anymore. It felt dense out here, almost jungly…so where were the night animals? Then, he noticed a low rumbling in the distance. From the direction of the lake.

Or maybe he was hearing a goddamn bear. The one thing that hadn't happened here yet.

"Jess?" he called, keeping his voice low. "Are you there?"

The grumbling moved to his left, where the darkness had turned patchy. Slightly illuminated lake-water played under an elusive moon. He bumped his foot against a rock and yelped. *Fuck.*

"Jess? Can you hear me?"

The grumbling was changing, growing higher. Could that be Jess? He found the sound impossible to pinpoint. Maybe she was sleepwalking… *and the lake has no bottom!* Then the sound changed again, became long and flute-like.

Someone was playing music?

He whirled around but could barely see anything. And his damned heart had lurched into a drumbeat to go with the flute. Stop it, he told himself. Like Jess said, this is a small town. Low crime. She had probably just gone for another walk…

Except the Jess he knew would never walk alone this late at night, no matter how small the town.

Screw the neighbors. "Jeeeessss!"

From between clouds, a finger of moonlight emerged. It illuminated the water just offshore, slightly to his left. To his amazement, a woman stood there, waist-deep in water.

Charlie's neck prickled. *No, can't be her.*

But it was.

Jess's back was straight, her arms relaxed in a natural position, palms down, as if gently touching the surface of the lake—

—and then he realized what else she was touching.

His knees buckled.

The palms of her hand pressed the top of…hair. Bright, curly hair.

Jonah.

* * *

"*Stop!*" Charlie screamed.

Heart banging, body trembling in outrage, he raced to the water and plowed in. While Jess turned to stare at him, her face as blank as granite in the moonlight.

Don't think about it.

What mattered was that turning her body had moved her hands as well, and Jonah popped free to the surface, sputtering, and bawling—and *alive.*

"Mommy...mommy...mommy!"

Thank God!

Charlie heard himself crying as he grabbed the boy's soaking wet shirt. With one mighty scoop, he clutched the shivering form against his chest. "You're crazy, you know that?" he screamed at his wife. "*You need help!*"

She mumbled something incomprehensible while Charlie turned his back.

He sloshed heavily toward the shore clasping the boy close. His jammies were dripping, and he shook violently, snot streaming from his nose. The child felt so light, so fragile and lost in his arms, that Charlie feared for him, feared for his sanity if not his life.

He began to run. Away from Jess.

How could she do this?

Near the house, he heard her again, calling to him as casual as if she had just woken up from her nap. But her last sentence was the last straw. It did him in. She said: "Hey, can you boys wait up?" and he spun around on the top step with a ferocity he did not know he possessed.

"Don't you come near this house unless you can explain yourself! Not one more step!" he hissed.

She stared up at him with that same blank expression. Maybe she hadn't heard. She looked so strange, her eyes open but twitchy, as if she had dived into REM sleep while standing wide awake.

Not that he cared. *I'm done with this.*

He knew he should call the police, even if that was too terrible to contemplate.

If this godforsaken town had any police. Why hadn't he seen any?

CHAPTER 28

"STOP YELLING," I SOBBED, AND nearly vomited for the second time in the last sixty minutes. "Please, Charlie. I can't think!"

The first spew had arrived without warning, the sick going straight onto my own wet shoes. My head had pounded then and pounded still, and not at the base of the skull. No accompanying memories either—in fact, no memories at all. I didn't remember this evening. I didn't remember what I had done or not done. I wished I could rip my head off my shoulders and be done with it.

Couldn't the husband...Charlie...see how scared I felt?

This thing he accused me of ... was unspeakable. And for him to say it with Jonah sleeping peacefully on my lap! Our son was not scared. Not of *me*. I felt violated—like a hospital patient tricked into surgery without anesthesia.

"I said I don't remember! What else can I do?" I cried, lapsing into hiccups.

"You can tell me what the fuck happened out there," my kind, gentle husband growled back. "I want to hear every goddamn thing you *do* remember, or I'm going to throw you in the car right now and drive you off this mountain to see a shrink."

Throw me? Charlie McCortney, threatening violence?

"I didn't do anything…I couldn't! Why don't you believe me?"

"Because I *saw* you, Jess. With my own eyes. If you were sleepwalking, you did it right into the lake! Into freezing cold water. And then you—"

"I wouldn't!" I reached out a hand to grab the saucepan on the floor by the couch. I had already used it once for puking. And Charlie had cleaned it out for me and brought it back. But he would not offer comfort. He acted like he hated me. Thank God poor little Jonah just kept on sleeping.

Suddenly, I threw up again. Then Charlie stood up, rinsed out the pot, and brought it back.

I wiped my mouth. "Okay. Charlie, l-listen. You have to believe me. I would never hurt my baby. I'm not a…" I could not say the word.

Murderer.

He did not look moved. "So, your clothes are wet, but you don't remember going in there. Or anything else a little over an hour ago. With your memory? Your *photographic* memory?"

That shut me up.

Was he right? Had I gone into the lake to drown my son? Charlie wouldn't lie, but…

NO.

Then why is this happening?

He saw me shivering and went over to the wall to crank up the heater. Meanwhile, Jonah just kept sleeping, his innocent head on my guilty lap.

I said, "I'd rather die than hurt my baby. Charlie, please. I'm scared."

"Not as scared as I am. Which is why we're getting out of here first thing in the morning."

"What? It's morning already."

"At first light I want us away from this misbegotten house. Out of Shy Moon Lake entirely."

I watched him stop his pacing to lean against the front door, as if guarding me from demons on the other side. **Lie if you have to.**

The thought—or voice—had come out of nowhere.

I carefully stood up and placed the sleeping Jonah on the armchair. Then I left him alone and went to the couch and grabbed a pillow and stood there strangling it.

"Stop," I whimpered to no one in particular; not really Charlie, not myself. Because I *was* losing my mind. I was convinced now. This must be a case of schizophrenia or bipolar, and—oh God! If I *had* turned psychotic and had really tried to—

There will be peace. Renewal.

"Jess? Jess, give me the pillow."

Charlie was extending his hand to me, extending it carefully, as to a wolf pup in the wild. "I'm not going to hurt you. I am not against you. I just want to help. Come on, give it to me."

Meekly, I obeyed.

"That's a good girl. Now, let's sit down and talk like reasonable people."

I nodded. My face was on fire. My breath came in gasps and sobs.

"My poor Jess. What in the world has happened to you?"

I shook my head. *Don't know.*

"We will need to go home and get you some help," Charlie said, with his own voice breaking. "Probably for all of us. But we'll figure it out together. I promise."

All will be well.

I hugged my arms to my chest while he fluffed the pillow a little and set it down. Then he sat, motioning me to join him.

"Now," he said in that same creepy voice: the doctor to the lunatic patient. "You can see why we need to go home, right?"

Stay.

"Right," I said over the ringing in my ears.

For a nanosecond, I was not sure where else to turn, which of Charlie's emotions to tap into. There were…so many.

I said, "Charlie…I'm really tired. From being pregnant…and sick. I know we need to go home—but moving is so hard. The stress."

"We'll manage," he said fiercely.

"I know. But…we need to do it safely. Not go crazier by rushing around so much that I—" *lose the baby*, my mind finished.

Charlie stared, hearing the unspoken words, his expression a disturbing brew of suspicion and fury and fear.

"My birthday is in a week," I added softly. "Just seven days. Please, let's not fight while we…pack…and make arrangements. I don't think we can take it."

There. I'd said it: *we*. Referring to Charlie and me, or the baby and me, or Charlie, the baby and me. Any of them would do.

Charlie's gaze flattened. "Meaning what? You'll go but not until after your birthday?"

"Well. I…how about we put the house up for sale and…and leave next week, after we're all packed. Like I said. Can't you wait a week?"

He squinted at me, with his brow furrowed. I looked back, promising him with my eyes.

"I don't know," he said at last.

"I *was* sleepwalking, Charlie." I hesitated, then pushed more words out. "I remember a little. It was…a terrible nightmare. About a fire—everything was burning and…that must be why I went into, into the water."

"You remember carrying Jonah?"

"I'm not sure. I—I can't tell you how horrible I feel."

Suddenly, he grabbed me by the shoulders. "Jess—I just want to go *now*."

"I know. I do, too! But I need…to calm down. Or—who knows what will happen?"

I touched his hand. He let me do it.

"Okay," he said. "We'll do that, then. Pack up and go asap. And when we get home, you will see a doctor. Multiple doctors. I will too, if it helps."

I held out a finger, and he hooked it with his. We sat there a moment, without words. Then he stood up, scooped Jonah into his arms, and head-gestured for me to follow him.

"Let's pile into our bed for now. We'll figure out the details after a little sleep," he said.

I crawled onto the right side of the mattress in the master bedroom, and Charlie lay stiffly on the left, with Jonah snoring in the middle. Then Charlie pulled the blanket on top of all of us, and I lay there, weighed down and suffocating, and longing for whatever it was that buzzed outside of the screened window.

Freedom.

CHAPTER 29

CHARLIE KEPT HIS EYES WIDE open for the few hours left of this endless night.

He didn't even try to sleep. What for? At least he rested: if you call growing less frantic resting. With the new light, he did become calmer. *Of course* Jess had been in some kind of trance, sleepwalking. What else could it be? The alternative was unimaginable.

She did not even like to harm bugs. If she found a spider in the house, she would use a piece of paper or a cup or whatever to shoo the creature safely out of doors. And Jonah? Jonah was her life. She would never hurt him; Charlie knew that.

Unless having a second child means she needs to get rid of the first?

What an awful thought. Evil. For a moment it shocked him. Talk about not trusting! Did he really believe that of the woman he loved?

No.

Jess *had* been sleepwalking; no doubt about it. His family needed to go home—this place was not working on so many levels. But he would give Jess her week. She was pregnant; let her take her time packing. Let her enjoy her birthday. Then they *would* go, even if he had to tie her up and throw her in

172

the back of the van. He would contact Mrs. Pattick about the house as soon as it was a decent hour. Get the ball rolling.

With those decisions cemented in his mind, he got up and made coffee. He carried a fresh cup of it onto the front porch and looked around. His heart, already broken, broke again at the lament of mourning doves. The lake twinkled fresh and pink. The air felt crystalline. No one else was out yet.

Except, he realized, their neighbor: Miss Rikki Stevens. She sat on her porch step watching the sunrise.

She didn't seem to have noticed him, which was good. He was in no mood to socialize. He slumped on his own front step and tried to forget she was there. But he couldn't help glancing over at her once or twice. In brown shorts and a reddish-brown tank top, she appeared earthy and sexy and quite likely damaged, a terrifying combination.

Then she looked at him as if catching him checking her out. "Hi," she called, fingers doing a little wave. He waved back without enthusiasm. She got up anyway and headed in his direction, a small smile on her lips.

Sighing, he put down his coffee cup to make small talk with a stranger on the worst morning of his life.

CHAPTER 30

WELL, SHE CAN'T QUITE PASS for a wood nymph, Charlie thought, watching the woman approach.

Wood nymphs are mythical creatures of water and mountain—and Rikki was lithe of limb and wearing that thrush of strangely colored hair in thin branch-like tangles. But she was way too sexually mature for any nymph. Not to mention that she clutched an ugly square Thermos in one hand, unfashionable sunglasses dangling from the other. And though she covered ground rather quickly for a person in an orthopedic boot on one foot and an Ugg on the other, she seemed to trip along too, at least on the inside. She stopped about an arm's length from him and said bluntly, "I'm surprised to see anyone else up and about. I always watch the sunrise alone."

"First time I'm out this early," he said, just as awkward.

They looked at each other and away.

Rikki said, "Oh. Well, I like to toast the new day. Orange juice and orange sky. Seems fittin.'"

To his surprise, she lowered herself on *his* steps, simultaneously tucking her clunky foot coverings under long gazelle legs. He glanced uneasily at his house and sat as far away from her as he could get without seeming rude. Rikki began talking about mornings, how sacred and secretive they were.

He thought she smelled faintly exotic, like musk. To his annoyance, he found himself more aware of this woman's cleavage than anything else. But then you can't help but see what's in your face, can you? He was human, after all. Despite feeling more like a zombie…

For a moment, they watched wisps of color and cloud roping night to morning. The sky seeped orange through threads of pink and added a spritz of surprise turquoise. Nice, Charlie thought tiredly, while somewhere over the lake a loon wailed. *I'm heeeere*, it called. *Where are yooooouuuu?*

"This is the only time I can be happy," Rikki was saying between sips. "I like solitude and wilderness. Nana hates the outdoors even if she sits on the porch all day looking at it. You know, the way you keep your friends close but your enemies closer?" Rikki lifted the thermos to her pouty lips. "Yum. Want some?"

What, share germs? He shook his head. "No thanks."

"It's homemade."

"I don't have a cup."

"Drink from the other side. I don't mind."

Why was he doing this? To be polite? He accepted the Thermos and took a taste. "Hey! It's spiked."

"Yes." She giggled.

"Alcohol first thing in the morning?"

"It's the only time I drink. This is my own secret ritual. Something my Nana doesn't know."

I'm heeeeere, keened the loon, directly overhead now. *Where are yooooouuuu?*

Another taste, and warmth surged into Charlie's chest. *The benefits of being a non-drinker.* Then Rikki fixed her gaze on him, and he felt a stab of confusion. He could see in those dark eyes a fevered aloneness. Despite being so artlessly attractive, she seemed friendless…as vacant as an abandoned house. Why? What was wrong with her?

And was the problem also true for everybody around here? Or maybe just the females…

"Early in the morning, I have a will," she said.

"As in Last Will and Testament?" *Dumb joke.*

But she giggled again. "No, silly. I mean a person with plans and dreams. I can't feel that most other times. Here, want more?"

Again, he accepted, thinking: Why not? Since Jess is so insistent on staying here a week and all, we might as well get a little friendlier with the neighbors…

*   *   *

"I have some more Happy Juice in the kitchen," Rikki said a while later. "If I go get a refill, will you take a short walk?"

They still sat on the step. The sky had grown bluer rather than orange and pink, and the Thermos was empty. The morning air was beginning to feel as sweet as a kiss on Charlie's flushed skin.

Then an image came to mind: of Jess waist-deep in the lake, her hand atop Jonah's head—and he recoiled. "No, I can't. I'm waiting for my family to wake up."

"It'll just be a few minutes, I promise."

"Sorry, maybe another time. What about your foot? Doesn't it hurt?"

"I'm supposed to exercise it. And it's safer to have company in case I trip."

He thought that was clever of her, making it seem unkind for him to refuse her invitation.

She added: "The thing is: I wanted to show you something."

"Show me what?"

"Wait, let me refill this. I'll be right back and explain." She took off with that remarkable agility—help not really needed, of course—and returned five minutes later with refreshed Thermos in hand. "Because you're so new, I thought I'd give you a little lesson on Shy Moon Lake," she said, standing there in her shorts and tank top, looking down at him.

Intrigued, Charlie stood up to stretch his legs. Behind him, his house slumbered on. He doubted either Jess or Jonah would wake up for quite a while. Still, he shouldn't take chances. "What kind of lesson?"

"The history…the kind only locals can tell you."

"Oh."

"Just ten minutes?" she said, with her big, guileless eyes.

His head buzzed; his gut churned. Truth was, he could use some insider information on Shy Moon Lake. He could also use a walk. He needed distraction: something, anything, to take away those images from last night.

On the other hand, none of this seemed real. What Jess had done last night, what he was doing right now… Maybe it *wasn't* real, and they had all gone insane.

He had better check on Jess and Jonah.

He excused himself for a minute to run into the house, through the living room and hallway, into the master bedroom. There, breathing harder than he should, he stared at them. Jess, mouth open and snoring—looking normal, not dangerous. Jonah, holding fast to his pillow, breathing deeply. Charlie waited a moment longer. They seemed complete without him, in the bed he should be sharing with his wife, in this new house he hated. With any luck—and for God's sake, his family needed a little luck—Jess and Jonah would never even know he had been gone.

He went back outside and told Rikki he would go for a very short walk.

*　*　*

"That way," Rikki said, pointing. She had abandoned the sunglasses but still cradled the Thermos.

"Before you start giving me that, ah, lesson," he said as they walked, "can I ask you something? Like, why doesn't the Internet work around here? And what's with all the warning signs on that wall?"

She gave a small chuckle. "Is that all?"

He tried to ignore the way her breasts swayed under her thin shirt. "Um, no, I'm only beginning. Why don't birds like to land on the lake? I've never seen anything like it."

"There's mystery around here, all right. You heard the legend of the lake?"

"You mean the star-crossed lovers?"

"Some say it wasn't a couple." She paused to take a sip of mimosa.

"What do you mean? They weren't lovers?"

"Or 'they' was singular. Just one person drowned."

They had reached the end of the lane. Ahead lay trees, shadows, bunches of sagebrush and manzanita. The tangle of dimness looked inhospitable, he thought. He said, "The other day, I got caught in a freak storm. It came out of nowhere, broke tree branches and almost blew me away. Then it just vanished. Do you remember a storm?"

"Yes, of course."

Bingo! He almost collapsed with relief.

"My wife and son were in the house at the time," he said, hoping not to sound disloyal, like he was complaining about Jess. "And she said she didn't hear a thing, not the rain, not the banging noises. Nothing."

"Yeah, that happens sometimes. Part of the story."

He said nothing. Waited for her to say what freaking story.

"I didn't go out because I *did* hear it," Rikki said. "And saw it through the windows. I knew what it was."

"Which is…?"

"Tell you in a minute. We're almost there."

The lane and row of cottages were nowhere in sight; the tangle of dimness had formed a sort of tunnel. This was obviously not a ten-minute walk.

"Pass the mimosa, please," Charlie said.

A MATTER
OF TIMING

CHAPTER 31

THE LOON CALLS A GREETING and lowers itself toward the surface of the lake.

I sit watching, my fingers swiftly plaiting my hair. The texture and smell of the braid pleases me: long thick strands warmed by the heated eye of summer, scented with sweet grass and the young yucca plant suited for the silky heads of newborns. The skin of my face feels supple from Jojoba oil, which also rids me of lines. I am lovely, the Earth Mother awaiting her lover.

The lover I continue to betray…

Suddenly I feel his hands stroking my braid. He is seeking reassurance. I must belong to him; and be as I appear. Having imagined he has found this promise, he returns his attention to my hair. He is fondling and kissing… then yanks down hard.

I cry out.

"You pain *me*," he whispers.

No one is present to witness the heresy that follows. No one sees him dragging me, half dressed—half and half—across dust and rocks. Toward the lake.

"Release me!" I pummel his face and shoulders with my fists, fighting to be free. "Release me—and yourself!"

He kicks me in the ribs before throwing me into the water.

CHAPTER 32

FOR SOME REASON, THE MIMOSA barely wet Charlie's throat. And the scent of wild sage had become so thick it clogged his nostrils.

He couldn't be this drunk, not so fast. His head felt like…like he had wet leaves stuffed in there instead of brains. His thoughts slowed stupidly. His tongue thickened; he could feel it growing heavier inside his mouth. Was this an allergic reaction, then? in a minute, his throat would swell like a frog's and he would fall into anaphylactic shock

Or maybe this Rikki woman had drugged him. And herself?

He couldn't quite remember why he was out with her in the first place. Why would he, nice-guy Charlie McCortney, traipse through the sagebrush with his hottie-nutty neighbor, partaking in her homemade mimosa—at the crack of dawn, no less?

Talk about crazy!

What if Jess does something to Jonah while I'm gone?

"I need to go." He handed Rikki the Thermos. "Sorry, just remembered something."

"But we're already here."

She gestured before them, where the path opened into a clearing bordered by primitive-looking trees with peaked fronds. Like what's on the back of a stegosaurus, Charlie thought distractedly. Once upon a time, dinosaurs must have roamed Shy Moon Lake. Of course, they had. Long before the Indians. Dinosaurs, Indians, white colonizers, and then tourists. *Ta-da.*

In the center of the clearing, a cluster of flat, tilted boulders also hunched out of the earth. "And these must be the handprints," he said. "I've heard about them."

Rikki scrambled onto the largest rock and drew her feet up under her hips, her shorty-shorts all but vanishing from sight. Her nipples stood out against the sweat-dampened fabric of her tank top. Red handprints seemed to dance around her on the stone.

Charlie tried to look only at the hands. "Since we're here, tell me the story or whatever, then I have to go."

She smiled beatifically. Earth Mother except sexy as hell.

"Okay. What we call Shy Moon Lake originally had some other name. I can't pronounce it. But the First People harvested acorns and ate rabbits and deer and fish and used reeds from the lake to make baskets."

Charlie sat on a boulder a few feet away, hoping his head would stop spinning. "Which tribe were they? The Kumaayay?"

"No. This was a small one, mostly unknown. Nana calls them Waatangay."

"Never heard of them."

"I told you, there's no official record."

"Then how—"

"Nana and I don't need to focus on that kind of history," she said, and he laughed.

"I wasn't aware there were different kinds of history."

"I am only trying to help you," she cried, looking hurt by his insensitivity. "But when whole groups of people are disrespected and then annihilated, we don't have the right to all of their knowledge. We can't even expect to say their real names."

"Oh. Okay."

"Nana's different, though. She's told stories my whole life."

Rikki paused, her throat pulsing at the base. She seemed to be fighting a different emotion now, wrestling with memories. For a moment, she shut tight her eyes. Then she opened them and cast their troubling brilliance into the muck of Charlie's mind.

"They had this tradition where the chieftain—usually a woman—settled conflicts, even with couples. Keeping everything peaceful and balanced. They had a sacred way to prevent misunderstanding from starting."

"And that was…?"

"A ritualistic dance. Men re-enacted the human sexual act from the woman's perspective, including giving birth. Of course, they only did it symbolically, not that it mattered when the settlers came along. They were so scandalized, the prudes. I'm sure that's why none of this is written down."

Right, Charlie thought. So, all you have is whatever.

Even though he was seated, little spots hung like dust motes in the sunlight. His throat still felt parched, too. But he did sense a strange sort of excitement emanating from this place; if he stayed very still, he could feel it in the warmth of the stone underneath him, see it in the dancing light of this lush new day, hear it in Rikki's rapidly changing voice. To his surprise, every vein in his body seemed to be awakening. His blood fairly thrummed.

What the hell was going on?

Now she was an insect, her words buzzing in and out.

"The dance helped men empathize with their women so they could better honor their Creator. See, women had *power* in Shy Moon Lake. Especially this one healer who was honored for her dual nature. That was a better time than now."

Oh wow, Charlie thought. Women with *more* power?

"You'll find under this rock, a cave with writing on the ceiling, describing that healer's triumphs and trials. It's sealed up, though," Rikki said. "Your most brilliant anthropologists will never find it."

How convenient...

"Luckily, Nana had the honor of going inside. Caves symbolize the womb, and this one told stories that have never been repeated."

Charlie blinked. It occurred to him that this healer Rikki had prattled on about—the one with the dual nature—might be important. He had better not get sick and miss out...

"The tribe also had another cave farther up the mountain. The settlers saw what was going on there and were shocked, of course. Horrified. A bunch of patriarchal Europeans watching a man pretending to be a woman having sex and giving birth? They didn't understand our ways, didn't revere our elders. Nana calls it the beginning of the end."

Wait. Had Rikki said *our* ways? *Our* healer?

Charlie rubbed his right ear. It seemed to have water in it. Unless the faint rushing was wind?

He opened his mouth to maneuver words around his tongue. It felt flat and heavy, a block of wood.

"Your, uh, Nana. Did she study this stuff?"

"No, she doesn't have to. I told you, certain women *know*."

Sure, Charlie thought. Like I know I'm drunk.

"Okay," he said. "So, the healer drowned and the star-crossed couple, um, drowned too. Which is why no one can go swimming and the birds are scared?"

"I didn't say that."

"But it's what you…think?"

"I think—no, I *know*—that those white men who raided everything and destroyed the holy dance got what was coming to them. On the same night. They were attacked and killed by a she-bear protecting her cubs. If that's not justice, what is?"

He looked around. "Wait. There are *bears* here?"

"Not anymore."

Good, he thought. He was the kind of guy who would walk right into a momma bear.

"Are you even paying attention?" she snapped, good and angry for the first time.

He nodded, trying not to panic. Suddenly, his throat was growing *smaller*. His esophagus constricting. Maybe he had Strep?

Surely, he would know if he had aspirated something and damaged his windpipe…

"That's how the cycle of divine retribution began," Rikki was saying. "With the revenge of Mother Earth and of feminine energy over patriarchal oppression. But the dances didn't stop. They just went underground, so to speak. Until…well, look here."

She gestured at the handprints. Charlie leaned toward them, trying to focus.

Okay, they were red. A little inside out and creepy too, but so what? What was he *really* doing out here besides listening to nonsense? Charlie stared at this woman's purplish hair and dark eyes—and longed for Jess. Would their marriage ever be the same?

He needed to go! Check on his family…

"Nana says the prints were made by a girl who betrayed her people. She sided with the townsfolk because she had been brainwashed into believing their moral hypocrisy. She led a band of angry white men to the cave, revealing its location to people she *knew* would destroy it." Rikki bit her plump lower lip. "There are different stories about this part. But…the men in the tribe, plus any woman involved in the ceremony, got murdered—even the girl who had helped. The handprints are made from some kind of paint, mixed with blood. It's a reminder, Nana says. A monument of betrayal and deception."

"Or bad luck," Charlie croaked.

She gave him a long look. "No one escapes justice here, Charlie McCortney. Like when the typhoid came after the massacre. Every single member of the marauding party died in less than a week. They died *because* of the massacre. Because of injustice inflicted on the People of the Lake, if you know what I mean."

"No. What do you mean?"

"The disease was *punishment*. Every single evil deed or thought perpetrated on those Indians came back tenfold."

"I bet…everyone got typhoid in those days."

"Maybe, but the white man's village was wiped out. It was their karma."

"I don't believe in karma," Charlie said as a ringing sound started in his other ear, the left one. He talked louder so he could hear his own voice. "No giant scoreboard in the sky. I mean; bad things happen to good people, too."

"But *you* know what it's like by the lake, don't you, Charlie?" said this strange young woman. "You experienced the storm. That freak storm you told me about?"

Her voice had blended into the sound of water. Trickling water. Where could *that* be coming from?

"Over and over, from the past to the present, betrayers at Shy Moon Lake get punished by their own actions—in a big way, and in no time at all. Because justice is *sourced* here."

"Sourced?"

"Yes. It is why a couple of us—you could say 'priestesses'—do rituals to balance the power. So that it doesn't…devour us."

Did she say *devour*?

Suddenly, on top of the dizziness and ear pain and trickling sounds, he also felt nauseated. In what seemed like slow motion, Rikki leaned toward him, offering him an unsolicited view down the front of her shirt. Her voice came out low and husky.

"The lake knows everything. It knows what it wants and moves us like puppets. Some of us can't handle that and try to leave. A few succeed. But most just stay whether they want to or not."

"Oh." He hesitated, gathered his bumping thoughts. "They can't leave?"

"*Things* stop you. Events, circumstances. Details—*coincidences*, some call it—force your hand. No one can be good enough to make the spirits happy any other way."

"Well...that sucks."

"Shy Moon Lake is *cursed*." She grabbed Charlie's arm, fingers surprisingly cold and sharp. "Think about it. Think about what has happened to you and your family since moving here. Haven't your mistakes come back to haunt you?"

He didn't answer. Couldn't.

"Like your wife and little boy. Hasn't a cold, crazy sort of justice happened to them, too?"

He jerked his arm free...and yet.

It *had* been a strange and terrible time for his family ever since arriving at Shy Moon Lake. First Jess's lie. Then she got pregnant, which was good... sort of. Except she didn't want it and had become unhinged. Which supposedly meant...what? That the lake had given her what she didn't want, because that was what she deserved?

Ridiculous.

"I don't believe in destiny," he said over the noise in his head and the water sounds—and over something else, he wasn't sure what...except a sort of fullness filling the corners of his bones, the spaces between his breaths.

"We're mortal and intelligent…so we seek…patterns. It's how our brains are…wired."

"Oh, Charlie. You don't believe your own eyes?"

"It's…superstitious claptrap."

"You haven't been here long enough, then. You haven't started *hearing* the lake. The trickling sounds and all that."

Shocked, he gaped at her. "What?"

"Because once that starts, it's too late. Though you can always hope."

He struggled to follow her logic: if she had any. "Wait. How did you know about the trickling?"

She said nothing, just smiled. Faintly.

"Christ," he said. "Are you telling me *you* hear it, too? Are *your* ears stuffed right now…like you're going deaf?"

"That's just how our hearing is here so close to the lake," Rikki said. "All the time."

He slid off the rock and stumbled backward, instinctively getting away from her. He had to escape this place and this story. Get back home and forget the notion that they were all somehow…linked…

Unless it was true.

What would he do then?

CHAPTER 33

"RELEASE ME AND SAVE YOURSELF," I command.

But this enemy—this love that has become The Enemy—is no warrior after all. He pushes me under the water again; I cannot breathe.

Sunlight fades: water consumes. I am clawing, struggling to rise.

To live.

I must compose myself. Remember who I am. And yet…I cannot submit. I will never allow this sacrilege to occur. Today is *not* a good day to die.

With the strength and will of all those who have come before, I push off the lakebed. This mortal form continues to fight; to scrabble its way toward shore. Rocks shred skin—face and arms and knees burn and bleed—until a sound intrudes: one I cannot place.

It is the cry of a babe. A babe in need.

No, not a babe. An older child, male, with fear in his curiously colored eyes, crying, "Mommy! Mommy, what are you doing?"

Mommy?

I look again, rubbing sand from my eyes. This bed…not a lakebed. I share it with Charlie.

The husband, who is not here.

And this boy, he stares at the pillow I am clutching with both hands.

I don't know what I'm doing. Why this pillow is raised high as if to…

I opened my hands, and the thing tumbled to the floor while my mind screamed.

Jonah. No! I won't hurt you!

Here we are One.

STOP!

"Mommy? Are you okay?"

"Yes, honey, I'm fine. Don't cry." With great concentration, I offered the child my hand, palm up. *Why doesn't it feel like my hand?* "Please sweetheart?"

He said nothing, just looked at it. Maybe he didn't think my hand belonged to me, either.

"Are you hungry? Should we make something to eat?"

Still sniffling, Jonah wiped at his nose. "You scared me," he whimpered.

"I know. I know I did. I'm so sorry. Mommy was sick, but I'm better now. I *am* better. It's safe." And this time I held out both my arms, praying for all I was worth—which was not much, I admit. *Please God. Please help him, if not me…*

Thank God my boy believed me. He came to me and hung on for dear life. We both did.

I murmured into his hair, "Jonah, be a big boy and listen. Can you listen and remember this…later and always, when you're a bigger boy and you think back? Can you do that for Mommy?" He nodded. "Good, I—" I kissed his sweet downy cheek "—have had some terrible nightmares lately…and it made me do bad things. Like in the lake. And I am so, *so* sorry I scared you. Nothing like that will ever happen again. I promise."

Because I have reached the bottom of whatever nervous breakdown this is, I added silently. I'll take meds if I have to or go back to the city and see a shrink, like Charlie said. Anything, anything at all, even leave Shy Moon Lake. *But I will never, ever hurt this child again. Do you hear that?*

I didn't know what, or who, I was talking to—and for the moment, did not care.

"How about French toast?" I asked Jonah loudly, over any voice and over the implications of hearing any kind of voice. "Daddy must have gotten up early, maybe he's taking a walk. So, you can help me cook. How does that sound?"

Jonah murmured his agreement, and we walked into the kitchen, where the wall behind the refrigerator remained blissfully silent.

No knocking.

I didn't know what that meant either, only that I had shut it up, too.

That, too, was enough, for now.

CHAPTER 34

"WHAT ARE YOU DOING?" CHARLIE asked Rikki—though he had heard her footsteps behind him, had felt her heat catching up to him, and he knew very well what she was doing.

His real question was: *Why? What do you want from me?*

He willed his feet to do something else. *Move again!* One step back in the other direction. Then another. But she reached out and touched his arm, and he caught the musky perfume smell of her hair. Over her shoulder, the lake gleamed. Sunlight pierced his eyes. "Look, I'm a married man," he blurted, this time so close he could feel her breath against his neck.

It was a wisp of moisture; a droplet of lake-water.

The woman simply stood there in the compelling light, like an offering. A Priestess of the Lake, he thought—and almost laughed.

Priestess? Rikki?

"Don't be afraid," Rikki said so low he had no idea how he had understood her. "I'm the one trying to protect you."

"You are?"

"Yes."

"From what?" his mouth said.

In the light from the rising sun, he saw shapes and shadows. He felt the ambiguity of time. Her face had thinned. Her profile was *noble*. How hadn't he noticed before? He squinted, tried to shield his face from the suddenly fierce rays…and found himself giving up somehow.

Putting down his hand.

The peace, this completely consuming woman and her stories…the intricacy…who could fight it? This was a place too rich for books or computers, where underwater shadows played like children. Shy Moon Lake had spun a magnificent, translucent spider web, too exquisite to destroy…

Yet how could anyone know this unless they had experienced it themselves? Maybe *that* was what the woman before him was trying to tell him.

"The descendants of those…Indians," he began. "Is there…a reservation somewhere?"

"No, I told you, they're all gone, at least physically. And no records. We only have our club. Which is why we re-enact."

She raised her slim arms and wrapped them like serpents around his neck. He put his hands on her waist. To stop her, to push her away. But her back felt hard and taut under his fingers. Her breath now misted hot on his neck. And her breasts pushed against him, full and warm.

"*You* feel the Lake, don't you, Charlie? You hear it, too."

This is ridiculous. I can't do this…

If his arms could not push, he would use his legs. Except his feet were trees, rooted into the ground. He realized, with sinking heart, that he did not really *want* to leave.

Even poets get depleted, he thought—and flashed upon this place on the night of the big ceremony. The male healer dressed as a female to recreate the sexual act in reverse, while the real women watched, ready to do it for real back at camp.

You're losing it, Charlie…

For in his mind he watched a woman who looked like Rikki and yet was not Rikki. Dancing naked except for a feather headdress, her long black braid riding her back like a whip. Then this magical creature of Shy Moon Lake leaned over the greedy blue waters…incanting spells in a foreign tongue while her thumb dripped blood into its hungry mouth.

Charlie shook his head. "Uh, excuse me? I—think I'm sick."

But his words just fell to the ground while the light…

"No. All is well," the priestess said. "We understand."

We?

He pushed on. "Do *you* have any…ah…Native blood? Is that why you're…?"

Her breasts pressed harder against his chest, their weight and movement as vivid as an icy lake. Her lips glistened with dew: Goddess as much as Priestess.

Just for a second, he thought, as her fingers entwined with his…lifting them to her breasts. The softness there, the resilience, seemed important. This nipple rising against his palm beneath the cotton of her shirt could very well be the most critical thing to happen to him in his life so far.

So what if his mind didn't belong to him? *My hand sure does…*

Then that thought disappeared too.

He found his most ancient, primal instincts, and followed.

CHAPTER 35

I COULDN'T BELIEVE CHARLIE HAD left the house so early without leaving me a note.

As soon as I'd fed Jonah and could think straight, I searched for a note in every room in the cottage, even the bathroom. Nothing. And that was odd. Charlie *knew* my history with vanishing husbands. He knew I would worry, especially after the horrors of the previous night.

Unless he wants *me to worry. Punishing me for scaring him?*

I did not want to alarm Jonah with my paranoia, so we settled in the living room for another rousing game of Chutes and Ladders. "I won again," Jonah hollered when his goofy-eyed game piece reached the top. The freckles on his nose—all four of them—stood out like fairy gold, and for a second I imagined us feeling happy again, playing games like this, in *this* house, with this pool of sunlight spread across the floors like a lazy old cat. If I did not grip these glimpses of contentment too fiercely, maybe they would stay?

Stay like my memories, I thought with a start. For I had not had as many memories lately.

I wonder why.

As if summoned by realization, a memory flitted in. Playing Monopoly with Dad in our cabin at Lake Ronkonkoma; he had not shaved and looked naughty in a yellow tee shirt and blue Yankees cap…his wedding band gleaming yellow like the shirt. "You match," I hollered, which distracted him from my slick move onto Park Place. "I believe your car is on my property, young lady," Daddy said gravely. "Time to pay the piper."

Pay the piper. July 15, 1988. Eight o'clock am. Same as today, except two decades earlier.

"I want Daddy to play too," Jonah said now, scattering the past.

At the same time, a loud *plop* sounded from the other room. Water dripping.

To my dismay, other drops followed like obedient soldiers: *plop, plop, plop.* Yes, the noise was coming from the kitchen. A leaky faucet? That would be new, sort of. Same story, different noise.

I scrambled up to check it out, and no, the kitchen sink was not dripping. Even the wall behind the refrigerator remained quiet. I ran to the bathroom. No leaks there either, just like there was no freaking note from Charlie.

Calm down, I told myself. This is not an emergency. But my ears felt weirdly full, too, distended with fluid. *What's wrong with this picture?*

"Mommy," Jonah said in a small voice. "What's the matter?"

With some effort, I focused on my son, his innocent face, his bewildered eyes, his wavering, high-pitched child voice. "Nothing…I'm fine!" I said. "But, Jonah, don't you hear that?"

"Hear what?"

"The dripping. Shh, listen."

He tuned in carefully, head titled. Finally, he shrugged. "I don't hear anything," he said.

I *had* lost my mind, then. Like Charlie, who imagined freaky, violent storms and believed me capable of harming my precious baby?

"Mommy, wake up," Jonah shouted, yanking at my leg. He stared up at me, white-faced. "You fell asleep! Why did you fall asleep?"

I was only beginning to figure out how to answer that when the front door opened. Charlie walked in.

"Daddy," Jonah said with obvious relief, and ran to him.

I waited another heartbeat to orient myself. Then I hurried to Charlie too, to slip my arms around his neck and get some comfort—when suddenly I stopped.

My husband smelled like the floor of a distillery.

*   *   *

"Charlie McCortney," I said, aghast. "are you *drunk*?"

He blinked at my question, his expression vague. "Uh, I had a little mimosa."

"Mimosa?"

"Spiked orange juice."

Charlie didn't even drink on New Year's. He had barely finished his glass of champagne at our wedding. What the hell was going on?

He looked at me anxiously. "I was, uh, sitting on the steps and saw our neighbor, who happened to have it in a Thermos."

"Which neighbor? You hate alcohol."

"It was the boot lady." He tried a smile. It didn't work. He added, "She was watching the sun rise."

"Oh. So, you watched it together? Drinking spiked orange juice?"

"Don't make it sound so sinister." He threw a look toward the kitchen. "Hey. What's that dripping?"

Thank God he hears it, at least. "I have no idea," I said. "It's not coming from any of the faucets far as I can see. Nor the wall in the kitchen."

"Jesus Christ. That's it; I'm calling back that plumber." Charlie reached a hand into his back pocket, then looked up. "Wait a minute. Where's my wallet?"

"Maybe you left it on the steps when you were drinking *mimosas* with that crazy woman," I said nastily, and walked away.

DEVIL IN
THE DETAILS

CHAPTER 36

"**WHAT HAVE YOU BEEN UP** to, traipsing about in those shorts—and with that boot, no less?" Nana demanded the moment Rikki opened the door of the screened porch. "Nothing too foolish, I hope."

"Just another offering," Rikki said breathlessly. Then she took a good look at her grandmother's face. "Oh my God, are you sick?"

"Don't change the subject. I asked you a question."

"But you look…" *Terrible*, Rikki finished silently.

Nana seemed smaller, drained of some critical life force, as if she had already departed emotionally and was simply waiting for her body to catch up. A body that, by the way, could no longer regulate temperature. The old woman swaddled herself in so many old sweaters she resembled a disheveled cat toy.

"Stop yipping and answer my question," Nana said. *"What are you up to dressed like the devil's mistress?"*

There was no point avoiding an answer; Rikki blurted out everything. She described seeing Charlie McCortney, their walk to the grinding rocks, and the seduction. Nana listened, barely rocking her chair. When the story was over, she grunted her disapproval. "And what makes you think this will get rid of them?"

"Because now he'll want to leave! He'll be too uncomfortable. They won't want to stay."

"Do you hear yourself? Lord, girl, don't you think? What makes you believe he won't just park himself here and expect you to put out on a daily basis? He is a man, after all."

"But Nana...he hears the sounds. He's scared."

"For all you know, you made things worse. You behaved in a wanton manner, which will be punished."

"I'm already punished! We all are. And *you* told me to get rid of them."

"Seducing the husband does not guarantee anything, except that *you* sinned," Nana said primly.

Didn't she remember her own counsel? The stories, visions, and predictions of calamity...along with rituals after ritual for mercy? And what about that last storm? It had clobbered Hannah Mason, who was probably the nicest person in town. Who next?

Nana.

Nana was old, yes. She had to die eventually. Yet Rikki's skin crawled at the thought.

Sometimes she wished *she* could die instead. Or offer herself up for whatever ridiculous or exotic retribution the Lake might fling at them: trip over a tree root and disfigure her nose or catch a skin condition that doesn't tolerate sunlight. Just thinking about it caused a burning sensation under Rikki's left arm. So, maybe I *will* be next, she thought bitterly. Either drop dead outright, or the Lake will treat me to more than a rash or damaged nose.

The Lake had use for young women. *Never forget that.*

"Nothing guarantees he'll want to leave," Nana was saying, "Or that if he does, he'll take the woman with him. And she must go."

Rikki set her chin. "Well, *I* think that if he cares about his marriage he will go and take her with him."

"If he cares so damn much, why was he with you in the first place?"

Because of the Lake. It's a cat with a mouse…

"We reap what we sow, Rikki. The end times are near." Nana closed her eyes. "I'm going to rest now. Leave me be."

Rikki disobeyed—an unusual thing. She stayed where she was, hugging herself, watching Nana. What else was there to do but keep guard while the old witch slept?

Oh God, I didn't mean that!

She wanted to rip the thought out of her own head. Even *thinking* Nana was a witch was evil. Rikki loved Nana. She needed her guidance. She needed her to live.

To her relief, her grandmother began snoring—and you can't snore when you're dead.

Once upon a time these snores used to scare the heck out of Rikki. She remembered worrying Nana would swallow her tongue. A very young Rikki had pried open Nana's sleeping mouth to check, only to discover that her breath smelled like onion soup. Dentures out, the old woman's mouth collapsed like an old plastic bag, the tongue clearly in view, flopping around.

After that, Rikki pretended Nana would live forever—or at least until they found a way to appease the Lake. Or get Below.

Below. What a lovely, tantalizing word.

"Nana?"

The old woman's eyes struggled to open. "What?"

"Nana, listen. I know you don't want to hear this, but I've been thinking. Maybe we should…try again, you know?"

Nana shook her head. Not even considering it.

"Why not? We haven't tried to leave in a long time. Maybe this time we'll make it."

"*No.*" Nana leaned forward, eyes snapped open and as sharp as a poison dart. "Not us. Not this family. Look at what happened to your mother."

"I know," Rikki said, though she didn't, really.

No one had ever explained it because no one knew. There was evil at the lake, and Rikki knew that better than anyone.

And evil must be fought with evil. Because nothing else was going to work.

CHAPTER 37

CHARLIE PATTED ALL HIS POCKETS. He even pulled them inside out, as if a wallet could hide in some tiny hole in the lining. Nothing fell out but a quarter and a stick of gum. Okay, he thought. My wallet is gone. Where? And when?

When I took off my pants to screw the neighbor.

Jess was still hovering nearby waiting for an explanation. Jonah was here too, watching. Jess's eyes had taken on a squinty glare. Jonah just looked interested.

"You're sure you took it with you this morning?" she said coldly.

"Uh, yeah. I think so. Must have fallen out," Charlie said.

"Oh really."

"Come on, Jess. It's not that unusual."

"Well, look outside where you were sitting."

"Right." He was only too happy to escape to the porch. But he found nothing down by the steps, no wallet. He returned to the living room, dreading what might come next.

What came next was more questions.

"Did you go anywhere else? Or did you just sit there getting drunk?"

"We took a short walk."

"Really. Where?"

"Near the lake."

"Everything is near the lake, Charlie. Where did you go exactly?"

"I'm not sure, I wasn't paying attention." He realized he was getting angry, too, the way any cornered rat gets angry. "She was telling me history. You know, local legends."

"Ah. And, what, you took your wallet out to pay her for the privilege?"

"Jess, If I knew where the thing was, I wouldn't be looking for it," he yelled, *just like a drunk*. Holy fucking hell, Charlie thought in disgust. It was amazing how easily a person could regress to adolescence. "Look, stay here with Jonah and I'll keep looking," he said, stalking out the front door.

"Be sure to check with Boot Lady first," she called sweetly from behind him.

As sweet as poisoned pie.

*   *   *

The second he reached the bottom of the porch steps, he spied Rikki sitting on the bottom step of her porch again, this time without the Thermos.

"Hey," Charlie said, and wondered if Jess was spying on him from the window.

In any case, he couldn't ignore Rikki, not after what they had just done together. She wore the same skimpy shorts as earlier, the same skimpy top and mismatched boots. Only her arms looked different. They were folded across her breasts as if guarding them from predators.

Was he the predator now? Was that the message?

With fierce determination, he kept a neutral gaze on her face. He avoided all thoughts of naked limbs and open mouths, or how the boulder had left smudged red lines across the triangle of muscle just above her tailbone...

Get a grip, he told himself. That was a mistake. A crazy mistake.

Aloud he said, "Got a minute? Can we talk?"

"Isn't that what we're doing?" Rikki shot back.

Not a very friendly reply, but he let that go. "I seem to have misplaced my wallet. Have you seen it by any chance?"

"No. Sorry."

"I'm pretty sure I had it when we were…together."

"Mm." Now she sounded like she had forgotten about their encounter entirely or didn't care.

He didn't care either, because he was a thoughtless stupid letch. But why had *she* been with *him*? She certainly didn't seem to like him too much. Her staring dark eyes looked impenetrable, without warmth. He did not want this strange woman to dwell on what had happened between them… but shouldn't she at least recall it in her secret heart…?

The whole thing chilled him.

He cleared his throat. "Well, if you see a wallet anywhere, you'll let me know?"

"Of course."

"And…I would like to apologize, Rikki, if I've caused you any problems. I know I caused them for myself."

"Oh, no problem on this end. My soul is clear," she said.

And her abrupt smile gave him another chill, this time up the back of his neck.

*   *   *

Charlie squatted near the grinding rocks, catching his breath. He was supposed to be in good shape. He was supposed to be a lot of things, like a good man, a loving husband and father.

What had happened to him? He really had no idea.

He glanced around, hoping to see his wallet. Instead, his attention kept returning to the handprints. They looked like cave paintings; nothing threatening about them, just echoes of the past. What *could* be wrong with a not-so-accurate drawing of rust-red, small female hands pleading with rock?

Help me…

He rose quickly and left the handprints for a proper search. Starting in the brush around the rocks, he scanned and analyzed one small area at a time, probing each color, each texture, each shape, for a rectangular black object hiding in the cracks, or camouflaged in clumps of dusty, pebble-strewn grass. And over the next ten minutes he found all kinds of junk: a black checker, a used condom (not his; he hadn't used one, he didn't exactly carry them around, damn that too), and a five-dollar bill. But no wallet.

Wait—hadn't he kept five dollars inside his wallet? Maybe it was around here after all. Unless Rikki took it.

Damn it, why was I with that woman?

She would have no reason to take his wallet. Money seemed not to matter to her. Would she dare use his charge cards?

His spirits felt about as low as they had ever been. They were like the handprints, tattoos of grief. Art imitating Life, or vice-versa…

Yet even now, even in these circumstances, the air here smelled delectable: a bouquet of wild sage that also reminded him of Rikki's ass. If there really is such thing as karma, I'm toast, he thought with a pang. And he missed Jess, the real Jess. He missed waking up light-hearted. Would that wonderful feeling ever return?

Screw karma, he decided with a sudden snort of derision. He would create his own destiny. From now on, he would avoid Rikki like the plague she was, make up his transgression to Jess, and get his family the hell out of Dodge.

Because staying at Shy Moon Lake had become a game of Russian Roulette.

CHAPTER 38

THAT AFTERNOON CHARLIE SEEMED LIKE a stranger to me. He paced around the house brooding over his missing wallet, avoiding all eye contract. Perplexed and scared, I kept my cool for Jonah's sake—and stayed away from my husband for my own.

Eventually Charlie took a long nap—no surprise there—and woke up in a slightly better state. He managed to get ahold of the same plumber as before, who actually came to the house again and did his job. The dripping noise everyone finally agreed they heard, had stopped. It was a miracle. The plumber said he didn't know exactly which pipe was leaking or *how* he'd fixed it, but I didn't care.

I was just relieved something worked. The little knives cutting at my insides eased enough for me to cook dinner. I made Jonah's favorite dinner: "fat spaghetti with small mushy meatballs," which turned out delicious. But when we sat down, I found I couldn't eat my own food. This was not nausea I was battling; it was something far more corrosive.

Like: Had I really tried to…to—*say it, Jess!*—to drown my son? How could that be?

The idea was ludicrous, a scene out of a thriller.

More likely, *Charlie* wasn't telling the truth. He wasn't behaving in such a normal way himself. Mr. Mimosa was no doubt mistaken about what he saw me doing in the lake. Maybe I'd been teaching Jonah how to swim.

No, not that either.

Forget it, I told myself; Jonah is fine. If questions don't have answers, don't ask them.

After cleaning up the kitchen, I went to the cottage's only bathroom and found it locked. "Charlie?" I said, knocking. "That you?"

"No," came Jonah's high-pitched voice. "I'm me."

"Honey: open the door. Why did you lock it?" My heart began to thump. Couldn't small children drown in an inch of water? "Jonah? Let me in!"

Finally, the bolt began ratcheting back. The door inched open, and my son gazed up at me, expression serious, small hands dripping. Behind him I glimpsed bright clumps of material in the sink. Jonah's stuffed menagerie— duck, turtle, Kermit the frog, and the beloved stuffed Shrek—had been flung in awkward poses, pooling so much water on the floor it looked like pee.

"Thanks for opening the door, sweetie. Could you tell Mommy what you're doing?" In the back of my mind, I registered the bedroom door opening and Charlie's footsteps approaching.

"Cleaning my animals," Jonah said in a grave voice. "'Cuz they feel dirty."

Behind me, Charlie made a strange sound in his throat.

"Oh," I said. "Is it, ah, working? Do they feel clean now?"

Jonah wrinkled his nose. "Well, Duck likes lakes better than sinks. Shrek and Kermit want mud. But they can't go swimming."

"I know, sweetheart."

Charlie said over my shoulder, "How about we bring your animals to visit the lake, buddy—even if they can't swim?"

I saw that his mouth had gone crooked; he was trying not to smile. I said, "That's a great idea. Tell you what, lovebug. Let's get you into some dry clothes and then the whole family will take that walk. Afterward we'll pop your animals in the washing machine for a good shine. There's water there too, right?"

"Right! And Daddy's coming?"

It almost hurt to hear the love for Charlie in my son's voice. What in the world would become of him if he ended up losing two fathers? *No, that can't happen. I won't let it.*

Charlie said, "Yes, Daddy's coming. I wouldn't miss this for the world."

Jonah let out a whoop of joy. "This is a good day!"

"Yes, it is," my husband said in the softest, sweetest voice I had heard in a while.

When his fingertips touched my cheek, it felt like a kiss.

CHAPTER 39

IN THE FANTASTICAL GOLDEN LIGHT of evening, Charlie herded his small family outside while Jonah chattered.

He liked the color blue best because lakes were blue—and why was pink for girls? Next, Jonah gleefully made mincemeat out of the name Shy Moon Lake: Scared Moon Lake, Mad Moon Lake, Tired Moon Lake, Fired Moon Lake (here Charlie and Jess exchanged two words: "*developmental phase*"). Then he spiraled into the Childhood Land of Non-Sequiturs. *How big is Shy Moon Lake? Why is the moon shy? Is it allowed to go swimming? Would the moon sink?*

When they found themselves on a spit of land covered with the coarse grains that passed for sand—the lake shimmering around them on three sides—Jonah's stuffed animals were freed from their prison. Charlie believed that kids and their toys were *supposed* to get dirty...what else was childhood for? And sitting in nature with his son and pregnant wife, he could almost imagine everything was fine again; that all the recent awfulness had never happened.

Then they headed back into the woods on a trail Charlie didn't recognize and ended up smack at the handprints.

This was the *last* place on earth he wanted to be—though he refused to envision Rikki in her shorts, or out of them. *Maybe I'll see my wallet this time*, chirped a voice in his head.

"See these hands, Daddy?" said Jonah. "They're small, like mine!"

"Yep," Charlie said. "An Indian girl made them long, long ago."

"How come did she make them?" Jonah asked, squatting to press down his own hands.

"No one knows." Jess sat on the boulder and placed her hands over Jonah's. "I love you," she told him.

"I love you too. More than any other Mommy."

Charlie placed his big hands over Jess's. "And I love you both of you, more than the sun and the moon."

They stayed there, arms bumping companionably, until Jonah pulled away. Then Charlie turned to Jess and spoke again, this time to her alone. "I'm sorry for this morning, Jessie. I shouldn't have gone off without leaving a note. And it was stupid to drink anything with that woman. I just made everything harder."

"Thank you," she said. "But I guess I have worse things to apologize for."

The moment was broken by a childish shriek.

"Mommy, Daddy! Look!" Jonah held up something in the purpling gloom.

Charlie's heart sank. *My wallet?*

"What is it?" Jess called.

"Paper," Jonah yelled back. "That's littering, right? Do ghosts litter?"

Charlie got there first to snatch whatever it was from Jonah's hands. The "paper" turned out to be a scrap of photocopied newspaper, badly charred around the edges and still warm to the touch. Which meant that someone had been here just a few minutes ago.

Probably Rikki...

Leaning against the same boulder on which Charlie had broken his vows to his wife, he tried to read the thing in the fading light. The paper felt crisp to the touch; ashes around the edge flaked away as he held it. Next to bits of unintelligible text, there was a blurry picture of a young woman. "What the hell," he mumbled. "Someone *was* here. Not a ghost, though."

"You said a bad word," Jonah said in a thrilled voice.

"Sorry." Charlie handed the clipping to Jess. "Looks like an article from the local rag."

She took out her keys and flicked on a tiny light. "It's the *Shy Moon Eclipse*. This town's version of the *New York Times*."

"Does it 'splain the red hands?" Jonah asked.

"No…just something about a lady from a lake family…who died bankrupt."

"An obituary," Charlie said.

"I don't know about that. It reads like an ordinary news item," said Jess.

"What's an 'obitree'?" Jonah wanted to know.

Jess explained while turning over the half-burned scrap. "And hey, there's more here. This is…about a different death."

"Cheerful," said Charlie.

"What I want to know is: Why would someone want to burn this? It's a fire hazard, not to mention littering."

Jonah looked around. "Mommy, I'm scared."

Charlie took the clipping back and shoved it into his pocket where his wallet should have been. "It's getting late," he said briskly. "Listen, champ. Hold onto Shrek and his pals, and I'll hold onto you. Deal? That way we'll get home as fast as possible."

*   *   *

The next morning while everyone still slept, the old-fashioned landline phone rang in the cottage's master bedroom. And the shrillness startled Charlie so much he almost fell out of bed.

Jess got to the phone first, just the way he had muscled his way to the burnt newspaper the night before. Charlie sat up in the dawning and watched her.

"Yes. Right. Oh, hi. How did you know this number?" She paused, frowning. "Oh. It is? I didn't realize."

Now Jess was glaring at *him*. Her red hair stuck straight up like Pebbles in the old Flintstones cartoons. He wanted to tear the phone out of her hand and hurl it through the window. Who used landlines, anyway? *Damn this place…*

He mouthed: "Who is it?"

She waved him away. "Oh…good. But…where? I see. Oh. Well, thanks for calling. No, that's okay. Bye."

He again mouthed: "Who?"—exaggerating the word so much he felt like a gasping carp.

She slammed down the receiver and whirled on him. "*That* was Rikki Stevens. The boot lady, as you put it."

"Oh shit," Charlie said.

"She called us so early because she has your wallet! Says you must have dropped it when the two of you were at the handprints. She found it there this morning on her daily walk."

"Ah. Okay. Jess, listen—"

But in a flash, she was off the bed and on her feet, fury blazing from every pore of her small body. "You listen to me, Charlie McCortney, and tell me the truth. Why did you go to the handprints with that woman—and why didn't you mention it last night? Come to think of it, how did you drop your wallet in the first place, Romeo?"

WATER RUSHING

CHAPTER 40

CHARLIE GAPED AT ME. "I was going to mention it. Only I didn't want to... ruin the mood."

"Oh really." With great effort, I managed to lower my voice. "So, why did the two of you go there? To the handprints."

"She was telling me about local legends. I told you. Don't you remember?"

"Not really. The whole thing is weird."

"I agree," he said, looking away. "But I was interested in what she showed me."

"Like showing someone your etchings?"

"Come on, Jess. She was a tour guide."

"Maybe the crack of dawn isn't the best time for that," I said coldly.

"Well, I was upset," he said, just as cold. "You and I had a hard night, remember? With Jonah in the lake?"

It was like being slapped.

I had not expected Charlie to throw this at me again so soon. Vague impressions rushed my mind so fast I felt sucker punched: soft, welcoming fog…and hunger for the water's smooth embrace. If I had wanted Jonah to feel it, too…was that so bad?

Yes, I thought. It was. It is. Charlie had been scared to death. He had screamed at me with hatred. My loving husband—hatred! *You tried to drown Jonah.*

I couldn't have done that last part, though. I was not capable of doing that.

Why would Charlie make up such a thing? For an excuse to act hurt and vengeful…or to traipse off with the neighbor? The whole incident was unspeakable. So, I shoved it into a box in the back of my heart and slammed the lid.

There: better already, except for my ears, which had begun ringing again.

"So yes," Charlie was saying, "I drank a little Mimosa when I shouldn't have. At least it wasn't scotch."

"What were the legends?"

"What?"

"The legends she told you. What were they?"

"Oh, stuff about massacres and karma and a bunch of superstitious claptrap. Nothing coherent."

"And your wallet? It just slipped out of your pants while she was talking?"

"There you go, sounding nasty again," he said, sounding nasty himself.

I tried a different tack. "Look. Charlie. I know I don't have the right to accuse you. Not after…whatever happened. But if your time with that woman was innocent, why did she call so early? And go on about *where* she found your wallet? Why didn't she just wait and knock on our door, like any normal person?"

"Because she's not normal. She's eccentric."

"Eccentric?"

"Okay, more like bat-shit crazy." He almost smiled.

"And that's the whole story?" I asked, smiling a little myself.

"That's the whole story. I swear it."

"You wouldn't lie to me?"

"Come on, Jess. You know how much I hate lying."

We shared a long, baffled look. How had two newlyweds—so compatible and in love—started tearing into each other like mad dogs in such a short time?

Charlie said huskily, "Jess…I *want* us to be okay. It's just that nothing has gone right here."

"Except I'm pregnant. Have you forgotten that?"

He looked at me speculatively.

"What?" I said, over the noise in my ears. The ringing had grown fuller…like the infection or whatever this was had swelled and traveling toward my sinuses. I shook my head and exaggerated a yawn, trying to clear the sensation.

"Jess? What's the matter? You look funny."

"Funny," I repeated, bewildered.

"Do you feel sick?"

"No, no. I'm fine. I'm perfect." And I was. Perfect. Complete. And I flashed on the rim of the crater-lake, water reflecting sky, fertile growth nearby. I could actually *smell* the growth.

One.

"Don't worry: a week will go faster than you think," I added, suddenly inspired. I almost felt sorry for him; for everything that he did not understand—and did not deserve to lose. "I promise. I'll call today for a doctor's appointment just to be sure everything's okay on my end. Then we'll celebrate my birthday and leave. Like we agreed."

Charlie was watching me with narrowed eyes.

"*And* we'll have a little family party the night before. Jonah will like that! Rituals like celebrations make changes less scary for little kids. Then we'll go. We'll leave Shy Moon Lake."

He mumbled something, words I could barely hear.

But it sounded like: *If it lets you.*

*　*　*

The next day I walked alone into town to consult the town's well-advertised—and probably only—OB-GYN. Charlie had not wanted me to go alone; I had insisted. What was Jonah going to do hanging around a bunch of pregnant ladies? Anyway, I needed privacy, I told him. Time to think.

Now, eyeing the country-goose-wallpaper in Dr. Bernard Nedly's waiting room, I did indeed think. I thought of Charlie tiptoeing through the tulips with Miss Eggplant-Hair, an idea never got less ridiculous; it was like imagining him in a skirt. Charlie and Rikki sitting in the tree, k-i-s-s-i-n-g...

He must have felt compelled to go with her. But why; to do what? Exercise? Sight-seeing? A little *je-ne-sais-quoi?* Why didn't he say, *No thank you, this doesn't feel right, and my wife wouldn't like it?*

Plus: his wallet had never fallen out of his pants before. Why now? Maybe he *wants* to sabotage what we have together. Maybe he's jealous.

Of the lake?

It was an odd idea and yet made perfect sense. Charlie knew how deeply all this beauty moved me. Okay, I should never have brought Jonah to swim in the lake. That would never happen again; my enthusiasm had frightened the poor child. But more than one person was clearly rotten in Denmark.

A nurse popped her head into the waiting room to beckon the only other woman waiting, who waddled over like one of the geese on the wallpaper. The doctor's table magazines lay spread before me on a low table: *Mother Goose, Home and Garden, Parents.*

No *Shy Moon Eclipse*, I realized, and remembered the newspaper clipping.

Why would someone *burn* death clippings near the red hands, which happened to be the place where Charlie had lost his wallet? How did all of it tie together?

I recalled, too, the jolly green innkeeper, Mrs. Spiro. She had claimed this town to have its own version of justice. Or maybe she meant its own version of crazy?

Then why, I asked myself, do I half want to stay? That's the biggest question.

My ears still felt wrong; stuffed, drippy, and popping. I was getting used to it, though—even found the constancy almost comforting, like I wasn't really alone when I thought I was…when I felt the loneliest.

"Mrs. Jessica McCortney," the nurse said at the open door. "The doctor will see you now."

* * *

"Good news," Dr. Nedly announced a short while later. "You are indeed pregnant, as you suspected."

We smiled at each other warmly, like old conspiratorial friends.

"I see that you're married," he said, gesturing for me to sit on his nice leather sofa. "Would this be a planned pregnancy?"

Nuh-uh. Nope. I nodded, and he beamed.

"Wonderful. When you bring your husband in, I'll share more information with both of you." Then Dr. Nedly went on anyway, about prenatal vitamins, exercise, relaxation, good nutrition, and morning sickness.

"I had a lot of that with my son," I said. "Nausea every day."

"Wonderful! Morning sickness is music to my ears. Tells me that the hormones are doing their job." He consulted his desk calendar. "Let's set up an appointment for next week. In the meantime, you can always reach out." When I didn't respond, he said, "Mrs. McCortney? Do you feel all right? You look pale."

I tried to sit up and found I could not.

"Remember to take it slow and easy," the doctor said, his voice strangely distant. "though second babies are almost always easier."

"I'd better go," I said in a rush. "Sorry, I didn't sleep last night. I guess I'm just excited and...uh..."

"Wait. Sit a moment, Mrs. McCortney. Please, you don't look well. I'll get you some water."

He opened a small refrigerator and handed me a cold bottle. I said thank you and drained it, marveling that it was too early to feel my baby's heartbeat with a stethoscope, much less with the palms of my hands...and yet. I knew someone strong grew there; someone eager to fill my life.

Bah-boom, bah-boom.

"Dr. Nedly?" I heard myself ask. "Could I be...carrying twins?"

CHAPTER 41

CHARLIE DECIDED TO TURN TO poetry while waiting for Jess to come home.

This would be his first time sitting down to write since their arrival in Shy Moon Lake. Hard to believe, but true. Composing usually anchored Charlie. It shepherded him through grief and fear and fatigue and anger. Even when a poem *didn't* fix things, it simplified the chaos; brought oxygen into the hot closed room of his head.

The *old* Jess would have wanted him and Jonah to accompany her to the doctor's office. The medical consultation would become a family outing and a fun one, since this was his baby, too, and Jonah's little brother or sister. But the *new* Jess had just babbled excuses and run out before Charlie could convince her otherwise.

So, here he was with Jonah, who cared more about re-watching *Shrek* than playing with his preoccupied daddy. Why *not* write?

After checking on the boy one more time, Charlie grabbed his beat-up leather satchel and slipped into the third bedroom of the cottage. This space had so far gone unused. The air was stale. He looked around, evaluating the light. Then he opened the window facing the lake. Sweet mountain air wafted in. He sniffed it, forcing his mouth to curve up in a smile. *Fake it till you make it.* There was a pile of junk in the back of the room, probably belonging to the previous resident. He poked around, found bubble paper and cardboard and hangers. Then he noticed a closet hidden behind the junk. He opened the door, and a three-legged stool tipped over onto his feet.

It was a rather small stool, as red as the handprints. He picked the thing up, pleased. It looked old-fashioned and uncomfortable, perfect for a poet.

Like a hair-shirt was perfect for monks?

He also spied an old traveling trunk in the recesses of the closet, and that startled him more than the stool. Who would leave behind such a substantial trunk? It looked like it had survived the Titanic. The lid was peppered with old-fashioned stickers and padlocks. He tried yanking the thing open; when that didn't work, he picked at the lock with the end of his house key.

Nothing.

Finally, he left that mystery alone. He carted the stool to the window, and withdrawing a writing pad from his satchel, unclipped his one-and-only pen—the Montblanc he'd inherited from his grandfather. He held it, cradled the weight of his pen, trying to remember his grandfather's face, the passion of writing, the joy and hope of creation.

Then Charlie began to write. To heal…

For inspiration, he imagined the cottage as an old soul with its own needs. Maybe his marriage had a soul too and was begging for help? Not a very cheerful notion, but there it was. The quiet little room exhaled dust mixed with lake brine…as he continued to grip his Montblanc.

Loss of Faith
Leaving no prints, it tears up floors
Leaving no sound, it has stolen my voice

Little by little, the stool Charlie sat on became more comfortable. Soon he wasn't even sitting on a stool. The pen moved without intention, but with certainty. He breathed deeper. His skin grew warm, his heart filling with something purer than contentment.

> *There, in the cage of your heart, a frantic beating,*
> *and words pressed against it, banging*
> *against windowpanes, trying to get closer*
> *to me.*

At some point, he had stopped evaluating his work. That was the best part. At some point, he *was* his work…

> *Unable to touch, it has chilled*
> *the places on my skin*
> *where you used to trace my name,*
> *brushing the air with musician's fingers,*
> *spelling a sigh that I alone have bent to hear.*

Little by little, the velvet scratches of his pen on paper merged with the waning daylight…and then Charlie heard a door close on the other side of the cottage.

His Montblanc stopped, poised. Waiting. *Is that Jess?*

After a moment, footsteps vibrated down the hallway, toward this room. Must be her.

Charlie glanced out the window at the lake, which appeared as calm as glass. He stood, pushing the stool out of his way.

The footsteps stopped.

He heard nothing else…and then…

Running water. Same as when he'd been at the handprints with Rikki.

Suddenly, Charlie threw down his pad of paper, his useless words, his stupid pen. He strode across the floor and flung open the door—

—and found himself facing a woman he did not know.

225

She rushed at him. He cried out in shock.

Her breath felt cold, her skin clammy to the touch. He tried to pull away, to see her better—and failed. The woman was dark, distraught. Writhing. Dressed in something soft, like suede, she pressed against him, against his lungs.

He sputtered, trying to breathe.

Two arms tightened on his shoulders…then four.

Who…what?

In panic, he fought her—*them*—off.

The room had grown so shadowy, he could not see, could not think. Through that watery sound—the horrible *rushing*—he did sense something else. Two somethings.

A woman with a braid. And a man wearing some kind of headdress.

Same face, two different bodies.

Or same body?

With all his might, Charlie yanked himself away. But she—*they*—wouldn't let him. The arms were eerily strong. He tried again with everything that he had—and jolted atop his stool.

Real hands *were* grabbing him. Jess's voice rang in his ear.

"Are you okay? Charlie, answer me! What's wrong with you? For God's sake, why can't you wake up?"

He blinked.

The noise in both ears had imploded—*PowPow*. In the dim light, Jess looked small, rumpled, and frightened.

"What…happened?" he said, voice rusty. "I was writing and—"

"And you nodded off! I know, I saw you. I don't know how you can sleep on that thing, but you were in a coma." Jess nodded at the stool. "Where did it come from, anyway?"

Damned if I know. Carefully he placed the Montblanc—the real one—into his pocket. He tried to focus on Jess's face. "Did you, um, hear anything? When you came in?"

"No. Like what?"

"I don't know." *Water. Dripping, running, rushing...*

"Well, Jonah was snoring on the couch. I didn't hear anything else, just the TV."

"Oh. Okay." He paused, got a grip. "Guess I'm tired. I dreamed, or thought I did. Anyway. How was the doctor? What did he say?"

"That I'm pregnant, of course," Jess said without smiling. "And everything is fine, far as he knows. Which isn't much, apparently."

CHAPTER 42

"STOP OBSESSING," NANA SCOLDED IN a shockingly weak, wobbly voice. "No one can go back, Raquel. Remember that if you want to survive."

She lay on the day bed that Rikki had hauled onto the porch so the old woman would feel more comfortable while still glaring at the lake—and watching for neighbors. *And* eyeballing Rikki, who sat on a chair leafing through the same old photo album, as if she could glean something more from the evidence that once upon a time, she too had been hopeful and sane.

Once upon a time, Raquel Finn Stevens had been bold. She had dared to make plans, to think of the future and plan someone else's.

"Those old pictures won't change a thing," Nana went on. "You committed a sin, but at least you had a reason. The best reason of all. Self-defense."

Rikki blinked, clutching the still-open photo album to her chest.

"Come now, no tears. Come here, Child," Nana said—another shocking thing.

Rikki stopped sniffling. She stole one last look at the picture of herself three months pregnant. In this photo, she wore a yellow maternity top. Her hair, the same purplish red, was turning brown at the roots. Those roots told the truth about who she was under the paint, under the pain. It revealed who Rikki had planned to be after her baby was born.

Until she had learned there would be two babies, not one.

The sound of rushing water had signaled the beginning of the end. Water first, then the Voice. **Come taste the water.**

"What are you waiting for?" Nana said now. "I asked you to come here!"

Obediently Rikki knelt by her grandmother's lap, pressed her face into the soft housedress…and began to sob. It started as a gasp and expanded into a wail, leaving her face wet with tears and mucus. Her fist hovered near her chin so she could plug it into her mouth the way she had as a small child.

Nana hesitated.

Then a marvelous thing happened. Her bony, claw-like fingers moved into a caress on Rikki's hair. And Nana murmured what sounded like endearments, in the universal language of grandmothers everywhere: soothing sounds that didn't mean much except…

"You *do* love me, I know you do," Rikki said into the lap of the housedress.

"Shh. There, there. All will be…as it must."

More soothing, which melted from those old palms into Rikki's skin and through her blood stream to her thumping heart.

Except, Rikki couldn't help noticing, Nana *didn't* say *All will be well*. It was never *All will be well*.

Or: *Yes, I love you, completely as you are and as life is here, right now and forever, no matter what goes wrong.*

Nana never said those things. She never gave more than a micro dose of sweet clarity.

"Shh. There now. Look at me," Nana said at last.

Rikki preferred not to look. If she did, would the rest of Nana's kindness flee?

"I like when you call me 'child,'" she whispered, wiping the mess off her face with her arm.

"We are desperate. You have to try something. Each time, we have to."

"I know, but...but..."

"You could *not* give birth to those babies. You had no choice. *I* was the one who should have warned you better. I was the reason you...went so long and had to take care of it yourself."

Rikki closed her eyes, remembering. The blood staining her bed. The awful cramps. The soul-searing fear and guilt and loss. "If someone else has to suffer, let it be me," she cried out.

"Don't talk nonsense," Nana said, lifting Rikki's chin. "I have another idea. Our last chance, so listen carefully. We don't have much time."

Rikki stopped crying and opened her eyes. She focused on the spark of life in Nana's rheumy eyes and listened as if her life depended on every syllable.

CHAPTER 43

"WHAT DO YOU MEAN?" CHARLIE asked me. "What doesn't the doctor know?"

"He can't tell me anything about the baby yet," I said. "Or how many babies there are."

"How many…?" Charlie opened his mouth and shut it again. "Jess. Did you really ask…?"

"No, I'm just kidding," I said hastily, knowing I'd put my foot in it. *Better off lying.* "I just asked about the sex. But it's too early, of course." I smiled. "At least he confirmed I'm pregnant. And so far, everything is fine. He wants to meet with us next week."

"Next week?" More alarm.

Oh crap. "We can follow up in the city," I said.

He finally smiled too, a little. The dimple I loved flashed at the corner of his mouth. I reached out, and he held me close, and as hugs go it was quite nice, though more than a little sad. Always sad now. It still shocked me.

Charlie said, "Hey, let's get out of this room, go to the porch, get some fresh air. If Jonah doesn't object, that is."

Jonah, snoring on the couch, did not object. I tucked a crocheted throw around his little-boy body and joined my husband on the darkening porch. This swing had been considerately left behind by the cottage's previous owners, as they had no doubt left the red stool Charlie had been writing on. I dropped onto the padded seat next to him, and we embraced again. I savored the scent of his shampoo—minty—along with his Charlie-skin, which today included a good layer of sweat. Over his shoulder, the lake smelled strongly, too: almost too fresh, like overripe fruit. A small tick of insect noise rose from underneath the porch. This was the Blue Hour, when day and night negotiated. Yet the crater-lake appeared dim and placid; a harmless thing stationed out there for prettiness.

Somehow, I knew that was another lie.

In my gut, I knew lots of things. I just couldn't explain them, even to myself.

Slowly, Charlie and I explored each other's mouths. With the white noise of nature as background, he cupped my breast then dropped his hand to my belly. "Hel-lo," he whispered. "Hard to believe someone's in there."

Two someones, I thought.

Doctor Nedly had indeed insisted it was too early to know, but he had said it with an odd tightness, almost as if he hoped I *wasn't* carrying twins. Which made no sense, either.

"Charlie?"

"Mm?"

"Do you ever think about justice?" I asked, with no forethought. I didn't even know *I* had been thinking about justice.

"What?" he said.

"Justice. Do you think about it?"

He looked at me, then shrugged. "I don't know. Depends what you mean. Justice as in the law? Or fairness in general?"

"Fairness. I mean, life isn't fair. We all know that. My question is: does it bother you?"

"I don't usually think about it. What's the point?"

That seemed amazing to me, not thinking about it. I hid my irritation. "The point is, it's not…right. Justice is…what love feels like in public."

"*What*?"

"I heard that on the radio once, during the last presidential election. And for the first time in my life, I get it. Justice matters! It's about the only thing that does." In my peripheral mind, I noted the same water sounds coming back, and stronger. I'd wondered about them, where they'd gone. Almost missed them, in fact, as if they had something to say, too. "Since life isn't fair, shouldn't we try to re-balance it?"

Charlie only appeared more confused. "Are you referring to me going on the Magical Mystery Tour with the neighbor? I thought I explained it to you. I thought—"

"Would you do it differently if you had another chance?" I blurted.

"Yes," he said without hesitation. "I sure would."

"Okay, then listen. We rarely get that second chance. Some things we can never change. The birth lottery, for instance. We can't help who our parents are, or stuff happening to us as kids. If we're lucky, great. If not, well…it seems random. I mean, why did my father have to die so young and healthy?"

When my voice cracked, it surprised me. I hadn't shed tears over my father in so long.

"You never talk about him," Charlie said.

"I know." I paused, gathering my strength—all I possessed already and all I had to borrow. "It was a freak accident. Daddy…was on a ladder, spackling the ceiling of our living room. And the cat—*my* cat—had one of those…cat moments. You know, when something startles them, and they jump out of their own skin and torpedo all over the room and climb walls? It would've been funny, except…"

"I know. Go ahead." Charlie's voice was soft.

"Dad tried to save the spackle stuff. He tried to regain his balance and fell and hit his head. It was just a bump, no big deal. We even laughed about it. *He* laughed. Later that night, we were watching the news. He kept asking how he could get the cat—Mittens was her name because of the white paws—on the evening news. Then my father went to bed...and never woke up."

"Oh, Jessie. I'm so sorry."

"A freak thing. That's not fair, is it?"

"No, it certainly is not."

"I couldn't even blame the cat. Mittens. If I gave her away, my father wouldn't come back. Though I couldn't look at her for the longest time. My point is: We *seem* helpless. Shit happens and we take it. But...what if we're wrong? What if we *can* make things better?"

Charlie waited, his face sad and puzzled.

"What if someone who's been cheated out of everything sacred—*out of life itself*—can balance the scales?" The rushing noises were so loud, I could barely hear my own voice. The tremor in my fingers had spread down my arms, my legs, my torso. Even my stomach tightened, as if the gift within were rapidly multiplying.

In the darkness in front of the porch, the wind picked up.

"What if," I went on loudly, talking over all of it, "we can remedy things inside one small space? Shouldn't we do it? Shouldn't we encourage justice to happen?"

Charlie held up his hand. To my dismay, I realized he was laughing.

"Jess, what's going on here? Why are you going on about this—"

"*Please*, Charlie, I'm serious. Answer my question!"

The laughter ceased.

"Uh, in that case...are you talking about vigilante justice? Or legal punishment?" he said.

"No. No. Not just that. Maybe I'm not explaining it right. Just this. If there was a way—if *I* found a way to make karma real, for example, to make sure there was payback for bad behavior; to make justice *more just*—shouldn't I use it?"

"Honey, are you okay?"

"Well, I *am* pregnant," I said, half-joking.

He didn't look the least bit amused. "Good grief. So, you're saying this conversation is about *hormones*?"

I shook my head. Not about hormones.

"Then to answer your question: No." Charlie's voice seemed far away, on the other side of the rushing river. I looked down at my fingernails. "I don't believe in karma. Life is not predestined or fair. We're just a bunch of tiny creatures on a speck floating in a vast universe. To quote somebody, maybe Carl Sagan. Or Dr. Seuss. Who gets to determine what's just, anyway? If it's God, then I have trouble with cancer babies and Alzheimer's and natural disasters. Or freak accidents. If an individual gets to arrange payback and make things supposedly more just—well, who's qualified to do that? Why should we trust him or her? Maybe everything would end up worse. Whatever seems fair could be misguided. Or evil."

For some reason, I was having trouble moving my lips. Charlie didn't seem to notice.

"Two wrongs don't make a right, Jess. Like you said. Getting rid of your cat wouldn't bring back your dad. It would just punish the cat. And the cat wouldn't understand. It behaved like a cat. Can we blame Mittens for not being a dog…or a human?"

"No," I said—or tried to.

"Life seems fairer when we stop searching for fairness. We do what we can by forming laws and policies, and then we live by the Golden Rule. After that, if we find the good in what is, we've accomplished a lot. You know: *carpe diem.* Seize the day and look for the positive. Or to use the vernacular, let go of what we can't change."

No, I thought. **Never.**

"Jess?" Charlie touched the hair at my forehead. "I can't hear you."

I strained to keep hearing the voice—that *other* voice—speaking to me underneath Charlie's.

"I said: *Drink the water,*" I gasped, and bolted from the porch into the house.

CHAPTER 44

SHE'S PREGNANT, RIKKI THOUGHT. LOOK at her!

Hiding behind a tall, half-dead potted evergreen on her own porch, Rikki watched the couple cuddle on theirs. The husband's hand stroking the woman's flat stomach. The intensity between them, as if the world had handed them something immeasurably fragile.

Yes, the new neighbor of child-bearing age is pregnant. With twins?

Clutching her own empty middle, Rikki withdrew into her own house. Poor woman, she thought, also retreating into her bedroom. There she felt a bit safer, though the memories slid into the room with her.

The day just ended had been normal at first. Breakfast with Nana. Chores. Shopping, including a trip to the pharmacy for sleeping pills, for herself this time. If Rikki had swallowed a couple of those pills, she would have slept through the night. If she had slept through the night, she might not have heard the Voice. The instructions.

Drink the water.

Now Rikki buried her face in the pillow, wishing she could smother her mind. The water sounds had been bad enough. Hearing and seeing and feeling freak storms and wind and sometimes a shape, a light, a shadow—or a root in the ground or a branch falling or a chip in the pavement tripping her, causing her to sprain her ankle—all of that was awful enough.

But that voice.

She could clearly remember the startling hardness in her belly—a pregnant belly, yes, but only three months. Not far enough along to harden like that.

Even if it held twins.

Even if doc had confirmed that Rikki was carrying twins.

How thrilled and scared and worried she'd been at the news! As worried as the doc looked.

Drink the water.

Of course, Rikki had known *which* water she was supposed to drink. Because of Nana and all the stories, Rikki understood that a woman of child-bearing age was doomed to revive past events—to *fix* them, even if she wasn't sure what those events had been, or what fixing them would entail, or why it mattered at all.

The Voice would direct her, step-by-step, until everything had been gained—and lost.

Yes, Rikki had known what was coming, what the Lake required of her. And so, the decision had come easily enough, at least at the time.

Later, folks called her desperate. Maybe she *had* been desperate when she terminated her pregnancy with one of Nana's old-fashioned wire hangers. All that blood. So cliché!

Yet she *had* evaded the Lake's demands. Rikki had lived, not died. Both she and Nana still lived. Terminating the pregnancy had been the right thing because it was *not* the right thing for the spirit of Shy Moon Lake.

Still, the whole conundrum pissed Rikki off. She loathed the fact that no young woman on this godforsaken shore stayed safe. Which also meant she was doing the McCortneys a *favor* by driving them off, just as she had done a favor for the family before them—the Thurstons.

Except the McCortneys were stubborn, cuddling on their porch. Not getting the message. Time to step things up, like Nana had said.

Maybe once the couple got away from Shy Moon Lake—*if* they managed to return to their lives Below—their new baby could be just a child. New, not ancient. Innocent, not tainted.

One, not two.

AN UNEXPECTED GUEST

CHAPTER 45

LATE THAT NIGHT WHILE JONAH slept, I began working on his room. I opened the ladder I'd dragged in with me, stuffed a few materials into the pocket of my robe, and had just perched on the ladder to hang plastic planets with strands of dental floss, when Charlie walked in.

He gasped. "Jess! What are you doing?"

The ladder shook like Jell-O. Charlie darted forward to grab it, and sheepishly I climbed down, robe tangling on one of the ladder steps. He helped me, pulling a thread from the already frayed belt. "Crap," I muttered, yanking myself away.

"Sorry to startle you," he said. "But why are you out of bed climbing ladders when you're pregnant?"

Good question. I had no idea why I was awake climbing ladders while pregnant. It just seemed important, to help Jonah settle in.

"I was…decorating," I said. "I wanted him to wake up to something nice."

He eyeballed the ladder. "This isn't even ours. Where'd you get it?"

"Uh, against the side of the house…but on the ground."

"*Our* house?" He scratched his head. "When did you notice that?"

"When did I notice what?"

"Good grief, Jess. When did you find this ladder outside our house? Was it before we went to bed, or after you woke up and decided to decorate Jonah's room in the middle of the night?"

The truth was: I didn't care whose ladder it was, or why or when. I only cared that these sweet little colorful planets go up now, while there was time to show my child how much I loved him.

"Honey: listen to me. Please?" Charlie face twitched, as if he were losing control of it. "We are leaving in a week. I see no point in hanging planets with…with—"

"—dental floss."

"Right." He almost smiled.

Then he folded the ladder, loudly and firmly, and left the room with it. Thankfully, Jonah still slept in the center of his bed: a pearl in an oyster of stuffed animals. I gathered the unused dental floss in one hand, crossed the hall to the master bedroom, shrugged off my robe, and was crawling into bed when my foot brushed against something under the sheets.

A lump. Stray socks or underwear?

I nudged the object again, then reached down to grab it.

Silky.

Frowning, I unfolded the red snip of material and stared.

My mind was unable to make a connection. This…*object* was neither socks nor underwear—at least not *my* underwear. In morbid awe, I continued studying the red silk thong that I'd never owned in my life.

Then I screamed.

CHAPTER 46

JESS'S SCREAM SPLIT THE NIGHT like a blade into flesh.

Charlie, who'd been outside dumping the mysterious ladder, nearly fell over himself scrambling back inside the house. He ran down the hallway and into their bedroom—where, to his surprise, his wife sat up safely in bed, still screaming.

Her face was blotchy, and she clutched something red. "What the fuck is *this*? You want to tell me, Charlie?"

"Huh?"

She rose atop the bed, waving whatever-it-was into his face. "What is this *thong* I found in our bed?"

Instinctively, Charlie backed away with a nervous laugh. A bewildered laugh. "What? I have no idea."

"Oh really!" Her voice was loud and crazed. But her eyes, thank goodness, bulged a little less; her face no longer looked epileptic. She hissed, "Then where did it come from? Tell me that before I grab Jonah and leave this house this second and never look back."

Maybe that's not such a bad idea, Charlie found himself thinking, while down the hallway Jonah began to scream, too.

CHAPTER 47

WE SPENT A GOOD TEN minutes comforting him—and managed to do it together, like good parents should.

"Mommy, I don't like my dream," Jonah said through sniffles and baby-like whimpering. "Our house was storming, and I was scared!"

Soothing my boy, memorizing his face, I waited till he had relaxed and slipped back into sleep. Then I turned to Charlie, pointing towards our bedroom.

Truce over. We need to talk.

I had thrown the hateful thong on the floor of our room, where it lay still: a puff of betrayal I nudged with my toe. "Charlie," I said, trying for control, for decency. "I want the truth. For Jonah, for me...for everyone. You brought that woman here? Into our house? You cheated on me, and you did it *here*?"

"No! I swear I don't know what that is." He had the audacity to go back to looking shocked.

"It's a *thong*. I don't wear them because I don't like the material crawling up my ass. Surely you remember that?"

"I can't believe you don't trust me."

"Well, if you're so innocent, tell me how"—my voice broke—"*how* it got into our bed."

"I told you! I. Don't. Know."

"And that's it?"

"Do you want me to lie? Okay, I used it to clean old DVDs." His jawline tightened; like he was about to break a tooth. "*I did not bring any woman in here.* I can't see *how* I could even if I wanted to. Jonah is with me whenever you're out. Or maybe you think I hustled the neighbor into this room to yank off her undies while our son is down the hall watching Shrek?"

"Whelp," I said, "there's still some lady's underwear in our bed. Though I doubt Miss Eggplant Hair is any lady."

His expression seemed to collapse. "Listen. Jess. I should not have spent one minute yesterday talking to that woman. It was…stupid of me, and I've apologized. I don't give a rat's ass about Rikki. You must know that. And I never, ever brought her into this house."

"Then how…?"

"Maybe it's from the previous owners. Like the ladder…and the red stool."

"Come on, Charlie. That's not an explanation."

He gave me a dark look. "I'm a cross-dresser, then. Is that better?"

Damn you, I thought—and stiffened. Pain snapped against my head, fast and hard: like two monster rubber bands. I closed my eyes, waiting for it to pass…and for the memories to start.

But none came. Not one.

Then the pain changed. It migrated…and lightened. My skull began to hum. My ears were ringing too, but that was par for the course. I pictured the crater-lake as the strangest thought popped into my head.

Drink the water.

Charlie said, "Jess? You okay?"

I lurched away, avoided his arms.

Down the hallway I ran, briefly into the kitchen then out the front door. His feet clunked after me; I heard him curse. Then he shouted something and grabbed my arm, and we tumbled to the ground. We fell onto dirt and twigs and small mean rocks. Was this the road? One of the paths? Why didn't I know?

And why was he making everything so hard? I pummeled this man I both hated and loved, with both fists, trying to get free.

Trying to get to the lake.

CHAPTER 48

CHARLIE COULDN'T BELIEVE IT: JESS was *fighting* him. Wrestling him right here in the mud like a mad sumo wrestler. How could that be? What was she afraid of?

"I won't hurt you," he yelled. "Quit fighting!"

But she continued stinging his shoulder, arm, chest, and cheek with frantic, ineffective fists. She doesn't know what she's doing, Charlie told himself—and realized *he* didn't know either. He could be hurting her.

So, he let go, and she collapsed with relief. Then he pulled his weight off by falling a little to the side while still touching her. Miraculously, she did not push away. Nor did she hit him, spit, or spin her head around like a thing possessed.

Instead, she began to cry.

"Why do you"—she extended her hand helplessly—"why do you keep stopping me?"

"Are you all right?"

"You *stopped* me! And I'm so"—another distraught pause—"*thirsty!*" Her hair was waving seaweed. Her bottom lip trembled as she pointed to something in the dirt a few feet away.

A kitchen glass. *Their* kitchen glass.

"You were thirsty," Charlie heard himself say. "You were going to drink lake water with that?"

She did not answer, just whimpered like a small girl. But he could swear he heard her thoughts. *Don't know. Don't know. Don't know!*

A raindrop fell on his face. Startled, he looked up at the dark gray sky. Multiple raindrops plopped down in quick succession—*ping, ping, ping*—as fat as a giant's tears. The house *is* storming, he thought with a jolt of adrenalin. Jonah's right. This place is a freaking swamp.

Then a keening started, just like last time.

At first Charlie didn't recognize it. A gust of wind kicked up, a few creaking branches…then this rising metallic *shriek* more like malfunctioning machinery than rain. The sky opened up and roared at them. He thought of a hurricane razing forests. A tornado devouring fields and barns. And instinctively, he leaned over to shield Jess with his body. At least they were in this together, whatever the hell *this* was. And Jonah was inside the house; safely sleeping.

They waited there together for what seemed like hours but may have been minutes. And when the noise had quieted, when he could open his eyes, Jess was staring back at him without expression. Her hair had flattened; she looked wild and frighteningly beautiful.

A sob broke in his throat. "Jessie, are you okay?"

She was cold to the touch. He kissed her hard, trying to instill her with warmth and love. Not fear. Never fear. Finally, she opened her mouth to accept him. For an amazing moment, they were on fire while pelted by cool rain. Charlie lost everything but her, the woman he had loved since the day they first met.

Ah, here you are! My Jessie…

He didn't hear the rain stop; only noticed it dripping in the trees, diminishing its rhythm. Then he knew the storm was over. The ground squished as he lifted his wet and mud-stained wife into his arms and carried her like a bride back to the cottage.

Jonah still slept. After double checking that the little boy was, indeed, breathing, Charlie carried Jess into the bathroom, locked the door behind them, set her on her feet, and peeled off her clothes. A crank of the shower, and the mirror fogged. Jess let him finish undressing her. Expressionless again, she stood before him, dirty but undamaged, at least physically.

He could only pray that she was intact mentally.

And maybe his prayers were answered, for all at once, she began to move. She undressed him, kissing the moisture off his shoulder, his chest, his stomach. She pulled down his shorts. One of them shoved the shower curtain aside; they stepped inside the deep old tub. The water felt shockingly ordinary as he washed her with soap and shampoo and shower water and she washed him, until not a drop of the rain or mud remained on their skin.

Then they made love, there inside the shower. Watching each other, smiling faintly, tears mixed with water…

Afterward, thoroughly cleansed and dried, Charlie put her to bed. He fetched Jonah and carried him into the big bed, too, where they all lay together in one exhausted lump, like seals on a beach. And against all odds, they slept all night.

At least Charlie did.

When he awoke, Jonah was still sleeping next to him.

Jess was gone.

CHAPTER 49

I OPENED MY EYES TO the darkness.

Must be early, I thought, before five.

Charlie lay wrapped around me like an overtight kimono. His breath steamed my neck; his right hand chained my waist. All remained quiet except for wind in the distance—and the water sounds that now seemed to live permanently between my ears, calling, calling, calling...

Part of me longed to keep him—and us—safely at the core of my being.

But I felt another headache coming on, and this time I knew there would be no laundry list of detailed memories from whatever years of my life.

No.

Those memories did not matter anymore: those shattered mosaics of a mundane life. Not when there was so much more here for the taking. So much more.

Whoooooosh.

Charlie's arm around me felt dead. I pushed it aside and scrambled to my feet and stood in the center of the room, fighting with myself.

I should go outside, I thought. **Now.**

No.

Leaning my head back, I stared at the ceiling—as if the water might be up there, too. "Leave me alone," I whispered. "Leave *us* alone, please!"

But who was I talking to?

I glanced around the shadowed room, the dresser, and the chair with clothes crawling all over it. Did I really expect an answer? What would the water tell me—assuming I was not stark-raving mad, and water really could communicate? *Noooooooooo, I won't leave you aloooooooooone.*

Water noises can't hurt you, I told myself. Just stop. Stop being such a wuss.

And so, I left Charlie slumbering while I went outside to sit alone on the porch and watch the lovely compelling Lake—and listen to what it might say next.

*   *   *

At seven-thirty sharp, I rapped quickly—*ratatatat*—on the door of *her* screened porch. I'm not a wuss, I thought. More of a warrior. Because I knew someone in that house would be awake and would talk to me.

I knew it in my gut and neck muscles, in the cacophony of watery sounds that ricocheted and echoed inside my skull to drip, drizzle, plop, trill, splash, and ooze.

The syrupy and sodden signature of Shy Moon Lake.

Talking to *me.*

I knocked harder, and the door of the porch opened to my touch. I stepped inside.

Stuff lay around like forlorn toys in a teenager's bedroom. A half-cro-cheted blanket. A stack of photo albums. A basket of socks, apparently clean—okay, forget the teenage metaphor. The porch smelled like an old person despite all the fresh air coming through the screens.

Something else, too, lingered at my nostrils: the scent—or heat—of emotion. *Her* emotions. Because suddenly I believed that the Lake was female. All females, at least here.

Footsteps approached from inside the house, and Rikki stepped onto the opposite end of the porch, raisin eyes boring into me. A chill raced from my toes to the crown of my head.

"What do you want?" she said in a low monotone.

I raised my hand to show her what I was holding.

"Want to tell me," I managed to say, "why and when you left your thong in my bed?"

* * *

She laughed without mirth, one of the darkest sounds I have ever heard. "I am not responsible for your pain," she said, as if that explained everything. Or anything.

"I didn't ask you about my pain. I asked about your thong," I said.

She just stared at the thong, at me.

"Say something," I hissed. "I know you don't love my husband. You don't even know him. And you can't hate me. You don't know me. So why are you doing this? Charlie and I have a little boy, and I'm—"

"—pregnant," she finished flatly. "I know."

I gasped.

Eyes glassy, she smiled—and I felt myself inhaling her mental torment the way I could inhale the fusty smells of this porch. Then, to my disgust, she reached out as if to touch my hair.

I leaned away.

"I did this for all of us," she said dreamily. "I don't expect you to believe me. But I did it for you *and* Charlie, for your family and mine."

"You…" My words died in my mouth. I could barely hear myself think.

The water....

"I had sex with him to send a message. Consider it a message from the Lake. For you all to get out of here before it's too late for you, too."

If I could only hear her properly—if I could hear myself think—I might ask questions, because something in her thin, humorless smile made me believe her.

This woman *had* screwed Charlie, but as a strategy to get us out of town. Away from the Lake.

I did not understand it, but I believed her. Both she and the Lake were my enemies.

Without another word, I turned and fled.

*   *   *

First, I stopped in a group of trees to bury the thong.

I did it without ceremony, without having decided to dig at the pebbly dirt and stuff the thing into the ground. Without thinking at all, I returned the degradation of my husband's ridiculous affair into the inhospitable sands of Shy Moon Lake.

Then, with the thong safely buried, I turned toward the cottage to face my life.

And I had just reached our porch, hands icy cold and caked with dirt, when Charlie stepped out to greet me.

"Jess—thank God! I've been worried sick. Where were you?"

I hesitated, savoring Rikki's confession. She had made a perverse sort of sense by explaining what she had done. Which did nothing to explain why my husband had done it, too.

"I want you out of this house," I told him in a voice that sounded strangely calm, even to me. "I've decided. Just go pack a bag and get the fuck out because I know what you did and can't stand looking at you. So, leave. **Now**."

CHAPTER 50

FORTY MINUTES AFTER JESS MCCORTNEY'S disturbing visit, Rikki had finished packing.

Steeling herself for the first of two heart-wrenching confrontations, she slammed shut Nana's ancient, musty-smelling suitcase and hefted the wheel-less monster to the parlor. The day before, Nana had announced she couldn't stand looking at the lake any longer. So, this morning the old woman sat in the parlor *not* looking at the lake. And this minor miracle twisted Rikki's heart almost as much as the hopeless watching had.

Yet she had to do what she had to do.

"I'm going now," Rikki said, chin up.

Nana didn't respond.

Maybe she had not heard. Rikki knew she should speak louder, with greater conviction. *Fake it till you make it.* "Nana? Don't be upset with me."

Still no response.

"If I get out safely—and I will—I'll figure out a way to get you, too. I swear it."

"Don't swear," Nana said.

"I'm sorry. But *please* say goodbye."

"Bah. What for? It won't work."

It was like being jinxed. Rikki felt as if she had swallowed a ball of yarn. Against her own resolutions, she began to cry. "But Nana…I can't just stay here waiting! I'd rather die."

Nana tilted her head, like the words held no meaning.

Rikki pointed to the suitcase. "At least I'm bringing Mama's shoes. Papa's *and* Mama's. I'll do a ritual on the road somewhere, pull over and find a quiet spot and pray that—"

"That what? Those shoes didn't help *her* none, did they?" Nana snapped.

"But…shoes are symbolic! Ever since I was little, you've said that the right shoes can help us walk out of a bad situation. You said it all the time."

When Nana finally raised her gaze to meet Rikki's, it was not a pretty sight; the despair, bitterness, and grief made her face almost ghoulish. "Goodbye, Raquel. Okay? I said it. See you in an hour."

Rikki hauled the suitcase off the floor like the superhero she wished she were and stormed out—slamming the front door behind her.

Take *that,* she thought at Nana's shout of protest.

*   *   *

A few people were moseying on the lane near the gate. Not lake people or townspeople but tourists from Below, as ordinary as toast. Rikki hated the illusion and the intrusion of seeing them for even a moment, but she did not hate the people.

Never the people.

She wouldn't wish ill on anyone: not an unfamiliar teenager listening to music on earbuds; or some old guy fiddling with his fancy camera; or a cheerful young woman in a UC Davis sweatshirt pushing a stroller *toward* the Lake, not *away*. Rikki did not hate them, just like she didn't dislike her pregnant neighbor.

They were just blind or stupid. And doomed.

As quickly as possible, while wearing an orthopedic boot and dragging a suitcase, Rikki passed the wall and onto Wells Road. She and Nana weren't crazy enough to park the family truck near the lake. No, siree. Instead, they kept the old battered Ford on *this* street, a happy coincidence since Rikki's best—or only—friend happened to live here, too.

Rikki always tried to accidentally run into Maria. Today, though, there would be no accident about it. Rikki needed to say goodbye to Maria or would regret it for the rest of her life (assuming she had one). Maria's parents were still both alive and well and sane. *Her* family did not complain of water sounds or unlikely accidents in sudden storms…or the Voice. Few people on the other side of the wall even knew about these things. That was their blessing.

No such blessings for my family.

A long time ago, after Rikki's mother disappeared, Maria had been cheered by the lack of a body. "Maybe your mom ran away to Hollywood, or joined the circus," she said. "You might get a postcard from her any day now."

"No, she's as dead as a doornail," Nana said at home the moment Rikki's father would leave a room. "She shouldn't have tried to go. I told her, but she wouldn't listen. You can't escape a bullet you've fired yourself."

One year after the disappearance—almost to the day—Rikki's father dropped dead in front of his six-year-old daughter. He had been climbing a ladder to mount a camera in a tree when he collapsed from what people later called a badly timed heart attack, but Nana called his "just desserts." People who live *here,* by this Lake, reap what they sow, Nana said. We don't get to mount cameras in order to see what's not meant to be seen.

Which is why I will get the hell out—crawl if need be—and mount 500 cameras in trees if I want to, Rikki thought. *And no one will stop me.*

Climbing into the truck, she focused on her heart chakra, colored a sweet pink rather than hot red. According to Nana, experiencing gratitude despite all the crappy happenings was key to placating the spirits.

I am grateful for the lessons the Lake has taught me. For Daddy and Mama, and all the others who have suffered before me. I am grateful for whatever family I have left. Oh, and for Maria, who has loved me all along.

"Hey, Rikki! Where you going with that suitcase?" cried a familiar high-pitched voice.

Speaking of Maria, here she was now—before Rikki could go to the trouble of finding her—halfway between the bright blue door of her family's home and Rikki's truck. The house was a whitewashed confection, with blue door, blue piping, and blue shutters; fairy-cute and childlike, not so different from Maria if she were not so fat.

Rikki and Maria had originally met in first grade, in Miss Billings' class, when Rikki did not have a mother or a playmate in the world. Maria had been a miserable thing, too. She was chubby already, and clumsy, as if assigned more than the normal allotment of feet. The kids of Shy Moon Lake didn't care about Maria's brilliant smile, just like they did not appreciate Rikki's colorful imagination or rich family history. Miss Billings spent almost no time talking to her two quietest, least popular students. Rikki had not received counseling after her mother's disappearance or her father's sudden death; counseling was just not done in Shy Moon Lake. Nor had sweet Maria Alvarez received medical treatment for her continued weight gain or her acne. Throughout the years, Rikki and Maria simply stayed together, playing and pretending and exploring. They told ghost stories at the grinding rocks and spied on the monthly meetings of the Shy Moon Lake Re-enactment Club. They made up their own endings, to everything. Then they changed the middles and beginnings too, to make life fairer. Why not?

In high school, the two friends decided it was time to attend those re-enactment meetings. No other kids were interested; mostly old folks ran the club. But from that point forward, it seemed like only old eccentrics *and* young misfits gravitated to the annual event that took so much time, money, courage, and imagination.

"I'm going Below," Rikki said now as her friend huffed up.

Maria's pink mouth fell open. "But…you always said it's impossible! And what about Nana?"

"I'll get her later. For now, Aunt Maddy will have to check on her."

"But…Maddy thinks Nana's nuts! And Nana hates Maddy. Plus, what about the animals?"

Rikki couldn't think about this, or she would be doomed, too. So, she said more confidently than she felt, "Nana will feed them. They'll pester her until she does."

"C'mon, Rikki! She won't even walk that poor dog. I don't think you can just decide to do take off and"—Maria broke off, struck by a thought—"hey, what about the festival?"

"Obviously, I won't be there. You take over."

"But you're the most…vocal person in the club. You *have* to be there!"

"Well, I won't be. Sorry."

"You should have told us earlier. You should've told *me*." Maria opened her mouth to add something else, then stopped. "Oh, never mind," she muttered, turning away. She waddled back to the blue door and opened it. "See you in an hour," she called before closing the door behind her.

See you in an hour?

Furious, Rikki got into the truck and fired it up; then she gunned the engine across the dirt shoulder and onto smooth pavement. She drove a short distance away before stepping on the brake to scream out her frustration: "Nana and Miss Saint Maria—you'll see!" She was strangling the steering wheel, then relaxed, wiggling her fingers to get the cramp out. "Well, Miss Maria, I think you're just jealous because I've finally found the guts to *do* something!"

Down-away, to one side, a couple of old women idled on porch chairs. Couples and families took nice, oblivious summer walks. Don't think about Nana, Rikki told herself. Except…what'll happen if she has an emergency? Will Maddy stay true to character and avoid checking? Who will put Nana to bed at night when she falls asleep on the porch? Will Nana catch pneumonia? Who'll iron her dratted sheets?

Can't think about it.

So far, so good. No flat tire, overheated engine, or closed road. What could prevent Rikki from leaving at this point? A bad gallbladder like the one that stopped Mama when she was young? Or a broken tooth, like Nana said had happened to Maddy? Certainly not a miscarriage, like the one that had, once-upon-a-time, defeated Nana herself.

No. Rikki was as healthy as a horse, teeth and all, despite her panic attacks. She never got a cold, could not remember her last stomachache, and was not pregnant as far as she knew. After passing the border of this godforsaken town she both loved and hated, she would be reborn. The Lake would disappear, out of sight and mind and heart.

Take that!

Past the very last street of town—shoe shop, manicurist, bar— the houses became sparser, less like rows of spying faces. The road grew bumpy. Trees lining the curbs bent like hands trying to block her exodus. She followed the road to the old-fashioned wooden bridge that looked transplanted out of a corny Western. Twenty or thirty yards beyond the bridge waited one of those moon-decorated signs she'd seen her whole life: "You are leaving Shy Moon Lake, a wholesome place to live."

Yeah, right! Come back soon!

Rikki gassed it again. The old truck jerked forward. As the bridge rattled beneath her, she started laughing and cranked up her stereo to hear an old song by Melanie: *"I've got a brand new pair of roller skates..."* Singing loudly, fresh air pummeling her face, she was fast approaching the sign when a shadow half the size of the pickup darted onto the road.

Rikki slammed on the brakes. Tires shrieked. The rear of the truck started to come around. She jerked on the wheel. The truck bounced, skidded, came straight again, and stopped.

Just beyond the sign, a deer paused in the road.

A buck.

Frozen, it gazed at her, fathomless eyes frightened and disapproving. Rikki's heart was thumping so hard she could feel her arteries squeezing. Here was a deer. Her personal totem. Soft brown fur, a blaze of innocent white, enormous round eyes boring into hers. The creature was speaking to her!

Stop.

Think.

Live.

The deer—*her totem*—had risked its life to communicate with her. And do it precisely at the "Leaving Shy Moon Lake" sign—before she poked a single toe over the border. Rikki sat there in the truck, breathing hard. What would happen if she ignored the deer? If she disregarded its message and tried to drive down the mountain? She heard moving water, too; felt it ooze into her consciousness.

Drip-drip, trickle, drizzle…whoooosh.

Then the buck turned and bounded into the woods, white tail a zig-zagging bolt. *There's no such thing as coincidence. If I leave, I'll vanish…like Mama.*

Just thinking of Mama brought back a flash of the old childhood terrors: the endless vigilance for signs and symbols, racking her brains to think of rituals that might hep—and eliminate the fear. Rikki drew her knees up around the steering wheel and pressed them into her chest, huddling the way she had so many years earlier when her father lay dying just a few feet from her.

Can't change it. Can't leave it. Can't beat it. Do what it wants!

She had never in her life seen the other side of that curve leaving Shy Moon Lake. Had Mama? Had she been murdered at the border at the exact moment she had been able to smell freedom? Or had she been eaten by animals…or something else?

Mama's car had eventually been found, but not her body. Never the body. If Rikki left too, would Nana ever know what had become of her?

Unlikely.

Rikki abruptly threw the truck into reverse and turned it around. Even if she stopped on Main Street for a little lunch, she would still be home in an hour.

Just like Maria had said.

And Nana.

CHAPTER 51

AFTER CHARLIE LEFT, I STRAIGHTENED up the living room, all the while repeating a mantra to keep myself grounded: *I am Jess, Jonah's mother. I am strong. We will go back to the city and feel good again.*

And the mantra worked, sort of. *I am* Jess, I thought as I entered Jonah's bedroom. A strong woman.

Believe it.

Jonah was still sleeping. Gently, I sat on the edge of his bed, kissed his downy cheek, and sang: "*Time to get up, time to get up, time to get up in the morning!*"

He didn't move.

"Come on, rise and shine"—*because now that I've thrown your Daddy out, we need to get the hell out of Dodge before I change my mind!*—"'cuz it's a beautiful morning. Jonah?"

In a sickening flash, I imagined *not* being able to wake him. Finding his eyes vacant, like my father's had been in the armchair that terrible night long ago.

No.

I shoved away the thought. "Come on, lovebug. Wake up!"

Jonah opened his eyes, thank God. He opened them and stared at me. "Mama," he murmured in a flat little voice.

"Hey bud, you okay?"

He blinked.

"Sorry to wake you. It's just that Daddy got a call and he had to go away for a while—work-related stuff. So, I wanted to talk to you, discuss our plans."

Jonah's blankness vanished. He scrambled to a sitting position. "Where's Daddy?"

"Don't worry, Daddy's fine. You'll see him soon."

"But where *is* he?"

Why do kids ask so many questions?

"He's doing grownup things, taking care of business," I said.

Which might not be a complete lie, I thought miserably. With a little luck—if we ever had good luck again—Charlie *was* taking care of business. Like figuring out why he'd screwed a perfect stranger in our own bed just because he was mad at me…

"Listen, honey," I said, caressing Jonah's cotton sleeve, his silky skin. "I know you're having fun here. We're all having fun. But our plans have changed. That means we need to get ready to go back to the city."

Jonah's bottom lip trembled.

"But…I l-like it here!" he said, to my surprise.

I had not known he felt so attached to this strange little place.

"Oh Jonah, I know, don't be sad. I'm sorry. It's just that… sometimes plans change."

Two tears dripped down his freckled cheeks. "Why do plans change?"

I caressed those red curls that had a life of their own. He did anchor me, my boy; to him, to myself; to the earth. To life. No matter what else happened, I was his Mommy. We would be okay—*as long as we move quickly.*

263

When I released him, Jonah gazed up at me, tears gone. And with the sun spilling over him from the bedroom window, nothing appeared out of kilter…except for the sight of my little boy suddenly shaking his head, back and forth, back and forth, as if winning an argument with someone I couldn't see.

"No," he said in that flat voice again. "We can't leave, Mommy. Not till you drink the water."

BOOK TWO:

The Sowing

"Justice is what love looks like in public."

— Cornel West

THE OTHER SIDE
OF NORMAL

CHAPTER 52

"OH BOY, YOU LOOK LIKE crap," Maria said when she opened her front door and saw Rikki. "Guess you didn't make it Below, huh?"

This was not the sort of reception Rikki needed right now. She pushed past her old friend, kicked off her sandals, and collapsed on the sofa. The living room was rearranged and uncharacteristically neat, not at all Maria's style or predilection. Her mother must be at it again.

"We need to talk," Rikki said. "I'm going to the re-enactment after all."

Maria lowered her bulk into the opposite armchair. "Of course. I mean, since you're here." She frowned. "You really do look awful."

"Gee, thanks."

"Did you catch something? From Nana?"

"You can't catch old age."

"Let me get you some tea." Maria began the eternal struggle to her feet, which Rikki couldn't bear to watch.

"Don't bother," Rikki said. "Please. I don't want tea. I want to talk."

"But it's peppermint."

"I don't care if it's the Holy Grail."

"I already made it."

"Why? Who were you expecting?"

"You," Santa-Maria said, clearly pleased at her own powers of deduction. "I knew you'd come back. C'mon, a little peppermint will settle your stomach."

"I *said* I don't want tea. You drive me crazier than all the rest," Rikki said bluntly. She didn't add how it felt oh-so-good to be here. Anyway, Maria knew. This was Rikki's second home. This was where they had played those games as kids: dolls, hide-and-seek, Monopoly, and finally what they only dared spell out—"s-e-x"—which was only intended to provide practice for when they grew up and had to do it with boys.

Maria never had done it with boys, far as Rikki knew. Only Rikki had branched out, trying various kinds of sex, even kinds she hated with people she couldn't stand. She'd also tried no sex at all.

"Rikki is worn out," she said at last.

Maria nodded sadly. "I think this whole thing has gone too far. Nana's done it to you."

"Oh really."

"Yes! Sometimes I—well, I see things differently now. Like I'm wearing new glasses. I mean, I'm not a perfect person either, but bad things don't keep happening to me or my family. *Good* things are starting to happen."

So, Maria was judging her now, too? "You don't live close enough to the lake," Rikki said.

"You always say that…but it's not scientific."

"And now you're a scientist?"

"This stuff is just…superstition. Everyone says so. Hardly anyone wants to listen to those old stories. They're tired of them, even call them 'crazy.'"

"Forget it then. I'll just remove my 'crazy' self from your presence."

"No, Rikki. Please." Maria clasped her sausage fingers together as if praying. "Listen. I'm doing better at the store. I've made friends, and people are nicer to me. I've even lost a few pounds. Can't you tell?"

"Yes," Rikki lied.

"I focus on the positive, and it works."

"I focus on the positive, too," Rikki said. "That's how I know this year's re-enactment won't be like the others. It will be an awakening, not just entertainment."

"What's wrong with entertainment?" Maria looked like a turkey all puffed up before it got its head cut off. "Mrs. Pattick keeps saying the festival should be light and healing—and people are starting to listen. She says it should be a place for us to spend money without worrying about—"

"What? Survival?"

"No." Another sigh. "Look, how about you spend the night with me tonight, after it's all over? Take a break from Nana, get away from everything without driving off in that broken-down truck."

Rikki gazed at her friend long and hard, as if memorizing her kindly fat face. "I don't think that will be possible," she said.

CHAPTER 53

DEJECTED AND ANGRY AND IN a state of shock, Charlie checked into Shy Moon Lake Inn.

Since the inn was located on the other side of the stone wall—only a couple of blocks away—he had expected to glimpse the back of his cottage. But due to the slant of the land, only the lake was visible from here. The cottages stayed hidden, as if they were something to be ashamed of.

For some reason, that troubled him.

The Victorian-style inn was indeed owned by Mrs. Terry Spiro, giver of weird potholders and wearer of bright sweat suits; Jess's description of the "gargantuan" lady had been very much on point. More importantly to Charlie, he found the inn quiet. He hoped to be able to think things through, *if* his brain still worked, *if* there was anything useful left to figure out. To his surprise, the innkeeper seemed remarkably incurious about him. She had practically accosted his wife, according to Jess, but now did not appear to recognize the McCortney name—unless she *had* recognized it, wondered what he was doing here with a suitcase and without his wife, and chose not to ask. Instead, she accepted his payment for two nights (he was a die-hard optimist at his core) and handed him keys to a lovely second-story room.

So, here he now sat, contemplating next steps. From this window, the white paint of the porch below hurt his eyes. This morning, as fresh as a slice of lime, seemed a reproach. Because *I'm* corrupt and stinking, he thought. Like roadkill.

How had his brand-new family reached such a low point? None of it made sense. Grinding rocks. Freak storms. Red handprints. Dubious Indian legends. The sound of water. Rikki Stevens. He couldn't even say who, or what, he was most mad at.

And how do you fight something you can't name?

Then he thought of the town newspaper, *Shy Moon Eclipse*. Jess had returned from the library fixated on that little gossipy paper. She had mentioned an editor who'd been quite the skeptic before taking himself out of public view.

Maybe the library, or that editor, would have a few answers for Charlie. He would write a little first—get the toxic stuff out of his head and heart—and then take a little walk.

Anything would be better than just waiting around for things to get better, or to get worse.

* * *

"How are you settling in?"

Startled by the voice, Charlie shot to his feet, Montblanc and papers scattering to the floor. The tall lady filling his doorway smiled, dentures as blinding as her white sweat suit.

"Oh—hi, Mrs. Spiro," he said. "Sorry, I didn't hear you knock."

"I'm afraid I didn't." She said almost coquettishly. "Your door was partly open, so I took liberties. Forgive me? This has always been such a friendly inn."

He managed a smile back and bent to retrieve his things. As he did, his own words on the top sheet of paper flew up at him.

I trusted you in the hollow of my throat
I trusted you in the soles of my feet
I trusted you in the naked skin
behind my neck
exposed.

"Goodness; let me help you," the innkeeper was saying. She had stepped fully inside his room now and bent to snatch the rolling pen. "This is my fault after all. Oh, is that a poem you're writing?"

"A bit of one," he said. Then he thanked her for her assistance and patted the pile of papers on his desk, away from her. *Guess she's nosy after all.*

"Please call me Terry. Mrs. Spiro sounds like you're addressing my mother," she said with an actual giggle.

He nodded, unsure how to respond.

"So," she went on. "Your room is to your satisfaction?"

"Very much so, yes. Thank you."

"Good! We do love having guests here. This is a very historic building."

"It's a privilege to stay here."

She wrinkled her forehead. "Are you feeling poorly, if you don't mind my asking? You do look a little pale."

"No, I'm fine." *Not.* Charlie cleared his throat. "I was wondering—do you happen to know Rikki Stevens? From the cottages?"

Terry Spiro pursed her thin aristocratic lips. "Yes, I know her quite well. She's active in the re-enactments, though I'd know her even if that were not the case. This is a small town, Mr. McCortney."

"Charlie, please."

"Charlie. I watched her grow up. Her Nana used to be active in the club, too."

"Sounds interesting."

She shrugged. "Rikki was one of the first young people to become interested. It used to be just us old fogies, you see. We had a nice event once a year and told stories of the ancient people who'd once lived here. We borrowed a few costumes and banged on drums. It was an innocent time. Nothing like the circus it turned into after Rikki got involved."

"Oh." Pause. "Circus?"

"She and her type always push for more, ah, *dramatic* interpretations— as if we can actually recreate the past. I believe it's called 'method acting.'" She shook her head. "Excuse me for sounding cynical. I don't see eye to eye with Miss Rikki. Yet she *is* persistent, as well as imaginative. I'll give her that."

Charlie nodded. He'd give her that, too.

"Funny you should mention the re-enactment," Mrs. Spiro added, though he hadn't been the one to mention it. "You do know it's today, don't you?"

"It is?"

"You haven't seen the posters? This is an important time for people like Rikki. Even if it's not quite the *event* she pines for. Still, it does mean a parade of people going past your place, since it occurs near the handprints. You know where those are?"

"Yes." *Unfortunately.*

"The actual re-enactment has become quite a process, as I said before. And no matter what, folks gather to watch. The show is free and in the open air, you see, originally meant to be a wholesome good time. You know, picnicking, everyone having fun."

"For kids, too."

"Well." She sniffed. "That depends on your perspective. Unfortunately, this whole affair does now include some dramatic dancing, with very adult themes. Less appropriate for children, in my view." She hesitated. "May I ask you something personal?"

Oh no, he thought.

"Do you know your totem?"

Charlie was at a loss.

"Because if you don't, perhaps I can help you."

"Ah," he said.

"I have been known to guide people in the right direction. The quest does not take long, and there are long-lasting benefits," Mrs. Spiro said.

"Really."

"Oh yes. Better health, intuitive wisdom, and improved relationships."

"I see. So how do you figure out my, um, totem?"

"*I* don't figure it out. *You* do, in my presence. You see, your animal symbol chooses you when you are open to it, and knowing your totem offers you the key to your nature. You'll be better able to recognize signs and interpret them."

"I see." Was everybody in this town out of their mind? Charlie wondered if he would ever know for sure.

She tapped the side of her nose, as if accessing private data. "The over-riding question is: are you a wolf, an eagle, or a bear?"

"Does it have to be one of those?"

"You may have a less common totem like an owl, a stag, a raven, a coyote—anything, really."

Rikki must be a raven. "And I would figure this out by...?"

"By concentrating, staying open to possibilities. If we meditate on it together, the truth may come." She cocked her head, considering. "Or do you feel like...a cockatoo, perhaps?"

With no small effort, Charlie said, "Well, no. I can't say I do."

"Cockatoos are flock creatures, Mr. McCortney."

"Charlie." *And by the way, cockatoos are not native to America.*

"Charlie. They are as loyal as dogs. In fact, they fight and kill if you try to hurt their family." She smiled knowingly. "*You* won't let anyone hurt your family either, isn't that correct?"

"Yes. That's correct." *Except me. Except me…*

"I thought so. And yet…I sense a great reluctance on your part. A wildness held back. Perhaps you are afraid of your animal spirit?" Another tap of the nose. "In the past you have been hurt by your own nature, I believe. Which makes it even more important for you to accept the qualities you can learn from your animal guide. We must all face our shadows, Mr. McCortney. Darkness, as much as the light, leads us down a path of deepening spirituality."

Charlie nodded, wondering how to find the path *away* from this conversation, this inn, and this town. "I see," he said again. "Well, thanks for the suggestion."

"You are very welcome."

"But I, uh, do have some…business to do today, and I would like to check out copies of the local paper. I heard the library isn't too far?"

"Of course not. Remember, this is a small town. It's a lovely building, too." The innkeeper scribbled down an address on a pad located on his desk. She added, "I won't be attending the re-enactment myself this year, out of protest, I'm afraid. But if you do choose to witness it, I advise you to do so from a distance."

Sounds like sound advice to me, Charlie thought, thanking her for the address—and already feeling as fierce and crabby as a goddamn cockatoo.

CHAPTER 54

JONAH WAS BEHAVING NORMAL, SO far.

I watched him every minute of the next few hours, keeping him close no matter what. He even came into the bathroom with me. Thankfully, my son showed no more signs of Otherness, uttered no more frightening comments like "drink the water."

Earlier, when I had asked him what water he was referring to—which water I was *supposed to drink*—Jonah had looked puzzled and did not reply. So, to be on the safe side, I avoided any water at all, even from the tap. We both drank milk.

Still, I couldn't shake off the dread that had settled inside my trachea like a chicken bone.

What was wrong with my baby? And with me?

I knew I should scoop him up and cart us out of here without bothering to pack—but that didn't seem right, either. The kitchen had so many unopened cans and dirty utensils. It took me a while to figure out which ones to keep. The living room was awash with blankets and toys and books, and our laundry hadn't been done in, what, a week? How had our stuff fit inside the van?

And if we left without Charlie, what would he drive? How would he get off the mountain, if he ever did?

This is what madness feels like, I thought—and recalled my eleventh birthday at Disneyland, when I vomited out the car window after riding the Mad Hatter's Teacups too many times. And my fifth birthday, when I lay in bed staring at the canopy overhead, counting its poles until I reached five, believing I would die when I turned six and ran out of poles to count.

These memories didn't surprise me. They were my version of normal. And yet...even my own unfurling history felt wrong somehow. Too brief and vague. Where were the uber-vivid re-enactments I knew so well and had always known?

No, I *wasn't* the same person anymore. And if I wasn't myself, who was I?

The motivation to hurry and escape this beautiful mountain was leaking out of me bit by bit, like air out of a balloon. Which meant I needed to do something to change this trajectory—or I might disappear in some way worse than death.

Think outside the box, I told myself. Think outside the box.

* * *

"Why do I need my stroller?" Jonah whined, leaning out the side of the contraption like a dog at a car window. "I'm too big!"

"You're fine," I said. "I won't belt you in."

"I want to *walk*."

"Honey, please. Just this once. You used to love your stroller."

"I was little then," he informed me, over-patient, as if explaining physics to a dummy.

He did sit back, though, and I felt weak-kneed with relief, for I needed to keep my son within eyesight yet away from that lake. His stroller seemed like the best bet. Meanwhile, the lake looked normal, too: normal-lake normal. I squinted at the placid water, marveling at appearances.

Normal. Ha!

After wheeling Jonah to the gap between lane and shore, I squatted down to face him. "Why don't you close your eyes and take a nap?" I said.

"I'm not tired," he shot back. He looked cranky.

I sighed.

"Okay, Jonah, I need you to do me a favor. It sounds funny, but I'm going to walk over there to the water for just a second. I'd like you to wait for me here, inside your stroller. Think you can do that?"

His expression crumpled. "W-why I can't go?"

"Because sometimes grownups need time to do grownup things. Don't worry, I'll be right there, where you can see me. And I'll be very fast."

"Why I don't *go* with you?"

I searched for a suitable story. "I'm just going to the water…to say a grownup prayer."

Jonah looked skeptical.

"You know how people pray alone sometimes? That's what I need. A moment to pray," I explained.

"I don't pray." Jonah leaned forward curiously. "Do I?"

"Sure, you do. We've prayed together." Once. Twice? I couldn't remember. "Some people call it meditation. They sit quietly and feel grateful or ask for guidance. That's prayer too."

He did not respond.

"You'll understand better when you're older," I said, feeling like a colossal hypocrite. How I hated saying this stuff!

But Jonah wasn't paying attention; he was staring at the treetops. "Mommy, did *you* make this world?" he asked in a small voice.

What? "Uh, no. I didn't," I said.

"Who did then?"

"Good question. Like I said, many people believe in God. Sometimes they use different names for God, or a guiding spirit. People have their beliefs. It's called 'faith.'"

"Oh. Do we have fate?"

"*Faith.* Honey: tell you what. Give me just one minute of grownup time over there where you can see me. Then I'll come back, and we'll go home and make lunch. How's that sound?" *Like bribery.*

"Macaroni and cheese?"

"Sure."

"With Daddy?"

"Not today, I'm sorry. Maybe next time."

Finally, Jonah nodded.

I smiled, handed him a sippy cup, kissed him, and hurried away. I kept looking over my shoulder, though, practically walking backwards. I needed to be sure he stayed put and did not panic. *I* needed to not panic, too.

The water lay as still as a prayer. No birds squawked overhead.

I cast another smile at my son before turning to the silvery lake. My mouth felt dry, as if my tongue had swollen. But I had to talk.

For that was my brilliant, desperate, "outside the box" plan.

To talk.

"*I know you are there,*" I whispered over the sock in my throat. "I don't know who you are, what you are, or what you want from me…or my family. But if you leave us alone…I'll try to help."

Help what? How? Who?

I inched forward until the edge of water tickled my toes. Cold! I reached out my right hand, extending one finger—my index finger—and touched the clear, fresh fluid. And I waited for thunderbolts.

Nothing happened.

Except my finger got wet, of course. Wet and cold. I withdrew it from the lake.

"Okay," I said. "Here goes."

I put the tip of that finger into my mouth. Tasted the lake water and swallowed the taste.

"There," I said to the empty air, feeling beyond stupid. "*I drank the water*. Does that help? Isn't that what you wanted? Will you leave us alone now?"

The center of the lake moved a little.

I stared hard at its glassy surface. Was it starting to ripple? No, all was still. Probably nothing had moved in the first place.

It is distinctly likely I *am* nuts, I decided. I'd experienced a psychotic break on the first day in Shy Moon Lake and couldn't remember. After all, the symptoms of mental illness include delusions, hallucinations, and not fully believing you are sick.

Check. Check. And *check!*

A few more seconds passed without mishap before I turned away from the lake. "Coming, honey," I called to Jonah.

He waved desultorily.

When I reached him, breathing hard, I felt more cheerful. "See, here I am! Was that long? Or was it only a minute the way I promised?"

"It was a long time," said Jonah.

"Oh. Well, sorry, bud. But I'm back now. Ready for lunch?"

He didn't answer. He was looking to my left, just over my shoulder.

"Jonah? What is it?"

"Mama," he said. "Why are there two?"

*   *   *

I whirled around to where he looked. Goose bumps rose on my flesh, my heart tripping.

Nothing. Empty space.

"Jonah? Can you, ah, tell me what you're seeing, sweetie? Tell Mama. Two of what?"

He hesitated, then said, "Two people."

His gaze still focused directly past my shoulder, speculatively, up and down. Then he screwed shut his eyes.

Someone is here right now.

"Jonah?" My voice trembled. "Can you open your eyes?"

He opened them and looked again. To my left.

"You…see someone?"

Nod.

"Is it…a man? A woman?"

He just cocked his head and sighed, and the sound was like wind escaping through trees. I couldn't see anything. How could my little boy?

It wants something.

"Why are you here?" I whispered to the empty space where Jonah stared.

"It's a lady and a man," my child said, his voice also a whisper.

"Wha-at?"

"A lady! With a braid. *And* a man."

I wrapped my hand around his small wrist. "You really see two people?"

Nod.

"Can you see *through* them? Are they…wearing clothes and"—I faltered, unable to believe I was having this conversation with my little boy; why hadn't I snatched his stroller and run for the hills?

"It's a lady and a man." Jonah made it sound like the most obvious thing on earth. "They're waiting. You had a drink, so now it's time to swim."

CHAPTER 55

"I **BELIEVE YOU MET MY** wife," Charlie said to Mrs. Collins, the librarian. "Jess McCortney? Petite woman, red hair? She came in here a little earlier this summer."

The woman blinked; her head tilting and bobbing; Charlie half-expected her to squawk for a cracker. When she didn't, he added: "We're new in town, and Jess said how helpful you were. You showed her back copies of the paper, *Shy Moon Eclipse.*"

Finally, the librarian nodded, smiling vaguely—as if in her line of work, she met dozens of petite women with red hair. But she did lead him to a back room stacked with old papers. "Take your time, Mr. McCortney," she said before leaving him. "I hope you find the answers we are looking for."

Had she said *we*? Answers *we* are looking for?

Charlie shook off the notion and got to work. And an hour later, he emerged from the room with his notepad filled with names and facts but his head full of questions.

He tried the librarian again.

"Mrs. Collins, I'd like to find the former editor Carl Roberson's family, if that's possible. I won't ask for private information, of course. But this is a small town, and I read his wife works at a bar called 'The Bottom of the Lake.' That can't be too far. Do you know if she still works there?"

Mrs. Collins looked down her nose at him for a long time. She seemed to be fighting with herself, weighing whether to answer his questions or simply tell him to go away. At long last, she nodded.

"You can probably find the wife," she said. "But her husband has been gone a long time."

"I understand," Charlie said. "Thank you."

Another nod, and Mrs. Collins silently pointed down the street to the right, like a scarecrow providing directions. And as Charlie was leaving, he heard her voice from behind him: husky, even choked.

"*Be careful,*" the librarian whispered.

CHAPTER 56

"HELLO, HANNAH," I SAID WITH phony upbeat friendliness. "Remember me? Jess McCortney?"

Hannah Mason peered out of her doorway looking startled and lost, like a Charles Dickens waif. Her lovely brown eyes were huge, sleeves of a big sweater pooled over her hands, the hem of an old-fashioned housedress peeking below the sweater.

I wondered if she remembered me. But how could she not? She *must* be able to recall the day when Jonah and I were rushed by a mob just because we had dared wade our feet in lake-water!

Unless, to her, mob-rushing was simply another day in the neighborhood…

"Oh yes, hello," she said at last, with a glance at Jonah, who tried to hide behind my leg.

I had no idea whether my child was playing shy or felt scared. I only knew *I* felt scared. "I hope this isn't a bad time," I said.

Hannah Mason shook her head. Then Jonah came forward, and her expression brightened. "Why, hello, young man! How are you doing today?"

"I don't want my stroller anymore," my son told her. "I'm too big!"

She smiled. "Oh, I do understand that."

"But I used it 'cause mommy made me," Jonah tossed me a betrayed glance.

"I see," said Hannah. "Thank you for telling me."

"You're welcome," said Jonah.

I cleared my throat. "We…uh, stopped by because I've got a bit of a dilemma and I remembered you said how much you love kids. I need a babysitter, only for a short while. I would pay you, of course. I'm sorry it's last minute, but you see my husband…he—"

"He left," Jonah put in helpfully. "I didn't say goodbye."

I cringed. But Hannah moved on, smooth and reassuring.

"It would be my pleasure to watch Jonah for you. My husband would enjoy it, too. He is the kindest man in the world. Would you like to meet him? *Stansey!*" she called over her shoulder. She caught my eye and blushed. "It's my nickname for him. Silly, I know. But Stan and me, we've known each other since we were kids. Stan?"

"Coming, hon," intoned a nasal masculine voice.

Stansey rolled up to the doorway. And yes, he was the embodiment of kind and ordinary; the town should elect him mayor. Every feature on his homely face, his shapeless body, spelled home and hearth, work, and community. He peered over half-glasses at Jonah and winked.

Jonah giggled.

At the couple's invitation, we stepped into a living room as cozy as a bowl of soup. Hannah showed me a closet stacked with board games and said, "We will be as happy as clams right here. I wouldn't dream of taking pay for the privilege of playing with your little guy."

"That's great," I said, now smiling for real.

This woman, more than anyone else I'd met in Shy Moon Lake, seemed like someone I could make friends with, if I stayed. Clearly, she was not the type to join any kind of mob rule.

And yet she had, hadn't she? She had at least witnessed the get-away-from-that-lake thing. Why hadn't she tried to stop it, called the police? Or even mention it now, to me?

Just the same, for this day, this moment, it was good to have an ally. I wondered why Hannah Mason had not had children of her own—and felt a flash of relief that I was carrying twins…as if that might redress some imbalance.

It was an odd notion.

"Enjoy your errands," she said after I hugged Jonah goodbye. "Have a productive day."

"I will certainly try," I said, and meant it more than she could possibly know.

Because today I was going swimming.

Screw the signs.

CHAPTER 57

WHY CAN'T LIFE BE FAIR?

Seething and heartbroken from her failure earlier in the day, Rikki hunkered on the porch steps, sacred box on her lap. Nana had acted all triumphant about Rikki not being able to leave the mountain, but that hardly mattered anymore. Just like it didn't matter that Nana no longer called this box "sacred."

Rikki needed to hang onto the truth. This box *was* sacred. It protected her most prized possessions. And now it was time to take them out again, to re-absorb their power.

First, she fondled the shape of the box itself. She savored the weight and details: rectangular, wooden, and covered with intricate engravings of parrots and trees and waterfalls. Then, reverently, she opened the lid. The raven had been Mama's totem: black, made from volcanic glass—obsidian. The stuff of the ancients. Rikki pressed her finger against the rock's shiny surface, imagining projectile points traded and used for warfare.

The raven moved her, maybe because it was also known as the Trickster.

In the box also lay a dozen small rounded obsidian teardrops. She fancied these tears originating from her father, from his actual tear ducts.

It was a strangely comforting notion she shared with no one, especially not Nana. Not these days.

With surprisingly steady hands, Rikki withdrew the deer fetish. Her mother had carved it out of porous volcanic rock called pumice; light enough to float in water yet abrasive enough to use as a sponge. When Rikki was little, Mama had said in her lush hypnotic voice: "You are alert and intuitive, like this deer. A fetish will remind you not to force answers, my little one. Read between the lines and peer into the heart of things. Look for causes rather than effects."

For a long time after Mama had disappeared, Rikki insisted on sleeping with the deer made of pumice. She bathed with it too, rubbing its magic onto her skin.

Her father preferred the black raven. He called it a bit of history he could hold in his hands. "Oh, but your father doesn't understand his connection to the Raven," Mama confided to Rikki. "Only women fully appreciate these symbols because we carry ancestral knowledge in our DNA. You see, in the beginning of the world, the Raven helped bring the sun, moon, stars, fresh water, and fire to the world—brought us out of darkness. That's why your father gave it to you. He doesn't know his gifts even if he intuits them."

Today's daylight spun webs onto the tips of the pines. Squinting against the brightness, Rikki put away her treasures. She closed the box, stood up, and carried it like a babe in her arms to the lakeshore. There, she knelt on the rocky sand, head bowed.

"It is time," she whispered to the Lake—already feeling less forceful, more deer-like. "Please guide me. Take me into harmony and acceptance."

Some people believed that to hear the voice of God, you had to know how to listen. Rikki held her breath and listened so hard she thought her veins would burst. But she heard nothing except for her Nana's words echoing in her head.

No one can outrun destiny. You work it like a puzzle.

Opening her box again, Rikki removed its most mysterious, sacred item: the long, thick, black braid. This was made of real human hair. Mama's? Nana's? Or did it come from Nana's Mama, the long-dead Omi? Rikki still remembered that impossibly old woman's face, the crevasses of grief on skin, the raspy voice, and long stories of ancient murder and mayhem.

If Omi had known the secrets, and this braid belonged to her…well, then it must contain Rikki's DNA as well as whatever lurked inside the lake. There had to be power inside this simple braid.

A bird cawed overhead. The raven, making its voice heard?

Rikki searched for a glimpse through tree branches. She needed to have proof of its message while she clutched the braid. And to her delight she did indeed spy a large black bird, magnificent against the azure sky.

Omi does know. Ask Omi.

Rikki closed her eyes. She was not yet sure of Omi's presence. Rikki noticed other creatures; oh yes. She could hear the voices of fish and frogs and turtles and water-snakes and a million crawly things: not audibly but in her bones. She kept caressing the braid so she could become an empath, and eventually she would perceive the vibrations of ancient music, the thump of drums as her ancestors danced their offer of honor to the earthly female.

What a pain in the ass, she thought.

Long ago, before the murder and mayhem, had life been fairer? If Omi had known the secret, why didn't she share it? Why all this prayer and meditation and ritual and symbolism? Omi could have written down what their family needed to know. She could have left Rikki a note!

Recently, Nana had had a vision and awoke to tell Rikki all about it. "I saw, clear as day, the cottages—all these cottages, except nothing looked right," Nana said. "They'd been smashed down and flooded, like broken reeds in the lake."

"And you think that's…the future?" Rikki had asked, her heart full of both awe and dread.

"I didn't say that. But I sure got that feeling."

"You saw…everything ruined? What about the people?"

"The land left was not fit for living, our town smashed and swamped. Looked

like the crater itself had collapsed."

Rikki also recalled—had never forgotten, really—the legend of the blanket, which Nana used to retell whenever little Rikki tried to dodge some obscure ritual.

In Nana's Blanket Story, a boy named Iktomi had been wailing that he was hungry when the all-powerful Great Spirit took pity on him. After receiving the child's warm blanket as offering, the Creator led him to a freshly killed deer. The child's prayers had been answered. He would not starve.

Except the kid got selfish about it—or merely human, in Rikki's grownup opinion. While kindling the fire, Iktomi could not help crying and complaining about the cold; he even prayed to get his blanket back ("*Indian-giver!*" young Rikki used to scream till Nana slapped her). Soon the boy abandoned his work, teeth chattering, to slip up the hillside and snatch the blanket he needed from a God who did not, in fact, need one.

This is an attitude problem, Nana used to explain.

As a consequence, the child's venison was gone—*poof*—the bones rattling, the blanket following the way of the venison, no longer available to warm him. The boy ended up with nothing before him but death.

What we sow we shall reap—and quickly because God is in a hurry! That was the moral of the story.

Still clinging to the braid, Rikki wondered how many of her people had been murdered over the years. Her veins contained the blood of both sides. Maybe everyone had joined forces to punish a singular scapegoat, just like Rikki had been a scapegoat her whole life.

She released the braid and went to work with the obsidian, moving it and then the pumice over her bare arms and legs. "I am part of the whole.

Like you, I come *from* the Lake and am *of* the Lake. The small and the large as One. Share with me your knowledge."

If she could not avoid her fate, then she shouldn't cringe from it either, she thought. Better to invite it in. *Who are you? Omi? What do you want? Speak!*

Abruptly Rikki unbowed her head, alert, like a deer sensing danger.

Invite it in…

She sat for another thirty minutes, opening herself up from the inside. Reaching for the darkness she had spent her life trying to escape. What ailed her was *gift*, not a burden. The re-enactment ceremony was a gift, too. These miracles would help her reach the esteemed spirit that haunted Shy Moon Lake.

She stood and gathered herself.

Like a woman walking into Shy Moon Lake, easing herself through the bright surface of things, destroying that reflection and all the illusions it held…and then sinking, sinking into the reality waiting below.

NO MORE BARRIERS

CHAPTER 58

THE WEATHER WAS BEGINNING TO shift. If I expected to bathe in that ice-cold lake water, I should hurry.

But I paused where I'd been walking and circled around first, evaluating the clearing, and the path, and the proximity to the road and parking lot and grinding rocks…trying to identify if *this* was the best spot. I did not dare linger too close to the cottages—didn't want to get mobbed again. And I would not inch closer to the gathering of that stupid festival; God forbid I get mobbed from that end, too. No, I needed privacy. That scrabble of bushes in front of this clearing would do.

The sky still appeared blue in most places: bland and unrelenting, like a flag of truce. But I didn't buy that, not for a minute. A storm was coming, I knew. A different kind of storm.

At the far, far edges of sky, between framing treetops, a darkening patch seeped into the blue. I kicked off my sweats and stepped in my bathing suit toward the lake. Still clutching my towel like a teddy bear, with water stretched before me mute and mysterious, I spoke aloud.

"I'm not scared," I said. Telling the lake?

Water lapped gently on the pebbled ground a few inches in front of me. A single crow perched on a reed, watching.

If I need help, I'll scream, I told myself. I can scream louder than the fifty neighbors who might come charging out of their seven cottages, probably brandishing garden tools as weapons.

Dropping the towel, I stuck in one toe, then my whole foot.

"Take that," I said aloud, and shivered, waiting for a response.

CHAPTER 59

"**EXCUSE ME—PAULA? PAULA ROBERSON? I'M** sorry to bother you at work, but would you have a minute to talk?"

The Bottom of the Lake Bar—smack in the center of town for some reason—seemed like another world to Charlie. People *smoked* here, a virtual sacrilege in California, not to mention illegal. And the bar lamps were yellow and shaped like the old-fashioned lanterns he had seen in the French quarter of New Orleans. The air smelled of leather and oil and a faint, not unpleasant musk that may have been cheap fragrance or the aroma of old saddles. Who could tell for sure with cigarettes everywhere?

Charlie glanced out a large bay window at the dolphin fountain. He didn't care anymore about Shy Moon Lake's charming, curious, or eccentric details. All he wanted was to quiz this tired-looking woman without getting her fired or getting himself thrown out on his ass—and then go home.

Not home to the cottage by the lake, but down the mountain and back to the home in the city. With or without Jess.

"Do I know you?" the waitress asked, neither friendly nor unfriendly. Her last name was not included on her name tag.

He introduced himself, and they shook hands.

"Pleasure," she said. "Since so many folks attend the re-enactment, I reckon I can spare a minute. What is it you want to talk about?"

"I'm new in town, and I've got a bit of a problem," Charlie said. "So, I was hoping to talk to someone who's lived here a while. And I read about you in the *Shy Moon Eclipse*."

Paula Roberson tucked a bar rag into her apron. She had keen, wide-set blue eyes and a stubborn set to her chin. If she was as she appeared—a hard-working woman whose husband had, by all accounts, simply vanished—then Charlie empathized with her more than she would ever know.

"I don't usually poke into other people's business," he added apologetically. "But some strange things have happened to my family since moving here. I guess I'm hoping for answers."

"Ah. Answers. From me? May I ask why?"

Charlie glanced around to see who else might be listening. The librarian had called this place one of the oldest townie hangouts. Maybe that explained its creative name (since, according to Shy Moon Lake's unwritten policy, any bar should have been named simply "The Bar"). Today, the "townies" appeared to be a couple of toad-bellied old guys, and one woman in outdated clothing, perched on bar stools. The entire scene gave Charlie a weird *déjà vu* sensation, as if he were watching "Saturday Night Fever" for the downtrodden.

"I live in one of the lake cottages," he said. "Next door to Rikki Stevens and her Nana. Do you know them?"

"What if I do?"

Someone came out of the restroom, and the jukebox flicked on. Barry Manilow began to moan.

"I guess I'm hoping for some…perspective," Charlie said. "You see, my family's time here has been difficult."

"So, you snooped around and found me?"

"Yes, ma'am. It started with your husband. I looked through the papers at the library and read his editorials. I can tell how much he cared…about this town."

"Yes, he did care. And you thought I would too? Because I'm his widow?"

Then Carl Roberson *was* dead.

"I'm sorry," Charlie said. "I wasn't sure. I thought that maybe—"

"He simply disappeared? Well, you are correct. My one great love did, in fact, disappear. His body was never found. Still, no point in hoping. I think I would know if my husband was alive."

Charlie nodded miserably.

"It's been two years. I should have grieved and moved on," the woman said.

"Not so easy," he said.

"No. Not easy at all." She seemed to gather herself; to stand taller and face him better. "To answer your question: Yes, I know Rikki, and everyone knows her Nana. Rikki is neurotically involved with that re-enactment nonsense. I suppose you've heard of it?"

"Their big event is happening today, right? I wasn't planning to attend."

"Good for you. The Visitors' Center might try to convince you if you stop there for information. Unless that silly little girl is working. She couldn't convince a firefighter to go to the fire station."

"Ah," Charlie said, at a loss.

"The posters have been all over town for weeks." Paula Roberson put on a sleazy falsetto. "Do you like Indian dances? Tom-toms? Well, they got 'em up the ying-yang. If you got kids, they'll love the fighting and dying, even when it scares the crap out of them!" She paused; energy deflated. "If you ask me, it's just a bunch of ignorant white people trying to get sensitive about history without asking the real questions. Look…do you want a drink?"

He didn't but asked for bottled water and chips. She served him without taking his money.

He said, "About this re-enactment. What exactly do they re-enact?"

The bar fell abruptly quiet—when did that happen? Barry Manilow had given up finding Mandy....

"I don't want to talk about the club," Paula snapped. "Let's just get to the point, shall we? I can see that you're all shook up, and frankly, so am I."

Charlie nodded, with his throat suddenly dry.

Paula closed her eyes. And when she opened them, they were wet. "Just please don't tell me," she said, "that your wife is pregnant with twins."

CHAPTER 60

WAIST DEEP IN WATER, I stopped.

A faint sheen floated on the surface. Under my feet, the lakebed slanted sharply down. Yet the temperature of the water stayed uniformly cool.

There is no bottom farther in. That's why so many people drown.

I could almost smell the oily sheen. Was it the lake's breath? Something lurked behind my nostrils. Something so verdant it verged on cloying. Twigs slowly drifted under the surface, just out of my reach; they had no doubt dropped from the trees or floated in from shore. I wondered about algae. Didn't all lakes have algae?

No fish here, I reminded myself. Like no birds. Where-oh-where are the crayfish, snakes, and bugs: fly larvae, spiders, and water beetles? *What about any goddamn living thing that's supposed to be inside a lake?*

Suddenly, I noticed my reflection in the water. Odd how distorted it looked. I raised my hand flat over the surface and saw two hands. I bent lower—and screamed.

A human hand broke the surface, reaching for my face.

THE WRONG PATH

CHAPTER 61

AS RIKKI ENTERED THE CLEARING used for their re-enactment—about 200 feet upslope from the grinding rocks—she waved hello to familiar faces and ignored the tourists. There were quite a few of them here already, more than she'd expected considering what had happened last year.

On the far side of the clearing, folks were almost done pitching the "Tent of Many Voices," such as it was. Rikki scowled at the painted figures on canvas; oh, how she hated these false messages! Who needs a line of Indian dancers chasing mobs of white men, especially now? The only thing true about that canvas "art" was the billowing of dust…and possibly the two figures portrayed as fleeing toward the lake.

To add insult to injury, the sellers around the tent were laughing, snacking, beginning to open cold bottles of whatever. Beer. The 'extravaganza' would not officially begin for an hour, but these "club members" lived with dollar signs *cha-chinging* in their eyeballs. Goods for sale spread over blankets in all directions for people who didn't care about them and would only lose them: crow beads, hollow metal beads, pony beads; and precious botanicals such as sage, homemade oatmeal soap, smudge sticks, and sweet-grass.

All "s" words, Rikki thought irrelevantly. How come?

With that same note of inner hysteria, she eyeballed the craft supplies also splayed out near the tent: porcupine quills, deer antlers, elk teeth. Clothing for sale like shawls, leather vests, "reservation" hats, and feathers. Oh, and children didn't waste any time getting underfoot. They ogled hand-painted fake eagle feathers, pheasant tail and plumage feathers, smearing their dirty hands all over everything.

Maria wasn't here yet. But that bratty teenager Kayla Dobbs was, carousing with her usual rabble of losers. A gaggle of teenage boys wore their shorts so low and baggy, their butt cracks showed. Nasty! And old Johnston Reed had turned up, unbending himself into one of the folding chairs set up for the decrepit and maimed.

Rikki didn't want him here in the thick of things, though she felt oddly touched by his attendance. Maybe the old geezer could represent Nana, who felt too ill today to attend anything—and which was safer for her, in any case.

Glancing at the nearest vendor, Rikki's stomach sank. "Patty Pattick," she said. "Hello."

The real estate agent glanced up and frowned. She'd been working on a display of brochures: 'Come enjoy Shy Moon Lake! Enjoy the Views!' She said: "What kind of trouble are you planning this time, Miz Rikki? Please do tell so I can warn everybody. We do not want you to ruin the festival again."

"I don't know what you're talking about," Rikki retorted coldly. "I don't ruin anything."

"Is that a fact."

"Let me ask you this. If you don't believe in the symmetry of re-enactments, why are you here? Oh, wait. I know that answer. To make a buck."

The old squirrel's cheeks reddened. "Everyone needs to 'make a buck,' as you say so disdainfully. It's called working. I sell people houses that happen to be for sale."

"Even when some of them need to stay unsold? You could just leave them instead of luring in new bait."

"New bait for what? Look, young lady. I am a rational adult. I don't go for all this"—a heavily be-ringed hand waved at the proceedings—"except as diversion. It's entertainment and good business."

"Good *business*?"

"Keeping this town from dying is my business. It's all of our business. We must support a thriving economy and sound cultural heritage."

"You know nothing about heritage!"

"Oh, and you do? Because of your crazy family? Or because you're so obsessed with play-acting?"

Rikki moved her mouth. Nothing came out.

That didn't stop Mrs. Pattick, who squared off, hands on hips.

"Last year was over the top, as I've said before. Tourists complained, and attendance dropped because of *your* eccentricities. No, let's call them what they are: *superstitions*. Paranoia. You go too far, like your Nana and her mother before her. This is not the act of a good neighbor. You are no longer a child. For goodness sake, when will you grow up?"

You ignorant old…grouse. Rikki had once read about the endangered sage grouse: bulging, sagging pouches, feathers, and long tail attached to a ridiculous puffball critter that makes meaningless whistles and pops. *Wish you were endangered, Mrs. Pattick!*

"Last year was good," Rikki said, chin up. "Not perfect but an improvement. And this year will be even better."

Mrs. Pattick eyed her sharply. "I don't know what you're planning, young lady, but I suggest you *not* do it. In your absence at meetings, the committee has scripted everything. We will allow you to stay, if you must. But we won't tolerate any misbehavior. *No surprises.*"

"Right. No surprises." Rikki reached into her pocket to touch Omi's braid as she stalked away.

Life had unspooled to its nexus. Time to prepare.

CHAPTER 62

"MOMMY," CRIED JONAH FROM WHERE he sat playing with blocks.

Hastily Hannah set down her teacup and scrambled to her feet "What is it, sweetie?"

Stony faced, Jonah stood up and walked a few feet to the front window. He still held a rectangular blue block. "Mommy!" he repeated to the paned glass.

He was such a beautiful little guy, red hair and white skin and eyes usually full of innocence and curiosity. But Hannah took care not to touch him right now…it was the look on his face. The vacuous stare. "Jonah," she said gently. "Don't worry. Mommy will return soon. I'm here with you now, your new friend Hannah."

He ignored, or perhaps didn't hear her.

She crept closer. "Are you thirsty? Would you like some tea? And cookies?"

Jonah waggled his arms a little, as if he were trying to dog paddle. Was he having some kind of seizure?

Or could he be hearing…*It*?

"Swim back," Jonah said, wiggling his fingers too. "Mommy, swim back!"

Hannah reached out and grabbed him. She held his squirming hand firmly in her own, whether he wanted it or not, whether it was advisable or not.

"That's enough, Jonah. Let's go away from this window and finish building your castle. That's a good boy, come with Hannah."

And then she shut the curtain. To protect him.

CHAPTER 63

TOM-TOMS BEGAN TO BUMP, ADDING a heartbeat to the buzz of talk and laughter of tourists, residents, and onlookers.

Next, the warbling voice of Pete Wiley—the old goat who was another one of Nana's contemporaries—rose into the air, apparently from the trees behind the Tent of Many Voices. Rikki stood on tiptoes to spot him. This is just *wrong*, she thought, noticing the elaborate sound system playing peek-a-boo behind the curtain. It's imaginary heritage because they annihilated the real one.

"A long, long time ago," said Wiley's voice, "this was a land of the People and their many customs."

Six would-be actors, dressed in fawn-colored fringed suede as members of the mysterious Waatangay, treaded softly into the clearing. Rikki tried not to look at their familiar faces. They paused at the makeshift amphitheater of boulders, lawn chairs, tents, and blankets, from which about 100 people watched. Then three of the tribesmen—all female—dropped to a squat. The other three, dressed the same as the women but obviously men, struck a pose. It was the frozen first step of their over-choreographed dance.

"As a People, the tribe grew and prospered in a life harmonious with Nature," Wiley's voice said.

The drums thundered while dancers reached for the sky. Arms curled inward. Up again: at the sky, toward the center, faster and faster. Hips and bellies undulated suggestively.

S-E-X.

All the adults in the audience—including Maria, who could be as dense as a redwood—stared mesmerized at such an obvious representation of the sex act. Townies in the crowd snickered. Tourists appeared both amused and startled. The children watching probably had no clue what was really going on. Certainly "the voice" wasn't about to tell them.

Where was Maria going now? She was moving within the crowd, dodging elbows, on her way to do something. Rikki had no idea what that could be and tried not to care. The truth hurt, but these days Maria immersed herself with people other than Rikki, people Rikki barely knew or had no interest in; club members who thought Rikki crazy or folks from Maria's stupid job.

Fine, Rikki thought. I don't need you.

Onstage, the dancers shifted into a circle. They changed places, faster, faster, again and again. Pound. Pound. Pound. Pound. *Climax.*

"Until one day…" boomed the voice.

The drums, having reached their thudding peak, ceased. A single flute note remained. The sound flew free, another bird escaping the lake.

"There was conflict among the People," said Wily Pete Wiley. "Betrayal and misunderstood young love, as timeless as the lake."

Oh, spare me your false-hearted theatrics, Rikki thought. The drums were thumping more hectically now: pDUM, pDUM, pDUM! And the circle of dancers in the clearing burst into chaos. A dark-skinned young girl with a long braid—that little flirt who hung out with Kayla…Victoria Something—peeled off from the others. Wearing an overtight suede shift festooned with cheap-looking beads and feathers, she approached the rock with the handprints, scrambled up monkey-like, and pressed her own hands against that ancient message.

There was a lull in the crowd. A. Big. Moment.

Afterward, the girl returned to the circle. She reached out a beckoning hand to the trees opposite from where Rikki stood. It was a signal to the woman's lover, hiding and waiting; the pseudo-actor who stepped out on cue.

Oh, and what a white guy we've got this year, Rikki thought bitterly. The alcohol-infused Jack Finnegan resembled more plumber than warrior, not that slutty Victoria What's-Her-Name was any kind of authentic Waantangay specimen. Nothing was as it should be. Instead, the re-enactment club was dishing out the usual version of what the town emblazoned all over its brochures. *See where the star-crossed lovers met their watery fate!*

Why couldn't today's white "lover" sport less of a gut? They could have found someone to properly play the part. They could have cared enough.

Now the circle of dancers shook their fists at the star-crossed lovers—or, rather, waved tomahawks made of sticks and duct tape. PTHUMP, PTHUMP, P*THUMP*! The female lover grabbed the man's hand to pull him away with her. They headed for the "lake," which was really a patch of dirt crudely covered with blue nylon tarp.

Voilà: our realistic stage set, Rikki fumed. No wonder our rituals never help! Well, today would be different.

Today *must* be different.

Then she saw Mrs. Pattick glaring at her and ducked back behind her tree, her bare skin goose-bumped with cold.

"They hoped to escape the judgment and ignorance of others," said Wiley. "To begin life anew and embrace love forever. Only the lake waters are deep and as unforgiving as those with cold hearts."

Rikki made a face.

The lovers on the blue tarp writhed to show their ardor—or maybe their pain. In parody of desperately misunderstood love, they fell to their knees. Rejected and mistreated by both the tribe and Outsiders, they would sacrifice themselves. If they could not live together, they would die together, just like Romeo and the other one. Juliet.

Not the point!

The drumbeat segued into another pulse of mournful flute. Then, actual silence followed for one beat, then two, before the whooping and wailing started again: dancers grieving as the lovers lay "dead" on the nylon lake floor. "Lost love is always tragic, yet love endures," said the voice.

As does hate!

Their show would be concluding soon, farce that it was. Rikki could not wait any longer. She lifted the thick black braid from her box, which was in a plastic bag at her feet. *Goodbye, Patty Pattick.*

Then she—Rikki Finn Stevens, descendent of Omi, whose real name was Abedubun, meaning "Light of Day"—stepped out from behind the tree and walked into the clearing. In one hand, held high above her head, she still held Omi's braid of hair.

In the other hand, she clutched a carving knife that belonged to Nana.

CHAPTER 64

WHEN I CRIED OUT, WATER rushed in my mouth.

No. Not water! My mind screamed. *If you stay under, you'll die.*

I gagged, pushing myself up and away. But that hand—human, skeletal, filthy with mud, twigs and God knows what else—clutched at my hair. It clawed my arms, my neck. The thing was a vice, a water snake…a crocodile. Inside this lake where nothing lived.

I managed to clear a space, gulping more air. And the water moved again…as a grinning skull bobbled to the surface.

My scream died in my throat.

A different hand shot up, with the arm still attached. Followed by a ribcage floating like a revolting boat. I managed to kick the whole lot of it, these broken bones of some poor soul.

Yet the pathetic, terrible pile kept re-attaching itself. Pulling me down.

Then a *third* skeletal hand floated up. Fingers flexed.

Ohgodohgodohgod.

I punched it out of my way.

The bones reared back, knocking loudly—and regrouped.

Time slowed; my vision narrowed. The sky dimmed. Rain pelted my head like tiny rocks.

No time left. No air.

Up became down. My chest was exploding, shadows flitted cruelly into illogical shapes. Spirals, chains, boxes…and a face. Oval. Long hair. Black braid.

Unfair.

Jonah, I thought. And Charlie.

But the light of my own spirit had shrunk to a pinprick. A collage of scraps flashed. Yellow bedroom with shag carpet. Thanksgiving at Grandma's. The new Andrew T. Morrow school. Honeymooning with my first husband on Catalina Island. The warm and heavy bliss of nursing a baby.

This life I had not loved well enough tumbled sadly past—

and disappeared, into the Gateway to Death.

CHAPTER 65

BELTING OUT A CRY SHE barely recognized, Rikki stepped onto the clearing—stark naked, waving the braid and knife.

Around her, the crowd gasped. Then they fell into shocked silence, as if they'd been squashed. Spectators, actors, re-enactment committee members, vendors, and tourists stared dumbly, trying to absorb what they saw. The dead "lovers" on the blue tarp reanimated and sat up, mouths agape.

"*I will not abide this farce any longer!*" Rikki told them, all of them.

From very far away, shouts began. Whistles and catcalls, too. Maria, face twisted in horror, approached rapidly on two fat feet

"That's enough, Rikki. Now let's just settle down," she said, as if the knife was fake, part of some new outrage on the agreed-upon re-enactment.

Or maybe Maria *did* know the portend of this moment—and intended to stop the truth. The transformation. Fortunately, it was too late for that, too. Everything would be lost unless *this* was completed.

"I was *murdered*," Rikki exclaimed in that voice that was not her own, had never been hers. "I WAS MURDERED."

She halted in the center of the clearing, calling to the weeping sky.

To the blood-soaked lakebed.

To the very *injustice* of life.

Tears of rain ran down her face. Drenched, shivering, she meditated on the thickness and familiarity of Omi's braid, while the traitors fled for cover…under the trees or the Tent of Many *Cowards*.

Only she knew there was nowhere to go. Not anymore.

"*You*—invaders! *You did this.* And *you*, the People. *You* did this, too with your hands or your silence. We are all complicit!" Her hand and body had become slippery; she could barely hold onto the knife. "Just know that there *are* no star-crossed lovers! There is only *me*!"

Her arm moved in a way that seemed choreographed but wasn't.

Like life.

And then the knife blade lowered until its point kissed her bare belly.

Overhead, lightning turned the sky briefly white. Thunder slammed down like a fist. She pushed, and the knife went in.

Exquisitely, painfully cold.

The tip of the blade persisted past her false skin…allowing the blood of truth to run down her legs like…a lost pregnancy.

Everyone seemed to be screaming now. *Yes*, she thought. *There is no going back.*

"My lovers crossed me, and their sins shall be collected," she murmured before falling—bloody and helpless—onto the muddy ground.

Shy Moon lives…

TOO MANY SIGNS

CHAPTER 66

"IT'S BEGUN TO STORM," PAULA Roberson said, her gaze diverting to the pub window.

Charlie had heard the thunder, too. Outside, the bar's awning flapped. Shimmers of light pulsed. Funny—it didn't look like lightning, more like hundreds of lightning bugs caught in jars. Drops of rain pelted the sidewalk. Rivulets streamed down the paned glass.

An old guy at the bar whistled. "Looky here, it's the end of the world again!"

There was laughter, loud, empty sounding. The guffaws of outsiders. Charlie wanted to tell them to shut up.

"The re-enactment," Paula whispered. "Guess they hit pay dirt this time."

And Charlie turned to her, feeling oddly angry. "What *about* twins?" he said.

She looked at him with obvious disapproval, so with effort, he lowered his voice.

"Please, Ms. Roberson. Why did you ask me about twins?"

Paula reached out and clasped his wrist. Her grip was strong, her skin cold. "I will tell you what I know, which isn't much. But I don't want to scare you."

"I can take it," he said, though half of him much preferred to close his ears to everything she said and run screaming for the hills.

Scare me? he thought. I'm losing my fucking mind.

CHAPTER 67

IS THIS DEATH?

Darkness bore down, crushing the core of me: the eternal I; the Watching One. I swam in the thickness of it, slowed, then ceased to occupy the space I had wished to claim. Drained of fluid, of want. Without time, everything is nothing; nothing, everything. And so, I no longer struggled, for there was no I.

No words.

Void.

Then, in the soupy darkness, sensation tugged.

Gently at first, I felt—or heard—the swell of water beating.

Ba-*thum*, ba-*thum*.

The lake had a pulse? Or…was that tom-toms playing?

Suddenly, my thoughts torpedoed up at me—all of it, the water, my family, the town, the fear. I saw time passing—mastodons paralyzed in tar pits—and was shocked by a firm, wet surface like sand forming under my belly.

The bottom of the lake?

But I have not drowned, I realized. I am alive. Pain skitters up my legs like rocks skipping water.

What is this place?

I push open my eyelids to stare upon dirty fog—and see a lakeshore. My bathing suit is in shreds. One breast protrudes, slathered in mud and twigs. A line of blood runs from my knee. My teeth chatter. And the soil beneath me is blackened dirt with dead grass and charred branches.

I raised myself on one shaky arm to look.

Everything around me seemed…unrecognizable. I couldn't see the lane to the cottages in the distance, or the ragged peaks across the lake. All things burnt lifeless…unless the sky itself was the horizon?

Maybe I wasn't on a lakeshore at all.

Could be I had landed onto the island in the middle of Shy Moon Lake. The *invisible* island, the one that didn't exist.

Nice trick, I thought. Nothing but tricks.

What have I done to deserve this? I asked the Universe, and the Universe answered back: **You betrayed Your People.**

"*But you brought me here,*" I cried out to the Spirit of Shy Moon Lake. "*Tell me what you want.*"

CHAPTER 68

"MOMMY?" CRIED JONAH, LOUDER THIS time. He did not glance at the curtained window but instead padded over to Hannah, eyes wide and blinking. "Mommy! Is she there yet?"

"She's shopping, honey, she'll be back soon," Hannah said. Dropping to her knees, she gazed into the little boy's blank stare. "Jonah, what is it? Tell me. What's wrong?"

"She's *not* shopping. She went swimming."

"Swimming? In the lake? Did she tell you that?"

"She went to the *island*," Jonah said, and he held out his hand. "Let's go find her."

CHAPTER 69

"ONCE UPON A TIME," PAULA Roberson said, "my husband met Rikki's great-grandmother. And he was never the same."

Charlie leaned forward. "Rikki's *great*-grandmother? Not Nana?"

"Not remotely Nana. Omi, as she was called, had taken to her deathbed by the time Carl got an audience with her. I still remember how nervous he was. Preparing questions and what-not. We'd been married only a year, in town for a couple of months. We'd moved from back east, you see, when his uncle passed and left him that hick newspaper. Oh yes, my Carl loved the quaintness of Shy Moon Lake! He loved the legends, too, at first. Everything was a story. Except when he tried to get the story *behind* the stories. Then all the tongues stopped wagging. So, he dug in, decided to track down the truth if it killed him. Damn, where are my cigarettes?" She broke off and patted her pockets. Charlie waited while she found her pack and lit up. "It's just not a break without one," she said, no apology in her voice.

Charlie said gently, "What did the great-grandmother say? And what does it have to do with—"

"Twins?"

He nodded, skin prickling from just the word.

"You've heard this before." It was not a question.

"Yes," he said. "From one of my neighbors. This nice lady named Hannah Mason. You know her, by any chance?"

"Yes, of course."

"Right. Well, she asked me about twins. And at that point, Jess—that's my wife—hadn't even confirmed her pregnancy. It was the day of that storm. Do you remember a big freak storm?"

Paula thought a moment, then shook her head.

"You don't? Really?"

"It's okay," Paula said, smoking.

"No, it isn't, not to me. Storms don't hit one street and not get noticed by people living on that street. I mean, the wind came out of nowhere. Literally. Branches blew right off the trees, like in a hurricane." *Her*-icane, he thought distractedly. It took him a moment to get back on track. "Hannah was terrified," he said. "We both were. Yet my wife...Jess...at home with our son...didn't know it happened. Neither of them knew. How can that be?"

"How indeed." Paula crushed out her cigarette. Charlie watched the wisp of smoke rise to the "No Smoking" sign below the smoke alarm on the ceiling. "There are a lot of strange happenings around here," she said casually. "So said Carl. And following up on those things was the death of him."

"I'm sorry to bring it up. But I—"

"Need to know?"

"Yes."

She shrugged and started her story. She didn't address the twin bit; rather began with a verbal snapshot of how, over the years, various folks had drowned or disappeared in the bottomless lake. Tourists, locals. Carl wondered why the bodies were never recovered. And what was up with those people living next to the lake? He described the cottage residents as particularly eccentric, superstitious, and unhelpful. Living all snug against the shore, they whispered things that outsiders considered spooky entertainment. Things

323

like unexplained voices and footsteps, strange watery sounds that came and went at random, along with spikes of emotion. Oh, and there were rumors of an island that somehow hid itself in the middle of the lake. *That* fairy tale was supposed to explain the tormented bird populations, freak storms, and—

Charlie snorted. It was a childishly triumphant sound, and Paula gave him a look.

"You want to hear this or not?" she said.

"I'm sorry. Yes, please continue."

"Okay. Well, Carl only ever worked for one paper. He wanted to honor his uncle by practicing good journalism. He was…an honorable man." Her eyes misted. "I just work in a bar. I guess I wasn't as involved as I should have been."

She explained how her husband had vowed to interview every life-long resident over the age of fifty. He asked rational questions of any rational individual who would answer them. Eventually, he concluded that the only place that really mattered—the area he *must* figure out—was on the other side of the wall.

That required his thinking outside the box, since those residents weren't exactly chatty. He had to go past the absurd signs again and again— and find someone who *wanted* to talk.

"Rikki was a kid when Carl interviewed Omi," Paula went on. "We were young too, in our early thirties. Rikki's mother was gone by then, her father dead. So, there she was, poor thing, stuck in that little house with Witch Number One and Witch Number Two."

Charlie smiled briefly. "The great-grandmother was mean?"

"No, she was more the good witch. Not gorgeous but all-seeing and full of visions. Actually, looked like a frail bird, bedridden but asking for little while the *other*—that Nana character—barked orders like a boot-camp sergeant. Carl had to get past *her*. He had to think of something. In the end, he got in to see Omi by claiming to write poems about the lake."

"Poems?"

"More like *channeling* poems instead of writing them."

Charlie's heart lurched. The hairs on his arms stood up. *Channeling poems. Like I did?* He recalled the being—*two* beings?—that had appeared while he was scribbling verses…before waking up to a terrified Jess.

Paula fiddled with her pack of cigarettes. "Carl told Omi that while he was writing, a 'mysterious Being' had come to him, put words on paper. 'Tell me who this Being is,' Carl asked Omi. I'm pretty sure he was bullshitting his head off. But she said she was pleased someone so gifted and attuned to the 'forces' had arrived. And then she told her own story."

"About twins?"

"About a man and a woman occupying one body, to provide great healing to the world. Except she—*and* he, for they were one, like a combined gender—was murdered."

Paula hesitated, then said in a rush, "And that, my friend, was the beginning of the end."

CHAPTER 70

I SIT CROSS-LEGGED ON A blanket in a reed hut, quickly plaiting my long black hair. Rolling the braid flat on top of my head before covering it with the great headdress—heavy, adorned with colorful beads, feathers, and bleached bones.

Then I rise.

Looking down, I see that I am a man, not a woman. This does not surprise me. It soothes a small quiver at the back of my heart.

A young woman slips into the hut. She wears a dress made of animal skin. She steps out of the dress and we draw ourselves down to the blanket.

I blink; the girl is gone.

I stand and unplait my hair, and realize that I am a woman, not a man.

A young man enters the hut. A white man. He speaks urgently as we lower ourselves to the blanket. More bared hips, more pressing and pushing, more lovely and strange human skin.

I blink again.

And now I stand waist-deep in the water of the lake, blood dripping from the slash across my throat. My lovers from the hut are in the lake with me, pushing me under, words vicious as vultures.

Everyone dies! Even Healers.

Not me. Not I. Not us.

NOT EVER.

CHAPTER 71

"MOMMY!" JONAH SHRIEKED THE MOMENT they stepped outside—and slipped like an eel from Hannah's grasp.

The little boy slid down the stairs, still screaming, racing pell-mell toward the water. "Momm*eeeeeeey*!"

Hannah cried "*No!*" and began to run, too.

Normally she was a gentle, inactive person. She was not prone to this. But now she chased this child so fast and hard, her muscles locked up. She ignored the pain—the *needles*—and kept going, intent on stopping him any way she could. Panting, cramping up, she reached out—and managed to grab the boy by the shirt, then tackled him to the ground like a linebacker.

Jonah writhed to get away. "I need to help Mommy!"

"No, no—your mommy has to help herself! I'm sorry Jonah. Stop fighting me. I'm not letting you into that lake."

She hugged him tightly, so tightly, breathing love into him with her arms. And eventually he calmed down.

He pressed his wet cheek against her throat. His small trembling body went limp.

"That's a good boy," she crooned, loosening her death grip. "What a brave little soldier you are."

Then she heard a noise: a kind of gargling from the direction of the lake. Quickly, she looked. And seeing his chance, Jonah twisted away again.

Hannah tried to stand, but the pain was sharper. She stumbled forward into the mud and fell hard, head smacking against something harsh and unyielding.

All went black.

CHAPTER 72

"OLD LEGENDS ARE ONE THING," Paula said, "and collective delusions quite another."

"Collective delusions," Charlie repeated.

"Yes. My husband had noticed an alarming pattern, he said. One that involved twins." She broke off, giving him a searching look. "I don't suppose your wife has done anything especially strange lately? Like, for example, trying to swim in the lake at night?"

Charlie recoiled. "How did you know?"

"I didn't. It's just an educated guess. That's what I mean by patterns. Big changes in personality are the first red flag. Little by little, Carl realized that every woman living in the cottages—every woman of childbearing age, I should say—started to do strange things. Sometimes violent things."

Charlie kept staring. He couldn't bring himself to mention what he had witnessed Jess trying to do to Jonah.

"And," Paula went on, "it turns out that every time these same women got pregnant, it was with twins."

"*Always?*"

"You can look up the data if you doubt me…not that there's a record." She laughed mirthlessly. "More importantly, as the pregnancies progressed, things went…bad. For everyone."

"Bad in what way?"

"Mental problems at first. Like I said: strange behavior. Moods. Hallucinations. Obsession with the lake, drinking its water or swimming to some island no one could find."

Silence fell between them.

"In any case," Paula said at length, "the pregnancies never worked. There were miscarriages or abortions and suicides or accidents. Not a single live birth of twins. And no happy women. Just haunted, damaged, fearful mothers-to-be who never became mothers."

"But…why? What can this have to do with a lake?"

"Omi's story had come from *her* great-grandmother, who'd heard it from hers. Something about the original tribes who lived here, and their healer. A person named Shy Moon. Shy Moon was murdered, according to Omi. Can't rest in peace. She needs twins to finished something or other. Or *he* needs them, I guess, for Shy Moon manifests both sexes. That's supposedly the source of the healing. Shy Moon was greatly revered, Carl said."

"But…why twins?"

"Maybe the dual nature of things? You know, good; evil. Man; woman. Life; death. Fair; unfair. It's hard to say. But Omi went on and on about the need for balance. At least that's what Carl told me." Paula Roberson shrugged and lit another cigarette. "These are campfire stories. Why should I believe them? Because Omi's family descended from the people involved in that murder?" She made a face. "I'm not a gullible person, you understand. But after my husband's time with Omi, he changed, too."

Paula was sucking the life out of that new cigarette. In between puffs, she kept talking.

"Suddenly, everything was about the damn lake. He got as obsessed and wacko as those women. *Had* to get closer, to tease out its secrets. Then one day, Carl started talking about…drinking it. The water. And going swimming."

"Oh no," Charlie murmured.

"Oh yes. He claimed to hear water noises…and whispering. He wanted to search for that island—just like those pregnant ladies. I tried reasoning with him. We fought, not that it helped. One day, while I was here working, my husband disappeared and never came back. It doesn't matter what anyone else believes, but *I* think he went to that island."

She crushed out her cigarette. Charlie watched her, dreading what he knew would come next.

"I don't need a dead body to know that my husband is gone forever," she said crisply, eyes as flinty as quartz. "So, if you love your wife, you'd better stop her from ending up the same way. Because she will, you know. She will."

BROKEN CIRCLE

CHAPTER 73

THERE WAS A LOUD BOOM—A car crashing into a garage door. Except there are no garages in the great outdoors, Rikki thought. Or in the great beyond.

Her eyes snapped open.

A heartbeat later, everything began to shake. Earth, trees, sky. The BOOM happened again, and someone screamed, "*Earthquake!*" Rikki pushed her upper body off the ground. Chaos was exploding, people running and shouting in all directions, calling for help. One of the festival structures crashed with a great fluttering. The big tent. Kids cried for their mothers. Rikki just draped an arm across her own bare stomach, felt the hot slick of blood there, and wondered if she would throw up.

Very little pain, though. That surprised her.

With the same peculiar, emotionless fascination, she watched the ground undulating. A small whale curved beneath the soil, diving and swimming, in almost liquid movement. She stood, lurched sideways, and clawed at a tree to steady herself. The bark stabbed back, under her fingernails. Fucking tree, she thought with no emotion, like some disembodied spirit.

She *should* be a spirit, damn it. Hadn't she sacrificed herself for the good of the town?

Blood painted her lower body, seeped from the long dark slit across her belly. It *wasn't* open like a mouth or door, though; nothing solid spilling out. How deeply had she cut? She couldn't see the knife on the ground. In another offhand observation, she realized she was naked. Shivering, teeth clattering, while trees tottered like drunks. A single bird twittered loudly, flinging its last protest to the sky.

Nana, an earthquake! Just like in your vision...

Rikki pushed off from the tree and managed to stand. She searched the ground for something to wear—branches, debris, a lady's stupid sunhat. Finally, she spied a burlap bag. It would do. She wrapped it as best she could around her middle and charged through stinging branches and bushes looking for a path. The right path. The one that would take her home to Nana, where she belonged.

But as she found it, she noticed the smell of smoke.

Fire? In all this damp? Tears swelled from her eyes. She'd never been so thirsty in her life. *Oh Nana, please be okay...*

In front of her, on the other side of this muddy path, a woman lay on the ground blocking her way. It was Hannah Mason, that sweet fool of a neighbor.

Dead.

No, not dead. Hannah raised her head, peered up at Rikki with a beseeching hand.

"*Get him*," Hannah begged hoarsely. "Please! I can't get up. I've hurt my leg."

Then the hand turned and pointed toward the lake, where a small boy was running toward the water.

So, the McCortney boy is going swimming after all, Rikki thought tiredly. If he does, he will die.

She glanced in the direction of the cottages. From what little she could see they appeared at least partially intact. With all her heart, she longed to leave this woman who was asking Rikki to help a child who was doomed anyway.

Precious seconds passed.

Rikki looked toward home one more time and sighed from the hole in the center of her being. *I was on my way home, Nana. Was going to bring you tea…*

Then she dropped the burlap bag and took off after Jonah, limping on her bad foot.

CHAPTER 74

"FUCK YOU, FOOT," RIKKI MUTTERED as she ran.

Her lungs and her belly were sore, too. But her bare feet, tripping and stumbling over brambles and rocks, felt like the real raw meat. And the boy… he was small, and he was fast. She couldn't stop, not even to catch her breath. He had just reached the water—sniffling, talking to himself—when Rikki stumbled on a rock and jolted forward, her arms flailing.

For a moment, she had no air. Then she found some.

"Jonah," she screamed. "You stop right there!"

He looked at her in surprise.

"You can't go in there! It's…d-dangerous! You're just…shark…bait…"

Jonah rubbed his fist over his eyes. Then he turned away. And the sight of his back straightening as he began to walk—*into the water*—dissolved what was left of her will.

She wasn't going in that water. Not for anyone or anything. Let him die. Let him die!

But he is so small, she thought. A baby. *Could've been mine.*

"Fuck," Rikki said again.

She was doomed…and it didn't matter. Nothing but this bright spot of little-boy life.

When she reached the water's edge, he stood only a few feet away, waggling his arms a little, mouth moving without sound. "Oh no oh no oh no," Rikki heard her own voice say. And she kept up the litany while she did it—she broke the barrier.

She went into the lake.

"*You're coming with me,*" she hissed and grabbed the kid by his waist.

He flopped. Water flew.

She screamed. He screamed.

Drops of water went into her mouth—in slow motion. She swallowed it, choking. Choking but not stopping. Her eyes ran, bile in her throat and water up her nose, as she held fast to the kid's shirt and hauled him one step, then another, and another.

When he finally went slack, she dragged him the rest of the way. Her own wet skin was freezing, her side and stomach screaming with pain, her feet burning…and her mind a roiling mess of triumph and fear.

You're safe, she told the boy without speaking to him. Stop crying. I won't hurt you.

*   *   *

When Hannah had first noticed Rikki Stevens stumbling this way down the path, naked and splattered with blood and trailing some kind of bag, she'd been too shocked to call out. Had the girl been assaulted? Or hurt someone else? Rikki had always been strange, yes. Hannah thought of animals cruelly caged in a tiny cell when they should be prowling free…until one day they break loose and kill everything in sight.

"*Help him,*" Hannah begged Rikki anyway, hoping and praying the young woman was in her right mind and intact enough to do the right thing. "I can't get up!"

The ground, or Lake, or whatever power surrounded this place, would not allow Hannah to help. What a surprise, then, to watch a filthy, bleeding, and naked Rikki gallop across rocks and pebbly sand into the water to catch Jonah. Hannah just prayed harder.

Oh God, don't let them drown!

Maybe God heard her, too. For Rikki scooped the kid in her arms, gripped him against her glistening, skin, and carried him from the greedy mouth of the lake. He kicked and screamed, of course. His small fists pummeled this savage beast that had stopped him from saving his Mommy. Probably he didn't even recognize Rikki as human. Hannah could hear the terror in his voice.

"Ma-ma! Ma-ma!"

Hannah simply sat up and waited, mute with gratitude, her arms open for this innocent child of someone else. And she held him tight the second she had him.

"I can't stay. I'll come back later," Rikki said, still standing there. She spoke in a voice less human than her face. "If I can."

Hannah nodded, humbled by her own prejudices. "Thank you, Miz Rikki. I have been wrong about you. I'm glad to learn you can be so kind."

"Me too," said Rikki, and turned away, no doubt toward home.

Buck naked but back straight. Like some ancient aborigine warrior out of *National Geographic.*

CHAPTER 75

AS CHARLIE HURRIED AWAY FROM The Bottom of the Lake, a single thought pulsed in his head over and over like the billboards in goddamn Vegas. *Gotta save Jess! Jess and Jonah!*

Thankfully, the rain had stopped. But the air felt dense and swollen, as if the storm planned to only rest a moment before exploding through the air again; he had better move fast. Charlie tried to map out in his mind the quickest route from Main Street to Wannasee Road, and from there to LakeEnd Way and the cottages. He tried an alley behind a grocery store, but that just led to a muddy lot behind the pharmacy. He scuttled over some boulders, darted down two more alleyways, crossed a street and somehow found himself at The Wall.

He ran past its stupid signs, through the gate, toward shore. He was dirty, his chest wheezed, and he didn't know where to go first.

Then he stopped, confused and disoriented. The ground was *shaking*.

An earthquake? They were having a fucking earthquake? Now? When he needed to find his family?

He tried to steady himself...tried not to panic. He wasn't going to break in an earthquake. Over the years he'd been in many a tremblor, some bigger than others. But the ground...how bad *was* this?

"Shit," he said, sprinting again. If Jess had dared to go swimming, would she take Jonah? Surely, she wouldn't drag him along again. *Or try to drown him....*

Barreling along the lake access areas, Charlie spied something blue in the distance, through some trees. A blue towel crumpled on a rock.

Jess's towel.

She really was here, then. Swimming. *Please let Jonah not be with her!*

He was alone at the water...no one in sight. And the ground still shook, rattling...stopping...rattling again. Charlie breathed in deeply, tried to right his head...and his eyes. He yanked off his jeans, jettisoned the socks and shoes, and plunged into the lake.

Icy and painful.

He had just begun to swim when he thought he heard something, some*one*: a sigh...a human sigh.

Ah*hhhh.*

It was followed by a trickling of water, water over rocks...and **If you go farther, you'll drown.**

Charlie blinked.

A mound of land peeked through the fog. An *island* in the middle of the lake. Carl Roberson's island? It was really real.

I'm a good swimmer, Charlie told himself. I won't drown. Because I don't believe in karma or ghosts and....

He dove underwater, pushing toward the island with everything he was, and wasn't.

CHAPTER 76

WHO ARE YOU? I ASKED the Being.

This was not a person before me, not substantial or insubstantial. Words did not apply, nor an image…just the purity of potential. Seed before flower. The kiss and stink of life and….

What is this place? Can't you tell me?

The hills were gone, just wheat undulating in a pinprick of endless, ripened fields destined to feed thousands…*of what*? I can't follow the spark. But form rises from no form…and wheat arises from seed and air and sun and death…as it should, as it should be. For we all feed the other…

This is my destiny, then.

Thank you. Thank you.

A mournful note arises. Flute or birds? Reed-like, the sound grows *wider*. Water surges like wheat…inside this miracle that has chosen *me*.

I feel the soft imprint of skin and fur, and glimpse strong nose, proud chin, fathomless eyes. This man / woman; woman / man. This yearning…

Shy Moon. It's you?

The wheat moves. Or is it water? I may not know the truth, but I can admire it. The symmetry.

It isn't fair, what they did to you.

Especially when you are a physical manifestation of all human division… when your sole purpose is to bring light into dark…and you were stopped—before restoration could occur.

You need another chance—marveling at the brilliance of it. **You need *me.***

The Being shimmers.

Hands that are not hands—they are the reach of life itself, the clutch of it and the release; the absurdity and beauty and that vile red in a place that has no color but oh, yes, it needs form—from my belly.

"*Ohhhh,*" I cried. **Ohhhhhhh.**

What has not begun cannot end. There is no division where there are no seams. No matter. Only the give and take of tides and moons and blood.

And the fields of wheat rustle louder; more frantic.

I sink to submission, pleased to sacrifice to this greater good that has no past, no future, only its own feeding.

Until I hear something else…a rattling cry of the twin of sacrifice: Human Passion.

"Jess? *Jess!*"

It was Charlie, screaming my name.

CHAPTER 77

SHAKING AND DRY-EYED, RIKKI PICKED her way through the shattered tapestry of her home.

She limped over creaking, broken floors, nodding at every sound, every image. The cottage partially intact, partially battered and crumbled. Broken China. One of the cats hissing from top of a shelf. Back arched, fur puffed up. Barking from somewhere deep inside the mess…

But Nana? Nana has left the porch? She needs to keep watch on the lake!

Rikki half fell into a bedroom—Nana's room, rarely used—and saw Peaches whining there by the bed. The form under the blanket next to the dog didn't make sense. Rikki had made the bed neatly herself. Who had messed it?

All that ironing for nothing!

She inched closer—and stopped, horrified.

Nana lay curled on her side, eyes open.

Staring at nothing.

A DECEPTIVE PEACE

CHAPTER 78

"JESS—DON'T! DON'T LET IT TOUCH you!"

I moved toward him, or think I do. Charlie. My beloved.

Then another name—the most sacred of all—emerges from the wheat to lodge inside my bursting lungs.

Jonah!

No! With a great blast of rage, the noble face before me begins to dissolve, collapsing into gaping holes...and the loathsome stench of decay.

It is vile.

It is real.

It is necessary...

"*Jesssssss!*" Charlie screams.

We won't go with you...

Something flies past me, and I scream. A *hand?*

The grotesque object passes through the translucence that is Shy Moon, turning it metallic red, like old blood.

I can actually *see* the color now. I can see water! *I can feel my womb opening, readying itself.*

Life giveth and life taketh away.

Life giveth and—**NO! NOT TODAY.**

"Help me!" He is waving something over his head like a club. A thigh bone? "Jess, help!"

With a hunter's cry, I rushed toward my husband—and reached for the same bone. Somehow my fingers found purchase, and my triumph broke free, soaring like birds.

We won't give you our twins!

Suddenly…or in an instant of four billion years…Charlie and I were at a mound of grinding rocks. Not in a lake, not in a field. The boulders looked like the ones on the lake shore by the cottages. This *is* real, I think. Is it the island?

"*Jess!* Stay here!"

Charlie's voice again. But his fingers felt wet and slippery; I didn't think I could hold on to them. If this *is* the island—it is sinking.

My thoughts snap into place.

Then my feet found my legs and my mouth moved as I willed it.

We will die together before you will get our babies—or touch Jonah, I told Shy Moon in her own language.

A wail of grief pierces my eardrums. It is a tsunami hundreds of feet high. A howl of loss winding around me like an umbilical cord around a baby's neck. I slapped my hands over my ears, wailing myself. And Charlie, bending over, doing the same…

…until the very fabric of night and day began to break and shrink… and disappeared into itself.

CHAPTER 79

STARING AT NANA'S LIFELESS FACE, Rikki let loose, but she did not cry. She *howled,* along with the dog.

She raged at a Creator she no longer believed in, one that had never listened anyway. She screamed at the indifferent universe; at a selfish, self-serving Spirit who had replaced justice with juvenile morality.

"Nana can't be helped now! Too late for the Stevens family...badbadbad*bad* family! Shy Moon has the last fucking laugh."

The dog whimpered, licking her hand. Rikki swatted it away.

She could hear voices outside the house. Residents coming to check on them...to take Nana away from her? *Haven't we suffered enough?*

Desperately, she looked around the room and realized what her grandmother had been doing before the earthquake. A suitcase lay open on the floor, stuff spread around it. Thick candles in a semi-circle. Old sepia photographs in frames. Small bowls filled with tobacco and herbs. Rocks and arrowheads and little stuffed dolls propped against books.

Rikki snatched up an old brown leather book and opened it, scowling at the old-fashioned writing. Was this Mama's diary? Nana's? Or Omi's?

Doesn't matter. Nothing matters, nothingnothingnothing...

Yet it was here. This diary did matter! Nana had thought so. Hoarsely, Rikki read aloud. She read the way Nana must have been doing, or trying to do, before the earth shook her away.

"*Kwaltup! Kwaltup! Mai Ma Me Yo?* Oh, Wildfire, go with me from this unhappy place. Here we cannot live happily and peacefully. The evil doing unto one so blessed must be undone or we will all be killed, and what happiness can this forsaken land then expect to witness? *Kwaltup Kwaltup…*"

She reached over to caress one of the objects—a figurine of a woman lying prostrate.

"O Shy Moon, our ancestors betrayed you and your gift, which was dishonored, summoning the ceaseless suffering of our own design. I beg you: find in your pain a shred of mercy for ours! And no longer shall you dwell near these cool forests, this secret lake, hiding your wearied, vengeful, feasting spirit on our foolish, hungry souls…"

Bending down, Rikki touched a sepia photograph of Omi as a young girl. Omi, who looked far more Indian than European, with that lovely thick black braid.

"*O Farewell, Shy Moon, thou child of the Lake,* make haste! Seek the happy hunting grounds of our fathers, for not many more years of misfortune can my family endure. Not many more years will elapse until we, like you, will be of the past; only dust and bones, and our human efforts to speak for us. Ah, my People! My People! May God give us—and *you*—rest and peace, which is all any of us may wish!"

It was getting harder to ignore her thirst. Rikki's tongue felt wasted; shriveled. She turned away from the diary toward the things propped against Omi's old books.

Pottery; a gourd; two beaded baskets. A braided Indian doll lording it over the rest.

And then: a wisp of fine dark baby hair.

Which baby?

Doesn't matter. The hair had been plucked without permission from an unknown innocent, to represent all the corrupted innocence over the years. Which makes your retribution as bad as the crime, Rikki thought bitterly. *Why can't you accept the unfairness of fate?*

Suddenly she stopped, struck by a new thought.

Go where Nana has gone, where Shy Moon can't find you.

It did not take long to pile the detritus of a life—of multiple lifetimes— in the center of Nana's room. Nor did it take long to find a box of long matches and light a-flame to Nana's cotton shawl, which in turn ignited the other useless belongings.

It did not take long for the conflagration to grow and spread. The room blazed in omnipotent yellow-white flames and devilish embers.

And it won't take long to die, Rikki thought, as she stood watching the fire, her palms placed gently on her poorly sliced womb.

Plunge into the dark to find light.

CHAPTER 80

THE UNFATHOMABLE NOISES HAD STOPPED. Everything had stopped. They were both dead.

Except Charlie felt a crushing weight on his chest, a harsh thump jolting him forward. Thump. *Thump.* Warm lips moved over his, and hot breath blew in. Moisture dripped onto his face. Sweat and tears.

Jess? *She* was saving *him*? From what—a heart attack?

There was no more rain, no fog, no fields of wheat—and no water anywhere. Where had it gone? This *was* the Afterworld, then. He didn't want the Afterlife. He had too much to do.

He wanted life in all its sloppy imperfections.

He wanted *Jess,* foibles and all.

Sourness rose in his throat. He managed to turn his head and vomit. He found his voice. "Jess? Wh-what happened?"

"We fought back. We both did," she said.

He could reach out and feel her, feel a patch of cool skin. He squinted against the strangely gray light, land, and sky—and thought he saw branches, skeletal, and a bird overhead made of bones…a flying carcass.

"But this place," he whispered. "Where are we?"

"It's still the island," she said.

"What?"

"I don't think the Lake wants us to die. Not together, not yet." Her laugh sounded bitter. "No star-crossed lovers stealing its limelight. I mean, what's the point without a pregnancy? Without *twins* to commandeer."

To his amazement, he saw his wife clearly now; she was pressing her hands against her bare belly. Then he saw something else.

Bright red blood seeping down from the inside of her bare thighs.

"Jess? You're bleeding!"

"Yes," she said, clutching her middle.

And as she fell face-forward, green began to seep through the trees. The gray netherworld slowly turned its face, and water reappeared. Charlie struggled to rise, lifting Jess with him. He propped her over his shoulder and waded into the frigid water. Then he began to swim into the silvery haze.

Everything felt wrong. Everything *was* wrong. But home had to be here somewhere, if he just kept going. Keep it ticking. Hold on and release, hold on and release.

He had to believe it was time to hold on.

As he moved forward, her breath became steadier. Other sounds also returned. Birds. Leaves rustling. Water gently lapping.

His arms ached. He kept swimming.

Eventually, to his nearly overwhelming relief, a quaint line of cottages appeared on the side of a tree-shrouded mountain.

And a wall. And a town.

Not home. But close enough.

LIKING IT HERE

CHAPTER 81

Fifteen Months Later

IN TYPICAL FASHION, I HADN'T forgotten a thing for our indoor holiday picnic. Not the marshmallows, the long branching sticks, the fire-logs, the hot chocolate, the cinnamon, or the whipped cream.

And so, Charlie, Jonah, and I sat together by our new fireplace in our newly renovated cottage, toasting marshmallows on sticks. We were happy to savor the autumn-scented moment rather than dwell on the baffling past or rather complicated future.

Jonah—who used to refuse to go anywhere near a fireplace—had just finished roasting his first marshmallow when the doorbell rang. "Don't answer it," he said.

I touched his red hair reassuringly. "I do need to answer the door, honey. Doors are for opening, not barring against the world."

So, open the door I did, to find Hannah Mason standing there, smiling, an orange scarf flung stylishly around her neck.

"Hi," I said. "Happy Thanksgiving."

"Happy Thanksgiving to you, too! May I visit the nursery, do you think?"

"Of course. It's still naptime, but if you could wait a few minutes, that'd be great. In the meantime, come on in. We're having a turkey picnic."

As soon as she entered the living room, Hannah bent to kiss Jonah's cheek. And our little kindergartener stared up at her, accepting the kiss. He had stayed away from people for a while, too—except for his parents. Thankfully, that was passing. I believed Jonah would be fine.

Despite everything that had happened to our family, I hoped.

Hannah turned to Charlie. "You've really done wonders with this place." She indicated the fresh coat of gold paint on three of the walls. "It looks totally different."

"Different was our plan. Different and bigger." Charlie sounded as cheerful as always. "It's nice how so many people are creatively re-doing their houses. Makes the cottages look more...substantial. Like places for year-round living, not just summer."

I glimpsed a flicker of pain across his face.

"Anyway. How's Stan?" he asked Hannah.

"Very well, thank you. The depression really did lift once we finished our remodel."

"I've heard that from so many people. I guess rebuilding is cathartic."

Another delicate silence.

I asked, "Any news on the Stevens' place?"

"Not yet. All that destruction...and so little of it salvageable." Hannah sighed. "Their family history just got annihilated. Why, if the neighbors hadn't responded so quickly to the fire, that poor woman would have been killed too." She lowered her voice, speaking with genuine sadness. "Imagine finding her on top of her Nana's body, naked and stark raving mad. She didn't deserve that. It's so sad."

"Yes," Charlie said. "Unbelievably sad."

We were all familiar with at least parts of the story: that somebody finding Rikki had fetched Doc Taylor, and Doc Taylor had done a heroic thing driving Rikki off the mountain to some place or other—no one was saying. But where she was currently living, medicated and probably harmless.

Doc Taylor never returned either, Mrs. Pattick made sure to inform us. He wrote letters, so supposedly he was fine. Then, to my surprise, Rikki wrote too—postcards. To us. Or me.

Did that mean *she* was fine? I didn't think so.

"Well, life does go on, doesn't it?" Hannah said. "I just wish the aunt— you know, Maddy—would say if there's any progress. She must know. She's just keeping her distance, as usual." Hannah paused, then said more brightly: "I like to think of all of us as getting another chance. Everyone, including that poor family. When Nana's house is ready, I'm sure Mrs. Pattick will sell it."

"Unless Rikki comes back." I crossed to the fireplace mantle to peek at the postcard leaning there. It showed a picture of the barren Death Valley in full knell of summer. Nothing alive, nothing thriving or growing. I didn't have to turn over the postcard to recall what Rikki had written on the other side.

I am free now. Are you?

Hannah said, "In any case, Rikki is much better off where she is. We can thank modern medicine for that."

Right. It didn't give *me* any satisfaction to think of that woman mad with grief and delusions and paranoia…and living in some inpatient facility writing cryptic postcards. I faced our guest and smiled. "Hannah, how about some hot chocolate?"

"Yes, I'd love that."

"And marshmallow on a stick?" Jonah piped up.

Hannah beamed at him. "Thank you, but no marshmallows on sticks for me, young man." She turned back to me. "And that visit to the nursery?"

"You stay here; the nursery will come to you."

"Wait, I'll help," Charlie said.

When we returned to the living room, I was carrying a bundle of soft yellow, and he was carrying the bundle of green.

"It's okay," I cooed to the tiny faces peeking through the tops of our bundles. "Everything is a-okay. We just have a visitor."

"Lordy, lordy! I can't get over how fast these babies grow."

"I know. They're both doing great."

Hannah settled back in her chair and opened her arms to accept the honor of cradling two tiny, flawless human beings. And as Charlie and I released the babies, I felt choked up with love and pride and something else I could barely identify: a wild defiant acceptance, perhaps, of whatever fate might throw at us next.

I also felt surprised by the sudden emptiness of my arms. As always.

"Ah, my little angels, here you are," cooed Hannah, who still hoped to get pregnant herself. "How are you both this fine evening?"

The babies didn't answer. The boy, a redhead, was almost identical to how Jonah had looked at that age. The other, the girl, had straight black hair and eyes as dark as raisins. Like her mother.

"I swear this little girl understands every word," Hannah marveled. "It's uncanny how alert she is! How alert they both are."

I nodded while Charlie poured hot chocolate into mugs.

"I'm so glad you named her Vida," Hannah went on. "It's such a good name for someone who has found life despite everything. Thanks to both of you, of course."

I nodded again and bit into my marshmallow. As much as I loved Vida, it was easier to *not* talk about her troubling origins—or think about that other baby: the unnamed twin I'd miscarried on that terrible night of the earthquake.

Thank God we'd been able to save at least one child: Charles Junior. And how very hard to believe that if I hadn't miscarried, I may have ended up with *four* children instead of three. When I had been so sure that all I could handle was one…

Oh, Fickle Fate, I thought. My whole life now felt as sticky, sweet—and just a little charred—as this marshmallow. And love? Love is a panoply of dark and light, sane and crazy, yin and yang.

Rikki, a disturbed young woman from any account, had acted bravely in the middle of her own loss. She had saved Jonah from drowning, according to Hannah Mason. Which also meant that a woman I disliked or hated had both ruined my life and saved it.

How was I supposed to make sense of that?

"Here," Hannah said, "I think little Chaz wants his Daddy." She handed Charlie his son and held out her arms for his infant daughter—his and Rikki's. My adopted daughter.

I watched Charlie holding Chaz, wondering, as I often did, where my freakish and somehow comforting memory had gone to. I still got flashes of my past in startling bas relief, just much less often, and in much less detail. Had trauma ironically corrected my Stress-Related Hyperthymestic Syndrome?

Or did the future matter so much more than the past that I didn't need to remember like that anymore?

These days I do need a GPS, like any normal person—or I would, if I ever went anywhere. My vision goes more or less in one direction: the future. The past is over. Dead and gone.

At least I *hope* Shy Moon is dead. I hope so for me, for Charlie, and for our children: our odd and oddly perfect little family.

Charlie has changed, too. His hair holds a surprising sprinkling of gray that looks good on him. He doesn't smile as often or as brightly as he used to, but his smile does grow deeper. We have gotten used to Shy Moon Lake and rather like small town living, though sometimes I don't understand *why* we like it so much.

Sometimes I wonder if I'm afraid to leave, afraid to even try. But Charlie says that's nonsense.

We are viscerally tied to this place, that's all. Plus, a few remaining mysteries do still intrigue, like that locked trunk in our spare room that Charlie and I haven't yet managed to open. Or the rare sighting of police cars patrolling on streets and birds landing on lakes. Things like that.

Oh, and by the way—there *is* such a thing as ghosts. Just no such thing as karma, instant or slow brewing. Charlie and I will make our own fate, come hell or high water—forgive the pun and the cliché.

Yawning, I reached for Jonah to cradle him onto my lap. Over this past year he had grown so much, so beautifully, that he was even more delicious than before. I still wanted to take a bite out of him.

Cannibal, I thought sleepily. Some things really do go on forever.

THE END